Red Talons

author	philippe boulle
cover artist	steve prescott
series editors	eric griffin
	john h. steele
	stewart wieck
copyeditor	anna branscome
graphic designer	jennie breeden
art director	richard thomas

More information and previews available at
white-wolf.com/clannovels

Copyright © 2001 by White Wolf, Inc.
All rights reserved.

No part of this book may be reproduced or transmitted in any form or by any means, electronic or mechanical — including photocopy, recording, Internet posting, electronic bulletin board — or any other information storage and retrieval system, except for the purpose of reviews, without permission from the publisher.

White Wolf is committed to reducing waste in publishing. For this reason, we do not permit our covers to be "stripped" for returns, but instead require that the whole book be returned, allowing us to resell it.

All persons, places, and organizations in this book — except those clearly in the public domain — are fictitious, and any resemblance that may seem to exist to actual persons, places, or organizations living, dead, or defunct is purely coincidental. The mention of or reference to any companies or products in these pages is not a challenge to the trademarks or copyrights concerned.

White Wolf Publishing
735 Park North Boulevard, Suite 128
Clarkston, GA 30021
www.white-wolf.com

First Edition:October 2001

The trademark White Wolf, is a registered trademark.
ISBN: 1-56504-884-9
Printed in Canada.

TRIBE NOVEL:
Red Talons

PHILIPPE BOULLE

Prologues: Wolf & Man

As soon as the caribou broke from the herd, it was done for. Fights-the-Bear charged alongside Storm-Eye, the rest of the pack coming up behind them. Storm-Eye leapt for the beast's flank and Fights-the-Bear pounced high onto its shoulder. Soon four other wolves were on it as well, bringing it down in a crashing mass of hooves and antlers.

Hare-Jumper yipped as the beast's thrashing legs connected with his side. Storm-Eye and Fights-the-Bear, the alphas, put an end to the prey's bucking with strong bites to its throat and guts. Soon the others were eyeing them hungrily as they feasted. Long-Runner got too close for Storm-Eye's tastes and she bared her teeth at her constant rival. Her throaty growl, raised hackles and curled lips quoted the Garou Litany better than any Galliard could: *The first share of the kill to the greatest in station*. Long-Runner dropped to the ground and yelped, submitting. Storm-Eye returned to her feast.

That winter night, their bellies full, the wolf pack slept deeply in Gaia's grace.

***

Mick double-parked his black SLK 320 in front of Club Release in South London, ignoring glares from some fool in the VW trying to get down the street. The line leading to the velvet rope was three blocks long, and he paid it no mind at all. The bouncer, a black man in head-to-toe Armani who outweighed Mick by at least six stone, gave him the standard baleful look from behind mirror shades, then moved the rope aside. Mick slipped a tenner from his black Prada trousers and handed it to him.

Inside, Stash was behind the decks laying out a two-step beat that had the crowd going wild. Men in thousand-pound get-ups swayed with women wearing ever-so-stylish dresses that revealed far more than they concealed. Mick walked through it all like a tiger in the jungle, sensed but unseen. Over the scents of sweat and pot and blow, he could smell the erotic combined musk of fear and arousal. He walked straight through the mass of dancers and wasn't even brushed against; everyone just unconsciously let him through. Some of dancers with maladjusted survival instincts, women and men alike, watched him with open desire. Moths to the flame, indeed.

He reached the small mezzanine overlooking the throng and opposite the DJ station. A leather booth was clear—of course—and he slipped in. The waitress was by with his Glenlivet in under a minute. Well done.

"So, where are you from?" The girl wore a Dolce & Gabbana that showed off her delicious figure, and she slipped into the booth beside Mick with only a glint of apprehension. Bold, this.

"Oh, many places," Mick said without looking at her. "Croatia, originally." His mind floated back ten years to when his mother and he had landed at Gatwick. Yes, little Mika Gerbovic had been a weak little brat crying for his dead Pappi. But that was before he came of age, before the Lady had awakened that dark spirit he carried from the land of his birth, before the change. But Momma hadn't approved of all that, of course.

He noticed that the girl was babbling something at him and he cut her short. "Let's go upstairs, shall we?"

The look on her face was pure delight. The VIP room at Club Release was the holy of holies of the garage scene, a place that grew legendary with each American movie star it turned away—and there had been many. The girl slipped out of the booth and extended her hand to Mick.

He took her by the arm instead, feeling the heat of her quickened blood. Yes, the change had been a good one, and Mick knew more was coming. The wonderful, barbed whisper inside him spoke of a liberation, of the land giving up its most glorious seed, the thing they all served. And that thing had such a beautiful name.

He led the girl toward the special wrought-iron elevator that led to the VIP level and looked down at the dance floor again. He wondered if anyone would ever find poor Momma under all that concrete.

Chapter One

"Jo'cllath'mattric."

Storm-Eye stood silently in the dense conifers and chill autumn air that surrounded the Hill of Lamentations, the sacred graveyard of the Get of Fenris who called the Sept of the Anvil-Klaiven their home. She was a visitor here, and hardly convinced the trip across the Arctic had been worthwhile, but this was where a sometimes-friend often spent his time at the caern and she had hoped to find him here.

Instead she had stumbled upon an ominous gathering indeed. Three Garou, all in Homid form, were at the hill. Two were native to the sept, and not just any Get: The man was Mountainsides, the recently appointed warder of the caern. The woman was Karin Jarlsdottir, the leader of the sept. Despite being a homid and a Fenrir, Jarlsdottir was also a moon-judge of no small repute. Storm-Eye, born under the half-moon just like her, had heard good of her among her own tribe, across the pole in what the humans called Canada. And the Red Talons were hardly known for facile compliments.

The third werewolf, also a woman, had just uttered that single dreadful word and collapsed into Jarlsdottir's arms. Storm-Eye recognized her as another visitor from across the Atlantic, an American Black Fury named Mari Cabrah. She had come here like many others to attend a grand gathering, but instead of heading home, she had accompanied a Get pack on an expedition deeper into Europe. They were to track down stories of a Wyrm-threat. That she was here, obviously wounded and obviously alone, could mean no good for the Fenrir warriors she had traveled with.

"Sweet Gaia, not them too."

The voice, barely a whisper even to Storm-Eye's wolf ears, came from a few yards away. If he hadn't spoken, Mephi Faster-than-Death could have remained hidden forever, even though it was him Storm-Eye had come to find. A world traveler and scout, Mephi was unsurpassed in matters of stealth, even among his tribe of Silent Striders.

More losses, Storm-Eye said without words as she approached her old companion. Born and bred of wolf, like every true Red Talon, Storm-Eye spoke in the language of wolves, with posture, gaze and movement. *Always, more losses.*

"I tried to warn them," Mephi answered in the oddly universal Garou tongue, a combination of human words and lupine movements that was one of many gifts from Mother Gaia to her favorites. He seemed defeated, filled with a deep sorrow that Storm-Eye recognized all too well. He too had traveled from this place with a pack to uncover traces of the Wyrm in Europe, and he too had returned alone, with tales of the pack's slaughter, of a corrupted river and a terrible Wyrm spirit stirring in the south. "I should have stopped—"

"Show yourselves!" The demand, half-scream, half-growl, came from atop the Hill of Lamentations. Storm-Eye silently cursed her distraction. She should have known the warder

Mountainsides, no matter how new to his duties, would not fail to notice intruders here. She and Mephi strode out of the trees, both knowing it wise to comply with an enraged guardian.

Mountainsides stood a fearsome ten feet tall in his Crinos war-form. His gray fur seemed to sparkle in the night, as if reflecting his own inner rage, and covered the upright wolf-man he had become. In each hand, he clasped a great Norse axe and his wolf-head maw snapped with terrible menace. Karin too had assumed the Crinos form, although she was smaller than Mountainsides and crouched near the stricken Mari to protect her.

An urge to stand and fight swept through Storm-Eye like an old friend, but she knew that was foolish. The warder was a warrior born and armed to the teeth. More importantly, he was within his rights here. This was Fenrir territory, their holy ground even, and as an outsider she had to show deference. She lowered her head and tail and then lay on the ground in acknowledgement of that fact. Mephi, she noted, although in Homid form, lowered his gaze and held his hands palms out, slightly away from his body.

"Enough, warder." Karin Jarlsdottir melted back to a human shape before attempting to speak any more. "These two are guests of the sept, not enemies."

Mountainsides scoffed for a second and visibly swallowed his rage before he too assumed his man-form. The two axes now appeared huge in his shrunken hands, but he seemed not to have any problem dealing with their weight. "Faster-than-Death, I know," he said, "but not the wolf."

Storm-Eye, she answered in a quick howl, *envoy of the septs of the Sky Pines and Caribou Crossing*.

"You are welcome here, Two-World Daughter," added Jarlsdottir. "But we have little time for introductions. We have lost the best of us, I fear, and we must prepare for the coming battles. Warder, ready the defenses of the caern and have those you can spare join me in the House of the Spearsreach. I'll gather the seers and our other guests."

Storm-Eye wondered at the Fenrir chieftain's use of her judge-name. Only her closest companions and those who had come to her for a ruling had ever called her Two-World Daughter. From anyone else, she might see it as an affront, but from Jarlsdottir, it was a sign of respect. The Fenrir then added, "Please, bring Mari to the Theurge Weaverguard. He will tend to her."

Storm-Eye glanced at Mephi and hoped he wouldn't make her do something that could only lead to trouble. Only one form could carry a wounded person safely and that was not one she found comfortable.

"It's okay," he said, "I got it." He gently took Mari from Karin Jarlsdottir and headed off toward the Fenrir seer's hut. Storm-Eye loped alongside, keeping her nose to the wind. They made quick time and soon Mephi was lowering Mari onto a rough bed in Toren Weaverguard's traditional home. The walls were engraved with Garou glyphs and Norse runes, epics of the spirit world and its defenders. When Weaverguard began examining Mari, Mephi commented, "I think she's in a coma, she's totally relaxed."

No, Storm-Eye barked. *She is still fighting.* How could he have held her close and not sensed it? Damn, blind Homid form! Her muscles may have been loose, but her heart was pumping like a thunderhead. The distinctive, subtle scent of determination and concentration wafted from her for any wolf to smell. She was totally focussed on a battle raging within her, holding back something mighty with all her energy. A fetish of some sort, made of two great wolf-teeth, dug into her wrist, further focussing her struggle. How could they not see? And how could Mephi so casually say she was grievously wounded, perhaps beyond help? This was a Get caern; the Litany's order not to suffer others to tend one's weakness was taken very seriously here.

"You're right," Weaverguard said in a warm voice that belied his tribe's antisocial reputation and his own powerful frame. His gray eyes gazed through Mari, just out of focus—the sign of a Garou peeking into the spirit world. "There is a Wyrm spirit clutching at her, but she is fighting it. I shall watch over her battle and lend what support I can."

"Oh, no," said Mephi and looked down at one of the reflective bands around his arms. He faded from sight as he stepped across the Gauntlet into the Penumbra.

Storm-Eye hesitated for a second and did the same, feeling the wisp-thin Gauntlet pass through her and seeing the spirit realm come alive around her. It was quite a sight. Weaverguard's simple hut grew to become a fortress in the Penumbra, its massive wooden walls towering over Storm-Eye and Mephi. The glyphs and runes now ran off into infinity and moved about the walls, guardians as well as tale-tellers. And in the center of the hut was the faintest outline of Mari Cabrah's reclined form. It was unusual enough for a Garou in the physical realm to project into the Umbra, but worse still was that within that outline was a sliver of evil. Only a foot long, the Wyrm-thing was still terrible to look at, a coiling black serpent with membranous bat-wings and a snapping, three-jawed maw.

"Oh no," Mephi said again. "It's them. We have to tell the others." With that he was back in the physical realm and when Storm-Eye followed, more slowly, she had to race to catch up with him as he ran toward the House of the Spearsreach from where Karin Jarlsdottir led her sept.

The Get were already down to business by the time they got to the hall. About a dozen Fenrir were standing in a circle, along with a half-dozen or so outsiders who, like Storm-Eye and Mephi, had come to Anvil-Klaiven for the recent concolation. That grand meeting had started as a trial of sorts and ended with a prophecy of three Garou packs fighting a mysterious Wyrm threat, the first two of which had now been all but destroyed. The Get were not taking it well.

"This has that Wyrm-humper Arkady's stink about it!" exclaimed someone Storm-Eye couldn't see, to the vociferous agreement of much of the crowd.

"Bjorn Storm-Singer is right, *Greifynya*," added someone Storm-Eye *did* recognize, "Arne Wyrmsbane's blood was already on his coat, and now Brand Garmson and the IceWind joins the list of his victims."

Storm-Eye did her best to suppress an outright growl. The speaker, a brooding youth marked by twin ram horns jutting from his brow, was called Cries Havoc. He too had been at the center of the concolation. An envoy to the Get from the Children of Gaia of the Sept of the Dawn, he had been asked to pay with his life for the death of Arne Wyrmsbane, the Get who had taken his place among the Gaians. Through some incomprehensible Fenrir tradition, he had symbolically paid that price and joined the sept in Arne's place. Storm-Eye bared teeth for a second in disgust—a mewling cub and an outright disgrace to the Litany, this one.

"We will avenge the IceWind and the Roving Wind packs," answered Karin Jarlsdottir in a calm but firm voice, referring not only to those lost with Mari Cabrah but those lost with Mephi too. "But if we act foolishly, we will only add to the Wyrm's victories." She sat on a high wooden chair, holding the great hammer that was the symbol of her position. Storm-Eye knew that many of the Get here were unsure of her leadership, that they balked at a woman commanding them. What human foolishness! Did not a wolf pack have an alpha male and female? Regardless, in this dark time, all seemed to listen to her, as was proper in a time of war. "The Fury Mari Cabrah managed to return from Serbia with a single word: *Jo'cllath'mattric*. Our blood died for this word, so we must know what it signifies."

The assembled Garou all milled about, searching their minds for some sort of answer. Storm-Eye hadn't had time to think of the word since she heard Mari speak it, but it scratched inside her mind like a sore. It had the stink of Wyrm-speak about it, but she had no idea if it was an incantation, a name or a corrupted breed of some sort. The Wyrm had many faces, after all.

"It's tied to the Tisza. It has to be," said Mephi. The Garou all turned their attention to him and he continued. "The Roving Wind pack fell fighting a group of Dancers who were calling out that river's spirit. It was totally corrupt, like a huge Bane or something. We got the pathstone we went after, but weren't able to stop the summoning. I saw the thing rise to snap a huge pattern chain and when that fell, Banes grew out of the land."

Unlike the IceWind pack, the Garou of the Roving Wind had not been residents of Anvil-Klaiven, but a wave of sorrow and anger nevertheless swept through the assembled Get at the mention of the death of brave warriors of Gaia. "Cabrah's fighting one of those things as we speak. It's inside her or something."

"That's nothing to scoff at," came a new voice. The woman was young and seemed out of place in the harsh Norse hall of the Get. Her clothes were everything Storm-Eye hated: pointlessly designed for some human aesthetic and made from Weaver-cursed fabrics. This was obviously one of those damnable Glass Walkers. "Most folks get a Wyrm thing inside them and it's game, set and match. If she's holding her own, she's even better than her reputation."

"Indeed." Karin looked at the Glass Walker for a second. "Julia, is it? From England?"

"Julia Spencer of the Old City Sept, to be precise." She smiled with what Storm-Eye thought was wanton disrespect, but Karin didn't bristle in the least.

"Our introduction was far too brief during the concolation." That seemed to defuse any tension between the two. "But you are quite correct, Mari Cabrah is a fierce spirit warrior indeed. She would have to be to stand by one such as Jonas Albrecht." The assembled Get exploded in raucous laughter at their chieftain's deadpan jibe at the American Silver Fang "king." Levity and sarcasm were not things Storm-Eye much cared for, but she recognized the value of bonding the sept in the face of mounting danger. "But if both the packs we sent out faced the same enemy, we must expect that enemy to respond."

Jarlsdottir's conclusion proved itself all too true when the ensuing silence was pierced by first one, then another powerful howl. The first warned of the Wyrm's approach, and the second called the Garou to battle.

The Sept of the Anvil-Klaiven was under attack.

Chapter Two

That winter morning, her belly still full of caribou meat, Storm-Eye woke to the warm feeling of Fights-the-Bear grooming her fur in the cold, sub-arctic air. She shifted contentedly and responded in kind. He was truly the finest of wolves, deserving the station of alpha like no other. She still remembered when he had earned his name, now nine winters ago. This was before her change, when they were still just littermates, both yearlings in their mother's pack.

They had killed a moose near a river and the alphas had been feasting when a bear appeared. It bellowed and pushed the wolves back to steal their kill, and it looked like the pack would let the great beast do so. But before anyone could stop him, her brother had leapt for it. A lone yearling should never have survived against an enraged bear, but he had timed his attack just right. Leaping onto the thing's back, he'd bitten deep into its shoulder and held firm. The bear's mighty paws couldn't reach the young wolf and the more it thrashed, the more the yearling's maw tore its flesh. The maddened thing had stumbled down the river bank, through the thin ice and into the cold water. To save itself from the drowning, the bear fled. The newly named Fights-the-Bear dropped to the snow to rejoin his family, and he received a large share of the kill. He had shown that same passion and fire last eve with the caribou.

Storm-Eye licked the dew from his fur. Winter was turning into spring, her heat would be coming soon, and this is where she belonged—a wolf among other wolves. She had done her service to the Garou

Nation, to tribe and totem. She had fought the Wyrm and the Weaver. She had seen packmates torn to bits by great Banes. She had tasted the bitter bile of fomori dying in her jaws. Now was her time to be a wolf, as she was born. As she was.

The pack moved from the clutch of tall conifers soon after first light. The yearlings yipped and played, establishing rank and reversing it with a speed reserved for the young. Hare-Jumper seemed no worse for last night's blow as he overturned his littermate and played at being alpha.

Long-Runner loudly barked her own dominance at the young wolves. When Hare-Jumper didn't respond, she pinned him to the scrub. He yipped submission to her, much as she had done to Storm-Eye at the kill. The two-year-old Dawn-Howler earned his name anew by starting the call. His warbling howl coursed over the rolling hills of summer, soon enhanced by Storm-Eye and the rest of the pack. *These are our hunting grounds*, they announced, *lands and prey are ours to roam and hunt*.

Miles away, Storm-Eye suspected, another pack was catching the last echo of the call and noting that they would hunt in another direction this day. And she hoped that perhaps the spirits of her brothers and sisters fallen to the Wyrm heard the call as well and smiled that their sister was where she should be. The Red Talons might call this land the Sky Pines Protectorate, and the humans the Northwest Territories, but for her it was simply home.

With a mighty shake, she threw the last of the dew from her coat and all such thoughts from her mind. Theory and regret were human crutches. She was a wolf. She looked down at the playful yearlings with pride and realized that, had Gaia brought her back here a moon or two earlier, she would have borne them. *Possession*, she thought. *Another human crutch.* The pups belonged to the pack and she was their alpha-mother. *Long-Runner's pregnancy be damned.*

Soon they were running again, and by the time the sun touched the western horizon, they were twelve miles from where they had slept. Fights-the-Bear led the pack down a hollow for some water and some rest, but not all the wolves followed. Hare-Jumper headed to the crest of the hill and his posture changed. *Prey*, he said, more clearly than any human ever could have. *A cow away from the herd. She hasn't smelled or heard us. She is weak.*

Storm-Eye tensed with excitement at the possibility of two good meals so close together. The others began to creep up to the hill, getting ready to follow their alphas to the kill.

But one alpha was missing. Fights-the-Bear stood by the small brook and lapped at the water. He ignored all for the satisfaction of refreshment and rest, it seemed. Hare-Jumper tensed, ready to run, and took a first tentative step away from his father and alpha. Fights-the-Bear turned and barked and his son jumped in fear. The elder wolf didn't run to pin his errant packmate and child, he just stared him down. Hare-Jumper returned the gaze for a few long moments, his defiance clearly communicating his feelings about the prey now escaping. Then he broke his alpha's gaze and lay down, in quiet submission. The others slowly made their way to the water as Fights-the-Bear wished them to. Yesterday's meal would hold them.

Later, when the pack was resting for a few hours, Fights-the-Bear spoke to Storm-Eye. In a few whips of tail and movements of his aging body, his meaning was crystal clear. *Hare-Jumper will make you good pups next heat.* That simple statement said volumes. Only the pack's alpha male would breed and that was now Fights-the-Bear. For Hare-Jumper to breed he would have to displace his father, and for his father to step down he would have to...

Quiet, Storm-Eye barked. *You will make the pups.*

I am old and tired, sister, he said, simply by lying down. *This thaw will be my last.* There was no sadness in his statement, no regret. Just acceptance. It was the wolf's way.

Later, as the rest of the pack slept, Storm-Eye paced. It was not right, she thought despite herself. She was as old as Fights-the-Bear, her last surviving littermate. Just because Gaia chose to give her the changing skin, why should he rather than she trot through into spring waiting to die? He had spent his ten winters caring for pack and pups, leading them on successful hunts and through bountiful summers despite the humans and their Wyrm-feeding ways. No Galliards would sing for him, and yet he was the one who followed Gaia's way. Was this the justice of the world?

Then her ears perked up to the damned sound of a belching motor and she caught a faint whiff of acrid exhaust. At that moment, she knew Fights-the-Bear would not die forgotten by Gaia.

Chapter Three

The Fenrir Anthem of War was a beautiful and terrible thing, sounding like nothing so much as the howl of a winter storm descending upon a lonely coastal village. Unfortunately, this time the village was the Get's own Sept of the Anvil-Klaiven and the storm would be the unleashed fury of the Wyrm.

Storm-Eye ran with all her lupine speed from the House of the Spearsreach toward the den of Toren Weaverguard. Karin Jarlsdottir had ordered her to defend the still-battling Mari Cabrah from the assault, and that was what she intended to do. The sounds of battle came from many directions, near and far, almost gleeful war cries competing with the terribly high-pitched shrieks of the damnable Black Spiral Dancers. Storm-Eye understood now why so few of the Get had been in Spearsreach—they had already set up a tight defense of the caern, one that was now paying off in Dancer blood and Fenrir glory.

She crested the hill nearest Weaverguard's home and her hackles rose. Two of the Gaia-forsaken things assaulting the caern were there, in their own corrupted version of the Crinos warrior-form. One was obviously female, rows of pendulous breasts hanging from her hairless chest, with a face so scabbed Storm-Eye wondered how she could see at all. The other Dancer, a male, had molted greenish fur and the membranous ears of a reptile. They advanced toward the low hut despite an assault by the frosty ground itself. Both were making slow progress as daggers of ice and frost formed around their feet with every step—surely the result of spirit guardians entreated by Weaverguard.

Storm-Eye didn't lose a stride. With one powerful bound, she sailed yards into the air and across the open ground around Weaverguard's home. Her rage boiling inside her, she doubled in weight and size as she flew, taking on the dire-wolf shape of the Hispo. She landed like an avalanche of fur and teeth on the male, knocking him to the ground with her momentum and snapping her own terrible jaws closed through his shoulder. His blood tasted of maggots and rot.

The female Dancer shrieked like breaking glass and raked Storm-Eye's side with her claws. The pain was a fierce burning; it only added to her mounting rage. Releasing the wounded male, she turned to face his mate, her bloody teeth bared. The Dancer held up her right hand, showing Storm-Eye her own blood on the barbed metal hooks that tipped the distended fingers where claws should be. Storm-Eye knew the male wasn't out of the fight yet, but now the female was the immediate threat.

The Dancer sidestepped, circling, trying to get Storm-Eye to move away from her wounded mate, but she was hampered by the spirits still fighting her. Each step was a labor, and when she glanced down to free her leg yet again, Storm-Eye pounced. She went right for the Dancer's throat, but the Wyrm-thing reacted in time to get her arms up to push the great dire-wolf off her. She paid for it with cuts and kicks from Storm-Eye's hind paws, but no more.

Storm-Eye ended up on the other side of her enemy, who turned and issued an ululating battle cry, twisting in an alien dance. This foul incantation seemed to push back the spirits and give the Dancer room to fight, room to kill. Behind her, her male companion was rising from the frosty ground, his left arm hanging limply from a torn and shattered shoulder. A great black tongue slipped from his maw to lick the gore that had splattered his face. Blood was running from wounds on Storm-Eye's own side, wounds that refused to heal. Alone against two Dancers she would have a fierce battle ahead of her, but Storm-Eye had never feared battle. And she was hardly alone.

First came Mephi Faster-than-Death, living up to his name as he darted over the hill in his sleek black Crinos form. The female Dancer—obviously the superior foe—noticed him despite her twirling and tried to strike out with her barbed talons. Mephi, even though he ran faster than any jackal or Garou had any right to, easily ducked under her swipe, spun, stopped suddenly and struck upwards. A Galliard and a traveler, Mephi was not reputed to be a great warrior, but his long Crinos talons opened the Dancer groin to throat in one fell swoop.

Next over the hill was Cries Havoc. He crested in Lupus form, howling a war cry all his own. The male Dancer tuned to face him, but it was far too late for the fool. Cries Havoc never broke stride but assumed his Crinos war-form. The small ram's horns on his wolf-brow, the sign of his unnatural status as the metis child of two Garou, grew with his frame. As a wolf-man, his horns were full and strong. He lowered his head and slammed into the Dancer, sending him flying across the ice field and into a clutch of trees—one of which actually swung a branch to receive the beast like an impaler's pike.

The silence after snapping, howling battle is always huge, and the three Garou stood there for a few beats feeling their rage ebb and flow. But the silence wasn't complete. It was pierced by a barely audible, twisted chirping, coming from near Mephi…*the female!*

Lying in a spreading pool of her own black blood, seemingly oblivious to the coils of her intestines draped over her lower body, the Black Spiral Dancer was singing again. Like it had the spirits of the glade, this song pushed at the Garou's hearts. As the bitch held up a length of rusted chain wrapped with wire and barbed hooks, Storm-Eye felt the wound in her side flare. All she could feel was that pain and all she could hear was the Dancer's song. It all seemed like screeching gibberish save for one terrible word that peaked the crescendo of the dark incantation:

"Jo'cllath'mattric."

Storm-Eye had just registered the barbed chain falling toward the frosty ground when the song was cut short by a great howl. Storm-Eye and the Dancer looked up in unison to see a hammer-wielding Garou in Crinos form literally fall from the sky. Storm-Eye had seen Karin Jarlsdottir in her war-form before, but then she had been crouched, defending the stricken Mari Now, she was a great mass of muscle and fury, slipping from the Penumbra high in the air to come down on the Wyrm-beast who dared threaten her caern and sept. Her hammer of judgment came with her, and there was no doubt as to the terrible finality of this wise-woman's ruling. Just as her clawed feet touched the ground between Mephi and the Dancer, she brought the hammer down, using every bit of her momentum to drive it through the invader's skull and frame. It hit the ground with a terrible boom like a mountain falling on a fly, and the Wyrm-bitch was no more. Storm-Eye could hear other Fenrir howling their Anthem of War in answer to the thunderous blow—they had obviously heard their *Greifynya* at war before.

"Inside!" Jarlsdottir barked at the Garou in the rage-filled growl of the war-form. She turned to lead the way, her silvery fur and great braid pocked with blood of fallen enemies. They left the Dancers' corpses to the spirits' tender mercies.

Once within Weaverguard's sturdy wooden home, the sounds of battle receded somewhat, although Storm-Eye was sure the enemy was not far off. The elder Theurge himself was nowhere to be seen, but Mari Cabrah lay where they had left her. Her tee-shirt and jeans were soaked through with sweat. Her eyes darted wildly under closed lids as she battled the thing within her. A rough-hewn necklace was draped around her neck—most likely a talisman or fetish placed there by Weaverguard to help her in her struggle. The wolf-tooth bracelet was still wrapped tightly around her wrist.

"Sideways," said Jarlsdottir as soon as she had scanned the house's single room. She held out her great hammer and the four Garou all stared at its reflective surface—somehow the gore of battle would not stick to it. Soon the physical world parted and they were in the Penumbral reflection of the caern. It was not a happy scene.

The great rune-covered walls of the Umbral fortifications rose around them, but the sky above was no longer peaceful. A great spiritual typhoon, the likes of which Storm-Eye had—despite her name—never seen, raged in the Umbral sky. Standing atop the battlements was Weaverguard, waving a great spear at the sky and the black shades that swept through it. Spirits of hawks and wolves and winds raced around him, doing his bidding and fighting against the encroaching tempest. In a second he had noticed their arrival and he leapt down to join them.

"This is no random attack, *Greifynya*," he reported. The Theurge was old and his Crinos muzzle was graying, but his eyes shone true and strong. Runes and glyphs across his fur shone with power as the spirit guardians he commanded strengthened him for battle. His body language spoke of the emotions bubbling within him: equal parts concern for the safety of the holy place he tended and thrill at the great battle to which all Fenrir were born. "These Wyrm-things are after something here."

"I agree," answered Karin, her voice somewhat clearer in the Umbra, despite her Crinos form.

"The Spirals in the physical realm seem meant to keep us pinned down while the spirits get what they came after. What are these things," she added sweeping a hand toward the black shapes in the stormy sky, "Banes?"

"Like none I've seen before, *Greifynya*."

"But I have," interrupted Mephi. "Those are the things that grew out of the blight near the Tisza. I...I think they may be here for me." To admit such a thing was a bitter pill to swallow for a Garou whose reputation lay in escaping from the Wyrm. If he had endangered the caern, his life could be forfeit.

"Or for her," said Weaverguard, indicating Mari's Umbral shadow. "The things inside her is tied to that storm somehow."

Storm-Eye, an outsider to this conversation, watched the roiling chaos in the Umbral sky above her. She could see the spiritual thunderhead fray and shred the shinning paths of the moon bridges that had linked Anvil-Klaiven to other caerns. And black things were raining down from there, spirits foul and hungry.

"There are plenty of possible targets. Have you been able to help her at all?"

"I've done what I can, *Greifynya*, but the battle is the Fury's to win or lose."

"You understate the benefit of your ministrations as always, my friend." Karin's toothy grin in the face of an assault on her caern was a testament to her fearlessness. "Now, back to the battlements with you. I'll join you shortly."

Weaverguard acknowledged the order with a small yip and sailed back up on the Umbral winds to the top of the great walls. Soon his attention was focused on what appeared to Storm-Eye to be a wolf spirit of some sort, but black and snapping at the Theurge like a Wyrm-thing. When she returned her attention to her companions, they were following Jarlsdottir back into the physical realm and she joined them.

The *Greifynya* was back in Homid form and picking up Mari in her arms, her great hammer set aside for now, when Storm-Eye stepped sideways. "Mephi Faster-than-Death, you've outrun these Banes before and I'm asking you to do it again, this time with cargo." Her voice was clear once more.

"Um…where?"

"Take Mari to King Albrecht by whatever route you can. Mari will be best able to fight her battle among friends and at her home; perhaps they can provide her some help as well. Also, you must bring word of the goings-on here to other septs. We will stand against the Wyrm as long as we can, but will need support if we are to bring the battle to it."

"Yeah, sounds good." Mephi took a length of flaxen strips out of his pack and wrapped them strategically around Mari to create a sling to help him carry her. She was cradled much like a baby in his long, thin Crinos arms.

"Go now. The warder cannot keep the moon bridges open much longer. Live up to your name, Strider." And with that, Mephi Faster-than-Death was gone.

I will go with him, added Storm-Eye in wolf speak, with just a turn of her head. She was almost out of the house before she heard Karin's command to stop.

"No, Storm-Eye, I have another task for you." The *Greifynya* gave the Red Talon a chance to turn back around before continuing. "It's possible that the Banes are here for Mari or Mephi, but I don't think so. There is another in whom they might be more interested."

She turned her gaze on Cries Havoc, who stared gape-mouthed at her. "But…"

"Get him to Antonine Teardrop in America," the *Greifynya* said. "Keep him safe."

Storm-Eye felt bitter rage grow in her and her hackles rise. How could the woman ask her to protect this fool? Not so long ago, when she had first arrived at Anvil-Klaiven, Storm-Eye had been among those calling for the metis's immediate and unceremonious execution, so weak had been the cliath's resolve in the face of pointless accusations. Now she was to *guard* him? It was preposterous! It was…

She glanced at Jarlsdottir, who had obviously read Storm-Eye's body language with ease and stared into her with cold, hard eyes. It was the order of the *Greifynya* of the caern that was her host. It was the alpha's command. And the Litany said the leader could not be challenged during wartime. Storm-Eye lowered her gaze in acceptance of the Fenrir chieftain's command and turned toward Cries Havoc. Unsurprisingly, this metis Child of Gaia—a walking violation of the Litany—didn't see things so clearly.

Philippe Boulle

"No!" he exclaimed. "I have to stay to defend the caern with the rest of you. This is my home now! I can't leave it."

"Cries Havoc," began Karin, her voice even but hard with suppressed rage, "the Stargazer Teardrop said you would be part of a third pack needed to defeat this threat. Without that third pack, many of this sept's best warriors have already died and I fear more will join them before the battle is through. I appreciate your desire to defend Anvil-Klaiven, but you'll do more good with Teardrop. So go."

"But—"

Jarlsdottir was in Crinos form before the others even saw her move. Her right hand went to Cries Havoc's throat and her left foot stepped inside and behind his right leg. She pushed forward, and he was flat on his back, her claws at his windpipe. "Go!" Karin growled.

Storm-Eye's tail wagged in admiration: For a homid, Jarlsdottir could communicate like a wolf when she needed to. The Gaian boy—and in this company he appeared a child despite his own bulky Crinos form—got up as soon as he was released and headed toward the door. He looked up again at the woman who had so thoroughly bested him, just before leaving.

"Be safe," she said, and then stepped sideways.

As wolf, Storm-Eye said to the boy and watched him shift into a thin gray wolf, still with small ram horns. *Follow*, she added and they headed outside, toward the Hill of Lamentations, where whatever moon bridges still held would be anchored.

They were still a half-mile from there when the air ahead of them tore open with an audible shriek. A nightmare thing leapt from the bleeding gash in the Gauntlet. It was shaped like a great wolf but seemingly made of pure darkness, highlighted by Bane-wisps crawling within it. Its eye burned a baleful green and in its maw it held a bloody shred of Garou flesh.

Storm-Eye recognized the pelt from the runes upon it.

Chapter Four

You will, Storm-Eye said in a language of bared teeth, fixed eyes and raised hackles.

No, answered Fights-the-Bear in similar fashion, locking gazes with her and raising his tail in dominant defiance of his alpha female. *It isn't our way.*

You will! Her growl segued to a loud bark and suddenly she was running and leaping, her rage fueling her drive. Fight-the-Bear leapt back to get a better position, but she was moving faster than any wolf should and by the time she hit, she had changed. The great dire-wolf Hispo form gave her at least a hundred-pound advantage and she bowled over her male like a pup.

To his credit, he did not submit easily. There were no high-pitched squeals, no suddenly bared throats. Fights-the-Bear growled and barked and fought like this great changing wolf was just another of many challengers he had faced over his many winters. But it was no use. In a few seconds she had him on his back and her great maw was around his throat, pressing in. Submission or death were his two choices, plain and simple. It was an easy choice.

I will, said his dropped ears and curled tail. *I will*.

Storm-Eye back off from her cowed male and shrunk back down to the form of a large reddish wolf. They had to get moving if they were to find their prey.

It took them an hour, but they caught up with the humans when they stopped their vehicle on a low rise. Storm-Eye's time among the humans told her the thing was called a "pickup," but it was just another Weaver-begotten monstrosity as far as she was concerned. Three men were standing around the thing, eating and chatting. Fights-the-Bear's ears perked up to the sounds, but he couldn't understand the words. Storm-Eye wasn't so lucky.

"Hey, Maurice," a fat little man said to his friend sitting in the bed of the truck. "You hear Shauna's back on the juice?" The man wore his long black hair in a single braid.

"Yeah. Shame, that is." Maurice, more slender than his companion, was nibbling at some pre-packaged foodstuff. "Hear tell she's been getting it from Old Hubert. Wish the Mounties would shut that fool down once n' for all."

"Liquor buys you lots of kickbacks," said the third man, stepping around from the other side of the truck. "Hubert's known that since we were all kids."

That one, Storm-Eye said with her gaze and her hackles, *the wolf-killer*. Even without her order, she knew it would be clear to her packmate that this tall man was the alpha of this bunch of humans. Not only was he fitter and stronger, but he walked with the stride of a man in charge. The others' sloping posture and slightly averted eyes spoke of deference, even submission.

"You think you can do anything 'bout it once you're chief, Gregory?" It was short-and-fat speaking again, his words blowing around bits of a sandwich.

"I ain't chief, Dorion." Tall-man Gregory flushed with pride at the mention of the word, though, and from far away Storm-Eye knew he would be. "The tribal council still supports Henry."

Philippe Boulle

"Henry's in Old Hubert's pocket and the council knows it," slender Maurice said. "Them Indian Affairs folks from Ottawa come sniffing around with the Mounties, the council will withdraw its support faster than you can say boo. And you're the only real choice after that, so stop playing all modest."

"Yeah, Gregory, we all saw you on television in Yellowknife talking about traditional hunting rights and all that. We know we owe you for the hunt, and we know you know. Y'know?"

Gregory turned and scratched his head for a second, then burst out in bellowing laughter. "Yeah, I know, you great big fool!" Soon all three men were guffawing like squawking hens. Storm-Eye moved forward, Fights-the-Bear right on her heels.

"Okay," Gregory said reaching into the cab of the truck. "Now that we scared away every animal within twenty kilometers, let's get started." He pulled out a large rifle.

Be ready, Storm-Eye said with tensed muscles and bristling fur. The two crept closer and closer to the humans, using the brush and low hills as cover. As the humans exchanged another pointless laugh, she broke left, running full tilt as if after prey.

"There!" Maurice exclaimed. "Look at that one, got to be almost two hundred pounds!"

"I think I've got a shot," said Gregory the alpha human, raising his rifle. Looking through the scope, he had a clear view of Storm-Eye—and not a hope of seeing Fights-the-Bear until it was too late.

"Watch out!" screamed the fat Dorion when he spotted the big gray wolf charging over the hill.

But the warning was too little, too late, and the beast was jumping and Gregory was falling. Maurice fired his gun, but not before Gregory's blood poured onto the ground. Dorion fired too, but it was even less useful as the wolf, too, was already dying.

A half-mile away, on a small rise, Storm-Eye turned from the carnage and headed back toward her pack's territory. The man called Gregory would kill no more wolves, and Fights-the-Bear would be remembered.

Chapter Five

Mick cupped his hands under the hot water running from the chrome tap. In the stark track lighting of his bathroom, every speck of dirt and grime was visible and he wanted to scrub it all away. Had to scrub it all away. The water turned from hot to scalding, sending steam billowing up from the polished porcelain sink. Perfect. He reached over to the small chrome toiletries shelf where he kept a vintage straight razor and other prized cleansing tools, and pumped the Neutrogena dispenser once, twice.

The orange gel dissolved into a white froth as he rubbed it between his hands, building up a lather. He closed his eyes and brought his hands to his face, working the suds into every nook and cranny of his perfect face. He used his middle fingers to work at the space around his nostrils, and his broad palms to slick the soap across his cheeks, then his throat. He moved up again, using all his fingers on his forehead. Satisfied he had scrubbed every pore, he lowered his hands to the water to rinse them. The suds were now a satisfying shade of pink. Neutrogena really was the best soap to wash up the blood.

After splashing water on his face and dabbing—never wiping, always dabbing—himself dry with a fresh white cotton towel, he passed his hand over the large mirror to wipe away the fog. His skin was just slightly raw from the scrubbing, but that would fade. He looked at the towel and saw that not a speck of red had stained it. Nothing started a day like a good cleaning, he always said.

Steam draped the mirror again, sending his reflection back into a gray haze. But in the haze, he saw things. And in the running water, he heard things. News, good news. People would be coming to him, people with whom he could truly play. Mick smiled at the thought and noticed a speck of bloody meat caught between his left-top canine and eyetooth.

He reached for the floss.

***

The beast stank of the Wyrm like nothing Storm-Eye had ever faced before, and she had faced many a twisted thing in her ten winters. The scent of blood and pain wafted from it like a cloud of flies from a disturbed corpse when it took a step forward. Things, Banes or other rot-spirits, crawled and swam through the darkness of its pelt and body.

Cries Havoc rose to Crinos form and readied for battle, but the thing stared only at Storm-Eye. It took another step forward and, if it could be said to have body language, then its posture said: *You are mine, little cub. Submit.*

Storm-Eye felt her own rage mount anew and this time she didn't fight it. The still-raw wounds on her right flank flared and added to her fury. The bitter pill of Karin Jarlsdottir forcing her to chaperone this inbred Gaian cub did the same, and she let loose. Luna's fire burned through her as her sleek lupine form bulked up in a split second. Forepaws stretched and distended into great furred arms, and soon she was upright in her mighty Crinos warform. Her senses tunneling in on the Wyrm-wolf alone, she pounced and soared the twenty yards to the thing with ease. Her terrible claws extended and her maw gaping, she let out a rage-fueled war cry and was on the thing.

It barely seemed to move, just followed her with its gaze. When she struck, her claws struck at smoke. Her talons, arms, and then her whole body went right through the wolf to hit the ground below. The Wyrm-thing dissolved into a brackish mist, the spirits within it swarming about like locusts.

"An illusion!" cried the metis, who had moved to join the fray.

He was soon proved wrong, though, by a searing pain in Storm-Eye's shoulder. The wolf rematerialized with its jaws clamped on that spot, trying to drag her down. Storm-Eye reached back with her left arm and grabbed hold of the thing on her back. Its fur was slick, as if it were covered in oil or the slime of rotted carrion, but she got a grip nevertheless and her claws dug in. She felt the bite loosen ever so slightly and pulled, tearing the Wyrm-wolf from her back and throwing it at a nearby tree.

The thing sailed through the frigid air almost calmly. It just let itself sail, never bucked trying to reestablish its balance or find footing. When it hit the tree, it seemed to disintegrate like packed sand hitting the ground. Suddenly it was a cloud of black smoke and crawling *things* and then it was gone, like a bad dream or a guilty memory. Cries Havoc whooped a cry of victory, but Storm-Eye felt no satisfaction.

Her breathing slowed as the rush of frenzy faded and questions flooded her mind. Was it dead? Surely not so easily. Where was it then? Would it come back? No longer in the fury of battle, she was keenly aware that she was wearing her warform, something she hadn't done in many cycles of the moon. Standing on two legs felt so foreign to her, as did seeing the world from so high up. She crouched to catch the scents on the ground and felt the fetish on her right arm tighten some around her biceps. Made from the twisted barrel of a hunter's gun, it held a moose spirit that hated human killers almost as much as she did. In her wolf-form it remained hidden by the same spirit, but now it was visible again. She glanced at it with her good eye and it reminded her of the human she had taken the barrel from. That had been a glorious hunt.

She shifted back to Lupus and shook away thoughts of the past. This was no time for reminiscence. She had to get Cries Havoc to safety—that was her duty to Karin Jarlsdottir and the others. She glanced at the Gaian metis and he took the wolf-form again.

They covered the last quarter-mile at full tilt, well aware that the caern was facing an all-out assault. The Fenrir and Black Spirals outdid each other with cries of battle, and the scents of fear, anger, blood and fire intermingled on the winds. Storm-Eye was happy to hear the resounding thunder of Jarlsdottir's hammer once more and she and Cries Havoc added quick yelps to the howls of appreciation that echoed from around the Fenrir lands. It was a cry of altogether another sort that greeted them when they got to the Hill of Lamentations.

"Bloody Christ on the Cross!" Julia Spencer, the Glass Walker who had been in Spearsreach was kicking the frosty autumn ground with her booted foot. "Just great."

Move, Storm-Eye said in a quick wolf bark. She then began readying to call upon the Lunes to grant her access to the moon bridge back across the Arctic to her home. From there, it would be a hard journey to Albrecht in New York, but it was doable. She had barely raised her voice in a howl of supplication to the spirits when the Glass Walker spoke again.

"Don't waste your breath, the bloody bridges are gone." Spencer's smallish face adopted an air—Storm-Eye was at pains to recognize—somewhere between defeat and defiance, with a hint of sarcasm. Humans were frustratingly opaque at times, and this one was made all the more so by the tinted glasses that hid her eyes and the bulky jacket that masked her body language. In fact, she wore a typically incomprehensible array of clothing. What did humans need with layer upon layer of clothing? How could you run or fight with your feet encased in hard rubber and leather?

"What happened?" Cries Havoc slid into Homid form to speak with the Glass Walker.

"You take a look at the Penumbra in that last hour? Not a pretty sight."

"There's a storm of some sort."

"Emphasis on the 'some sort,' horned-and-charming. I've never seen anything like it and it's driving the Lunes mad. The bridges got swallowed up just before I could get to them. So I, like you, am quite stuck." Again, Spencer's words were defeatist but her body language defiant.

"What about Mephi Faster-than-Death?" Storm-Eye spoke in Garou tongue, better suited to questions of the sort. Who knew how well this young Walker would read a wolf.

"Tall, dark and jackal? Carrying off a woman in his arms like a fairy tale? He made it onto the last bridge before the storm rolled in. No idea if he's okay or not." She looked off into the distance and kicked at the ground. "Hope so. But we're all out of luck."

"No." Storm-Eye looked at Cries Havoc. "We will go overland. Over the ice."

"Over the ice." Cries Havoc swallowed. "To Canada."

"You realize there are rat-faced Dancers out there, right?" Spencer butted in. "And there's no pack ice here, so you'd have to make it into Finland, maybe Russia. That's insane. You'd have a better chance standing and fighting with the Get or even facing the storm and the—" She looked around, grappling with an idea. "The two of you are up to a row if need be, right? I mean, you can fight?"

Storm-Eye just looked at her, her posture rigid and her hackles rising. She ignored the pain from her injuries, neither of which were in any rush to heal.

"I'll take that as a yes, then." She took a small black disc out of one of her heavy coat's many pockets. It flipped open to reveal a small mirror. "Let's go, then." And they stepped sideways into hell.

The storm they had seen high above the caern before was now sweeping across the ground like unleashed fury. In the Penumbra, sacred lands like caerns could be grand indeed, and Anvil-Klaiven was no exception. The Hill of Lamentations on which they stood was now a vast mound, with great stone markers indicating the graves of Fenrir heroes. Those graves stood empty, their occupants waiting for the Apocalypse in the afterlife.

Storm-Eye knew she should also see the high rune-walls of Weaverguard's fortress and the fiery glow of the sundered Anvil of Thor that gave the caern its name. Instead, the raging tempest was all she could see. The grave markers disappeared into the roiling mass of clouds and flashing, maddened Lunes before they reached their apex. Everything beyond the hill was embroiled in the storm.

"Hold me down!" Spencer said, her clothing billowing in the Umbral wind. "Hurry!"

Cries Havoc turned to Crinos and grabbed the homid woman with his left arm, the claws of his free arm and feet digging into the ground for purchase. But Storm-Eye knew it wouldn't be enough; the wind seemed determined to loosen these intruders into its domain. She flowed into the war-form as well and grabbed Cries Havoc by the arm. Her other arm found purchase on the nearest grave marker and she held firm with her not-inconsiderable might. Still the wind was strong and getting stronger.

"Thanks!" The Glass Walker, now at least somewhat secure, reached into another of her many pockets and brought out a gray plastic tablet of some sort. Storm-Eye couldn't quite see what she was doing, but she felt Cries Havoc tense at the sight. A flash or light, a spark or ember perhaps, shot up from the tablet.

Storm-Eye, her claws fighting to keep their grip on the stone, nevertheless looked up. The storm blotted everything out. Except, every few moments, the clouds would swirl in such a way as to allow a glimpse of the Umbra above and beyond the caern and the tempest. Once Storm-Eye saw the red star that some said warned of Phoenix's coming and the final battle. Other times she saw the faint shimmering regularity of the Pattern Web, the Weaver's mad entrapment of reality. And that shimmering, or at least a strand of it, seemed to be getting closer.

"Get ready!" Spencer yelled over the increasing howl and took on the Crinos form. She was sleek and thin for a Garou, her fur brown and gray and hidden under some clothing attuned to herself, but the change in size was enough to make Cries Havoc almost lose his grip. "Sorry," she said somewhat sheepishly as she found her own purchase in the ground.

That was when Storm-Eye became aware of the clicking noise and looked up to see a horror of a different nature than any Black Spiral Dancer or Wyrm-wolf. The thing was the size of a large dog, with a bulbous and silvery body. Its spindly legs were articulated gears and made of chrome. Its many eyes were black lenses and its small jaw a drill. From its swollen abdomen came a shimmering thread on which it descended from the sky,

Philippe Boulle

weaving with its hind legs. A Pattern Spider. A Pattern Spider at a caern. It landed before them and gripped the ground like a satisfied crow over a corpse.

Before she could act on her mounting fury, Storm-Eye heard the Glass Walker yelling, "Climb! Quick!" With that she was ascending the Pattern Web and Cries Havoc, the fool, was climbing too. Storm-Eye had no choice but to follow.

The ascent was surprisingly easy at first. Although the web whipped back and forth in the Umbral wind, the worst gusts and the spirits they carried always seemed to miss them. Storm-Eye was no expert on spiritual matters, but it seemed to her that the Wyrm things were avoiding the Pattern Web. That worried her all the more.

Time, like distance, is quite flexible in the Umbra, and Storm-Eye could only say that it had been a long time when they finally cleared the storm. It was not a progressive transition through ever-decreasing densities of cloud, but a sudden emergence, like breaking through the surface of brackish water into clear air. Looking down, Storm-Eye could see the roiling mass of the storm still raging, although it seemed to be miles below now. Looking up, she saw the Umbral sky, complete with the crimson omen-star and the other white points of the firmament. And the Pattern Web, now much clearer but somehow infinitely far away, despite the fact that the thread they were climbing was clearly linked to it.

It was then that the trouble started. First, little crawling things emerged from the web between their fingers, weaving tiny strands that bound them to it. Storm-Eye pulled her hand away instinctively and snapped the threads with a yank.

"Keep moving," the Glass Walker Spencer said. "Don't let them tie you in." Tearing away strands with each handhold, they continued their climb.

"Well, here they come." Spencer pointed ahead of her on the strand, where bulky black shapes were descending toward the Garou. "Looks like quite a bunch of them."

"What are those?" Cries Havoc had a hint of panic in his voice.

"Hunter Spiders. They defend the Pattern Web against threats to its integrity." She looked back with something akin to a smile. "Threats like us."

"We have to leave the Web." The solution seemed simple to Storm-Eye, although she had no idea what leaping blindly into the Umbra would entail. Surely nothing good, but it seemed like a better idea than facing off against more and more Pattern Spiders. "Now."

"Not just yet. If we—"

"Look!" Cries Havoc pointed back down the strand below Storm-Eye, or maybe it was behind her, because gravity seemed not to have much meaning here in the spirit world. She turned, half-hoping it would be more Hunter Spiders, or maybe the raging Wyrm-spirits of the storm coming up to swallow them anew—anything except what she knew it had to be: the Wyrm-wolf, running out of the storm along the thread as if it were a well-worn path. Storm-Eye did her best to steel herself for battle, shifting to a half-stand on the thread, still pulling and flexing on her legs to stop the ever-weaving Pattern spirits from binding her in.

"Well, that's a bit of luck." Spencer ignored the perplexed gazes from her companions and brought out her small tablet again. Storm-Eye could see it was some sort of Weaver-thing, with a glowing screen that displayed images. She used a small stick or pen to activate it while holding it in the palm of the other hand. "That should do it. In three…two…one… *Voilà*."

Suddenly, the Pattern thread on which they were standing went somewhat slack. When Storm-Eye saw the reason, she couldn't help but smile. Behind the Wyrm-wolf, coming up the strand it had just woven and swallowing it up again, was the Pattern Spider Julia had summoned. If the Wyrm-wolf ran like a breeze over hard ground, then the Spider undid its work like a gale-force wind. It closed the distance to the wolf in a few seconds and a bizarre battle ensued. Wisps of black Wyrm-smoke and mad strands of Pattern thread mixed into a knot that boggled the mind.

"That'll take care of the Web at Anvil-Klaiven, but we've still the Hunters to answer to." The Glass Walker snapped some of the threads around her ankles, waved absentmindedly up the thread, then returned to her tablet. "I'll get us out of here, if you'll buy us a bit of time."

The lead Hunter Spider was getting very close indeed. Six of its eight jet-black barbed legs moved along the thread with ease, while the front pair extended forward. Those last ended in shinning blades and claws, snapping open and closed. Storm-Eye scampered past her companions and raced to face the Weaver-thing.

Brother Moose, she called silently, *lend me your strength*. She felt the gun barrel around her biceps tighten, loosen and shift as the spirit inside it woke for the first time in over a year. The fetish crawled down to her forearm and she felt her muscles swell with the spirit's power. For just a second, the sense of wolf and pack faded and she was bull and herd. Surrounded by hundreds of her own kind, she wielded all their strength and power.

Her awareness returned to the task at hand just as one of the Spider's barbed talons was swiping for her. She ducked as best she could on the thread and avoided the first swipe. The other fore-limb came in then, stabbing straight towards her chest. Instead of dodging again, however, she grabbed the limb just behind the blade, stopping it from plunging into her chest. She shifted her weight and felt the power of her fetish flow as she pulled with all its might. With a metallic screeching sound, the limb pulled out of the spider's joint, taking a chunk of the thing's clicking insides with it. Storm-Eye threw the thing off into the Umbra and the Weaver spirit retreated by a few lengths. *Thank you, Brother Moose.*

Of course, the Hunter Spider was a long way from out of commission. Its glowing blue eyes focused on Storm-Eye as another limb unfolded from within it. The Garou readied for another attack, very conscious of the other Spiders coming down the thread behind the leader.

"That's it! Let's go."

Storm-Eye glanced behind her. A thin, shimmering line was arcing from out of the Umbral sky toward them. A moon path. Thank Gaia.

"Jump for it!" yelled Spencer, and they did.

Chapter Six

The silky thread pulled at Storm-Eye's side as the graying Glass Walker pulled the suture through her flesh. His gray hair and salt-and-pepper beard framed a frowning, wrinkled face that spoke of long years of struggle. His green eyes bulged behind magnifying lenses that further distorted his appearance.

Julia Spencer, the young Glass Walker who had got them out of Anvil-Klaiven, appeared at the doorway. "All's well, Geoffrey?"

"So, you invited a Pattern Spider into a Fenrir caern, my Julia?" The old man's focus never wavered from his first-aid work. Spencer leaned against a nearby wall in the converted series of lofts the Old City Sept called home. "You do realize we Garou have laws against such things, don't you? Perhaps you've heard of a trifle we call the Litany?"

Storm-Eye suppressed a comment as the old man moved from the wounds on her side to those on her shoulder. She was lying on an elevated metal table, and felt very much out of place in her wolf-form in what amounted to a modern field hospital.

"You know, Taylor," the young Glass Walker answered, "what you're doing looks a lot like tending another's sickness." The paraphrase of the Litany was well-played, but it brought Storm-Eye's hackles up too, because she was the one allowing it to happen.

"Not the same, dear Julia. Even the Talons and Fenrir make allowances for patching up wounds to carry on the battle." Storm-Eye knew how slight those allowances were, although she felt that fulfilling Jarlsdottir's direct request qualified. The Glass Walker male, who had introduced himself as Geoffrey-with-a-G Taylor, didn't seemed perturbed at all. "There's no excuse for threatening a caern like that. None at all."

"I'm sure you would have done much better as envoy to the concolation, Geoffrey. Is that your point here?"

"My point, Julia," he said and pulled a stitch tight enough to make Storm-Eye flinch, "is that sending a cliath pup to do an adult's job was a mistake. The boss sees that now." He smiled darkly.

"And what makes someone an adult, Geoffrey? Jumping at shadows and licking the boss's arse? That why you're here with us instead of with the rest of your crew in Hastings?"

He dropped the needle and thread altogether. "Listen, little pup! I'm ready to—"

"Enough!" Storm-Eye sat up and stayed in Lupus, barking in the Garou tongue. "Staying at Anvil-Klaiven was threatening the caern because the Wyrm-things were after us. Julia Spencer acted boldly but rightly: The Spider was recalled and the Pattern thread undone. The caern is safer for her action than it was with us stranded there."

"I wonder if the Get will see it that way."

"That is for Jarlsdottir to decide, not you." Storm-Eye stared at Taylor, daring him to challenge her judgment. Spencer and Cries Havoc stayed where they were, the tension of the moment freezing them in place. It went on for several minutes.

Philippe Boulle

"Switch to Homid or Crinos," Taylor finally said, glancing down, "so the sutures heal up. That'll get you where you're going, but those Wyrm wounds aren't mending anytime soon."

She leapt off the table and felt her muscles grow into the dire-wolf form. Skin grew and stitched itself around the sutures and fur pushed through the places where it had been shaved. The pain of the Dancer and Wyrm-wolf's wounds was still there, but lessened somewhat.

"Or Hispo will do, I guess." Taylor turned to his tribemate. "You make really nice friends, dear. Come this way, the boss is waiting." Taylor led them out of the infirmary and onto the mezzanine that overlooked the Glass Walker caern's inner courtyard. The whole place, as far as Storm-Eye could tell, was inside a large building with openings above to allow in what sunlight this city provided. There was some sort of garden in the lower courtyard, although she would never think to call it natural. That was where the moon path had led them and it seemed like there were many other rooms surrounding and overlooking it. Everything was clean and polished, looking something like a valley after a fresh snow, before even the hares have had a chance to lay down tracks. But everywhere were walls and confines. Even the courtyard was hemmed in on all sides by concrete, steel and glass. There was no hiding the Weaver's presence.

They arrived in a clearing at one end of the garden, where several other Garou and some human Kinfolk where gathered. The Kinfolk marked themselves by staring at Storm-Eye, a great dire wolf stalking alongside three humans. They all sat on the lush grass, and had laid out several tablets like Julia's, only larger. These featured keys and buttons that some of the humans tapped at with dizzying speed.

"Welcome to the Old City Sept," said a red-haired woman looking over the shoulder of one of the tablet-users. She spoke in Garou, to the visible consternation of several Kinfolk. "I trust Geoffrey has done his finest stitching, Storm-Eye. I'm Nicola River-Runner, the supposed elder of this motley grouping. You may all wish to come and look at this. We seem to have a guest."

Storm-Eye and the others traipsed over to the group of Kinfolk and looked at the screens on the tablets. She had to force her wolf-eyes to focus on the flat images so that they were clear, ignoring the Glass Walkers prattling on about the glories of "wireless networks," whatever those were. On the Kinfolk operator's tablet was an image of the sad concrete of the city outside. A black vehicle was at a corner.

"That's a block away. The Mercedes has been there for thirty minutes. We just sent a pack out."

***

Mick pressed the CD control keys on his dashboard until he found a nice, mellow beat. That he had never noticed this converted warehouse truly bothered him. Until that scratching, delicious voice inside had led him here, he couldn't remember ever seeing it, and he'd spent many a long night driving around these very unfriendly streets looking for new venues and the occasional playmate.

That just wasn't, well, normal.

A security guard came out of the building and walked toward Mick's car. Interesting. He couldn't see them, but he smelled others moving around the rooftops and lanes. More interesting still.

"Excuse me, sir," the guard said when he got up to the window. He was wearing a light uniform, carrying a policeman's club and a two-way. "Can I help you with anything?"

Mick smiled and breathed in this one's wolf-musk. "Yeah, mate. You work in that block there?"

"What can I do for you, sir?"

"Well, I organize dance evenings and I'm looking for a new space." The best lies were always close to the truth. Mick handed the poor boy a business card. "I was wondering if the space would be to let for a day or two. You know, for a party? I pay well."

"No, nothing for lease, sir." The guard didn't take the card and gave Mick his sternest look. "You might have more luck farther on."

Ooh, frightening. Mick smiled and put the car in gear. "Well, I'm sorry to hear that. I'll try farther on."

Once he had turned the corner and the guard was out of his rearview, he glanced down at the pure blackness that pooled on the car's floor, and at the feral wolf grin within that darkness. "Soon, pet."

***

"Seems clear, over." Little Tim Bolyn, the Child of Gaia who'd been on guard duty that night, sounded frustrated over the radio. "Just a promoter or something."

Storm-Eye glanced at River-Runner and saw a look of concern on the woman's face. She thought she had heard of this woman once or twice, a Fianna warrior who ran with Glass Walkers. Apparently she'd risen to leadership, and without losing her warrior's instincts.

"All right," she said into the communication device, "but let's keep on our toes. Blake, see if you can follow our man for a few blocks just to make sure he doesn't circle around again. Over." She turned to one of the Kinfolk and added, "Mac, be a dear and check his number plates with DVLA, will you?"

The assemblage broke into more activity, and Nicola River-Runner rose from her crouched position on the grass. "Go on to your offices, everyone, I'll brief our guests."

As the various Garou and Kinfolk headed for rooms overlooking the garden, River-Runner summoned the two newcomers and Julia to her side. "How were things at Anvil-Klaiven when you left, Storm-Eye? Julia's told me some of it."

Storm-Eye, still in her massive Hispo form, sat near the sept leader. She showed proper deference, but no submission. This sept stank too much of Wyrm and Weaver for a Red Talon to be comfortable. She used wolf-speak, perhaps to test this homid. *Not good, but the Fenrir fight well. The caern holds but the battle is fierce.*

"That's the news we're getting from the Sept of the Night Sky, as well. The Margrave and Jarlsdottir seem to have kicked the Wyrm where it hurts, for it to lash out like this." Apparently wolf words were no problem to understand, although the Fianna continued in Garou herself.

"And the Sept of the Dawn?" Cries Havoc's voice croaked somewhat when he mentioned his birth sept.

"I've been in contact with Dawntreader, and we're readying a response. He sends his best."

The things may be baiting you, added Storm-Eye. *Weakening the defenses of other caerns so they too can be attacked.*

River-Runner smiled. "You've the makings of a leader, Talon. That's why it's taking time to strike back. If we try to open moon bridges, we may just get a face full of Banes for our trouble. Thankfully, the Wyrm has picked some well-defended caerns to lash out at."

We must get to the Stargazer Teardrop. In Albrecht's lands.

"So Julia told me earlier. But I don't think travel by moon bridge is terribly wise. Until we understand this storm phenomenon a little more, Dawntreader and I think it's best to limit bridge use. Crossing the pond doesn't strike me as being very cautious."

But we must get there.

"I agree, and I think Julia is just about ready with an alternate route."

Storm-Eye hadn't paid much attention to Spencer moving to one of the larger tablets and tapping its keys as River-Runner and she spoke. Now, the Glass Walker looked up with a satisfied grin. "Three tickets on the Concorde. Heathrow to JFK in under four hours."

Chapter Seven

The wolf pack was moving south when Storm-Eye found them again. They stretched out in a line following the scent trail of a moose through the spring snow. The yearlings bringing up the rear heard her approach and looked up excitedly, barking their recognition for their elders to hear. Long-Runner and Hare-Jumper turned and brought the pack together then. What had been a sleek line of hunters became a rolling little ball of excited pups and more cautious adults.

Storm-Eye kept her firm gaze and solid stride as two yearlings ran to her and licked her maw, hoping for regurgitated food. She finally shook them away when she saw Hare-Jumper still, his tail high in a dominant stance.

Fights-the-Bear is gone, Storm-Eye proclaimed in a few movements and fewer sounds. *He has killed one of our enemies and we will sing for him.*

She raised her head to the darkening sky and let out a great mournful howl, a howl she knew as the Dirge for the Fallen. It praised those who died for Gaia, sending their names to be carried by the spirits of the wind and the stars and remembered forever. Although Gaia was always listening, songs sung with genuine heart and by the whole pack were best remembered. Storm-Eye quickly realized she sang alone.

The yearlings paced back and forth, caught in a cage of their own anxiety. Some were tense, hackles raised but tongues hanging, saying *This is wrong* with every ounce of their beings. Others seemed to submit to nothing at all, lying prone on the ground, whining quietly.

You say Fights-the-Bear killed a rival, said Hare-Jumper in a quiet growl, *but we heard man-killer shots and man-screams. I don't understand.*

Storm-Eye walked slowly toward Hare-Jumper, the wolf who she felt would become her alpha male, fighting back frustration. *No,* she yipped, *not a rival wolf. He killed a man.*

It was as if she had dealt a blow to the large gray wolf, he recoiled so violently. *Why did the man attack Fights-the-Bear?* His question, given through quick pacing and mounting anxiety, only augmented the younger wolves' own tension.

He didn't, Storm-Eye barked back. *We hunted the wolf-killer man and we killed him.*

Hare-Jumper's head dipped low and his lips curled back. His hackles rose to their full heights and an angry, dangerous growl came from somewhere deep inside him. *This is wrong. Leave.*

No. Storm-Eye's answer was simple and loud, her form swelling to the bulky Hispo that could flatten the entire pack. Rage bubbled within her. *This is my pack and you are my mate.*

You are a skin-changer, Storm-Eye Kills-the-Man. We are not. It was Long-Runner, the eldest female save for Storm-Eye herself. *Your ways are not ours. You do not belong with us.*

I am alpha! Storm-Eye growled, her four hundred pounds of muscle and anger tearing to get free. *Submit!*

No, Hare-Jumper and Long-Runner answered together. They both stood strong, ready to fight, ready to die. Storm-Eye could easily kill them both. It would take only the release of her burning rage and the terrible Crinos form would overtake her. No two wolves could stand against an enraged Garou. It would be so easy....

Storm-Eye turned and ran, heading north. She did not look back.

Chapter Eight

Ever since they'd been at Heathrow, Storm-Eye had been struggling not to scream. Bad enough she had had to assume her Homid form, weak and deaf and with the nose of a newborn pup, but now she was about to board some Weaver-made contraption that would take them across the ocean.

She swallowed and her throat was desert-dry. She tried to push the panic down a notch, telling herself she had known of these airplanes for years. She had seen them pierce the sub-arctic sky. She had even come close to several with her pack. Her kind considered her a scholar of humankind, after all.

But to actually get into this oversized metal arrowhead! Every instinct in her body, furless and encased in too-tight homid clothes, raged against this. It was folly!

"This..." she began, and cursed herself for the hundredth time for using the Garou tongue. A bloated human woman, fatter than any cow Storm-Eye could remember seeing, gaped at her, hearing only an animal grunt in her speech. Storm-Eye paused and resumed in whispered English. "This is a bad idea."

"There's no other choice," Cries Havoc answered quietly. He was wearing a woolen cap that did a passable job of hiding his horns. Hopefully the same spirits Julia had summoned to get Storm-Eye's twisted metal fetish past the humans unseen would also help with his disfigurement. The two of them were sitting in a corner of the British Airways waiting room for Concorde passengers, while

Julia got one last errand done in something called the Laptop Lounge.

"If we wish to get to America," the Gaian continued, "this is the fastest way."

"It's wrong. Reliance on the Weaver is wrong."

"Julia knows what she is doing. You said so yourself to that foolish Geoffrey." He sipped from the bottled water he had ordered from the waitress before Julia left.

"That fool was goading her for position, but he had a point. Summoning a spider like that was a great risk. Taking so many risks can only lead to eventual disaster."

Julia slipped into the third seat at the tiny round table they occupied. "You two might want to keep your voices down, I think you're scaring our fellow travelers." She nodded to their left, where a human boy was staring straight at them. Julia resumed in a low whisper, "I do have some good news, though. I checked my e-mail and it seems like an American friend of mine is in New York on business. She's agreed to give us some help once we land. Our seats are all taken care of and we should be ready to board any minute now."

***

When the British Airways man's voice came over the intercom announcing boarding of the Concorde for New York, Mick glanced at his watch. Good old BA, right on time. He dropped his perfectly folded copy of *The Times* into a fancy trash bin, and went to the line.

The three of them were only a dozen or so passengers ahead, looking very much like fish out of water to his eyes. He could feel his briefcase wriggle slightly, and whispered a quiet "Easy, pet," to keep it in check.

To think he had felt blessed before. This went so much further than the simple change and blood and strength. Now he had an agenda. Direction. A plan.

First, he and his new pet would take care of the three little cubs ahead. Then he would bring their skins to the Lady. The same Lady whom he had only ever seen on the night of his First Change, but who now called him to America. And then, then it would be the day of Jo'cllath'mattric.

He smiled easily as he handed his boarding pass to the attendant. She looked delicious, but he was so excited he wasn't even hungry.

Yet.

***

Storm-Eye—or "Rebecca Sterling" according to the US passport Julia had produced thanks to her spirit allies—had had enough. The cold mechanical humming of the plane's engines. The endless comments from others about going faster than sound. The panoply of pointless entertainments on the small screens everyone seemed to be unfolding from their chairs. The huge quantity of alcohol everyone else on the plane seemed determined to imbibe.

She had miraculously been able to sleep at one point as the exhaustion of the last few days crashed in around her. But that had only led to dreams of being carried away along a great river, over falls and towards rocks that looked and smelled like the maw of a great black wolf. She had woken up near panic and Julia had had to talk her down from changing forms and tearing this Weaver thing to pieces. She could still taste the fury in her mouth.

Now they had finally landed—and what a joy that had been—and were out of the Gaia-forsaken thing, but things had gone from bad to worse. John F. Kennedy Airport seemed designed explicitly to enrage Storm-Eye. Everywhere she turned were crowds of humans milling to and fro, evenly divided between those who were utterly lost and those who pushed through them like bull moose charging through brush. Everywhere people yelled, children screamed, and droning, incomprehensible, mechanical voices mumbled from somewhere above. If ever there was a herd that needed to be culled, this was it. And to top it all off, Storm-Eye's ears were killing her.

"Deep breaths, Rebecca," Julia put in. "We're almost out of here."

'Almost' meant another half-hour pushing through human sheep, putting up with a pathetic little beagle sniffing their luggage, and fighting to get a dingy yellow vehicle to take them away. From there, it was a sea of other vehicles and concrete troughs toward concrete canyons, then through another press of bleating, stinking humanity and into a dingy train that clacked its way farther into the urban blight, sometimes on elevated platforms, sometimes in long dark tunnels.

Storm-Eye's borrowed clothing was soaked with sweat—another human weakness—by the time they disembarked and headed into the underground station. Although it stank of rot and rust, and light was hard to come by, at least there weren't many humans here. Storm-Eye finally took off the ridiculous dark glasses Julia had insisted she wear to cover up her unseeing left eye. If she needed any more proof that humanity was basically a species of parasitic sheep, then their practice of covering wounds of battle was it.

"Nice shiner, *chica*." The speaker was a woman, or at least a girl, dressed in baggy pants, an oversized shirt and a further oversized green coat. What appeared to be long black hair was incompletely tucked into a brimmed cap an odd shade of orange with a caricature of some sort on it. She was sitting on the only still-functional bench in this train station, some chunk of processed food in her hand. She extended the foodstuff toward Storm-Eye. "Snickers?"

Storm-Eye suppressed an urge to flow into Lupus right then and there. Instead she sniffed the air deeply. Even with the nearly useless nose of her Homid form, she drank in this woman's scent: Garou.

"Carlita?" Julia lowered her own sunglasses so that she could peer over them.

"That's bigsis745 at planet-dot-net, to you." She popped the rest of the chocolate bar into her mouth, chewed it vigorously and swallowed with an audible gulp. "Yummy. I take it these sourpusses are the buddies you told me about?"

Julia glanced around the empty corridor of the empty station. "Carlita, Bone Gnawer of Tampa,

Florida, may I present Cries Havoc, Child of Gaia of the Sept of the Anvil-Klaiven, and Storm-Eye, Red Talon of the Sky Pines Sept."

"Jeez, you sound like a Fang or something." The Bone Gnawer reached into one of the large pockets of her drab green coat and came out with some more candy. She unwrapped a small piece, and threw it up in the air. It landed in her open mouth with a pop. "Just call me Big Sis, 'kay?"

Julia seemed a little stunned and took a minute to respond. "Right, Big Sis. Regardless, thanks much for lending us a hand. I'm glad you happened to be in New York."

"Happened is right. I've got more n' enough crap to deal with in Florida. If it wasn't that some fool back in Tampa got hisself on the wrong side of a river spirit and couldn't make the trip up, I never woulda been on my way." She threw her arms up and Storm-Eye noticed a large, rough dagger hanging from her waistband. "Whatcha gonna do?"

Storm-Eye took a deep whiff of the air, more out of habit than anything, and the small hairs on the back of her Homid neck stood at attention. The dark, familiar stench registered, and the skin on her shoulders and arms puckered into gooseflesh. She went with it, and reddish-brown fur pushed through the pimples. Her legs and arms stretched and she took on first pounds then hundreds of pounds of muscle and fury. Her clothes, never attuned to her form, strained and tore, going from ready-to-wear to rags in a second as she shifted to Crinos. Her senses finally flooded back, if not to their lupine heights then at least to something more than the deaf stupidity of humanity. The stink was clear and strong. "Wyrm."

"My clothes..." Julia said, staring at the shreds on the subway station's dingy floor.

"Wyrm!" Storm-Eye repeated between clenched jaws. An order. The other Garou finally got it and they all assumed their war-forms, crouching against the low ceiling. The cramped spaces didn't seem to bother Carlita. All dingy-brown fur, coiled muscles and bared fangs, she hunkered down and drew her large fang dagger. They all tried to find the source of the stink.

"There!" Cries Havoc launched forward after a slick shadow. The metis ran toward the subway platform from which they had come, rounding the corner after the shadow. He howled with rage and battle.

Storm-Eye knew it was a trap even before he was out of sight. She turned onto the platform just in time to see him rake his claws at the Wyrm-wolf they had last seen near Anvil-Klaiven. Its sight sent chills through her, enough that the warning she barked came too late.

Cries Havoc's claws sank into the shadow before he could react, connecting with nothing but the tile and concrete of the platform. "What? Damn!" Then, with only the faintest jingling, a length of chain sailed from another passage and wrapped itself around the young Gaian's neck. Storm-Eye could see the hooks and barbs on the chain's length bite into Cries Havoc's pale gray pelt. But she could do nothing but let out a quick howl, because the great black wolf re-formed then and was on her.

The Wyrm-beast was all too solid when it hit Storm-Eye, slamming into her with the weight and power of a bear. The impact sent them both careening off the platform and onto the rails. She used the momentum to push the wolf-thing off her and quickly tried to gain a sense of this new battleground. Water running from a rusted pipe caught her attention and she saw just beneath it a diamond-shaped sign with a lightning bolt on it. Storm-Eye realized it meant one of the rails was dangerous, electrified. Thank Gaia, she hadn't fallen on that!

The Wyrm-wolf moved closer step by step and Storm-Eye returned her full attention to it. It was treating her like a moose or other prey animal, she realized, slowly closing the distance between them, hoping to make her run and expose a vulnerable flank or rump. The key was not to run; the wolf would stop just before it got within striking distance of its prey's defenses. So Storm-Eye waited, letting it get closer and closer, waiting for the right moment.

Now. Just when the Wyrm-wolf took another step, she leapt. The ceiling of the trench was high enough for her to get a good jump and she came smashing down on the thing. *Garou are not prey!* she howled as she fell on her enemy. Her claws bit deep into the black, cold mass of the thing. She felt, more than heard, it scream. But then it was flowing like mist around her again, and before she could move it had re-formed behind her. It clawed and scampered up her back, just as if she *had* fled, and took a good bite hold.

Storm-Eye felt the bite's sting, but knew it would get far worse if the wolf-thing got the change to pull and shake and tear at her flesh. She tried to back against the side of the trench, but it held firm. It squirmed just outside of her reach when she tried to pull it off as she had during their first battle. Out of options, Storm-Eye pivoted on one great Crinos leg and fell, back-first, onto the rails.

The current running through the third rail struck the wolf-thing first and it emitted a terrible screech, along with the smell of burning tar. A few seconds of that and the thing broke apart into a smoky mass of ash and stink. Storm-Eye rolled to avoid the rail herself, with only limited success. But a few burns and shakes were well worth having hurt that damnable thing—and hurt it she had, she was sure. She tensed for a moment waiting for it to return but it didn't. *Licking its wounds*, she thought. It would be too much to ask for it to be dead.

But driving the thing off had taken time, more than enough time for others to have fallen as well. She leapt out of the trench and ran to the second passage. And stopped.

Cries Havoc was hanging from a long chain dangling from the stairwell at the end of the corridor, his neck and one squirming arm tangled in the black, barbed links. He held the chain itself with his free hand, desperately trying to release the pressure on his windpipe. Storm-Eye ran to help him and looked up the stairwell to see what was at the other end of the chain. There, some forty feet above her, a black

Garou in Crinos form was perched on a railing, pulling Cries Havoc up. The werewolf's fur was an oily, too-perfect black, and its ears were long and pointed.

"Oh, wonderful," purred the Black Spiral Dancer in accented English. "More playmates."

Chapter Nine

Storm-Eye's rage carried her far on the first cold spring night after she left the wolf pack. Flitting between the sleek quickness of her natural wolf-form and the terrifying power of the Hispo dire wolf, she followed scent trails between pack territories.

This was how lone wolves survived, she knew, stalking the borderlands between established packs. Unlike most loners, she could defeat a whole wolf pack in combat, but she didn't want that blood on her hands. No, the borderlands also hid the paths taken by her other kin—the changing skins, the Garou—to get to their holy site. The Caern of the Sky Pines was neither large nor elaborate as these things went, but few things associated with the Red Talon tribe were. In the crook of a river still covered in ice rose a clutch of pine trees far taller than any others this far north. They rose so high that they touched the sky, the Galliards sang, and the moon-seers confirmed that the wind and star spirits favored these great trees. Harm to them would be a great offense, and so the Garou guarded them well.

In the shades of these great evergreens, the Red Talons of the Sky Pines Sept held their moots and honored their totems. For six winters after her change, this had been Storm-Eye's home. Here she had learned the ways of the changing skin, the Litany and traditions of the tribes of Luna. She had watched in rapt attention as Scents-the-Truth had condemned the traitor Wyrm-Rutter, trying to learn everything she could from the aging elder who shared her moon sign: Philodox, the judge.

When the trees came into view over the horizon and Storm-Eye caught the scent mark that so clearly announced *This is Garou land*, she tried to think most of that moment. She failed, and her mind went to a time three winters later. She and the rest of the Summer's Sun pack had stood against Wyrm-Rutter when he returned with his damnable Black Spiral kin. There had been many monstrosities that day—bloated Wyrm-boars that spat maggots and blood, the twisting Bane that the traitor kept as a pet—but the Black Spirals were the worst. Garou who had surrendered to the great devourer, who had become that they were born to fight.

The battle had been terrible that summer's night, and the losses had been great. Wyrm-Rutter and the others had withdrawn with a great deal of Garou blood on their hands, but the caern stood firm. That this supposed victory, which had cost Storm-Eye so much, still earned her much glory had never been much consolation.

She missed them still.

She realized she had stopped running, standing within the scent-laden buffer zone between the sept's territory proper and that of the various Kinfolk wolf packs that surrounded it. There, with the marks of various Garou and wolves wafting through the still morning air, she had been lost in remembrance. But it was not her own deed she was here to mark. She tilted her head back and began to howl. *Storm-Eye once called Judge-of-the-Trees comes to the Sky Pines*, she called. *I carry the story of a hero of Gaia to be sung to spirits and Garou alike. Who guards this caern?*

We do, the answer came, first in one voice, then in a lupine chorus, *the Pack of the Brightest Star defends this place against Wyrm and Weaver.*

We do, came a second melody of howls, *the Pack of Six Winters also tends the trees of the sky spirits and keeps them from harm.*

Storm-Eye ran along the river bank toward the river and the tall pines near it, and soon enough several wolves were coming down to greet her. The first was the apply named Talon cliath Fast-as-the-Gale who jumped at her playfully, showing off his status as a full Garou adult without actually challenging Storm-Eye's status. Others soon joined him, including the Wendigo Philodox Listens-to-the-Night and the Talon Theurge Speaks-for-the-Trees. Notable in his absence was the Pack of Six Winters' eldest, the Galliard Heard-by-Gaia, also the sept's most senior lore-keeper.

For the next half-hour, Storm-Eye frolicked with the other lupus Garou, running about the bawn and spilling over each other in mock battles like pups establishing rank. It all very wolf-like, save that as Garou she was clearly welcome on this territory. A lone wolf entering another wolf pack's territory could expect an altogether more deadly reception, she well knew. Even those descended from homid stock were welcome at the caern so long as they integrated with their lupus cousins—Storm-Eye happily remembered the proud Uktena Ahroun who had been unable to play on all fours and stormed off in a huff.

The sun rose high in the sky as the werewolves reintroduced themselves, but eventually they got down to business. In the process of establishing that she still ranked high, though not highest among the Garou of Sky Pines, Storm-Eye confirmed that Heard-by-Gaia was absent from the caern. She had heard no dirge sung for the great moon howler, so doubted he had fallen in battle. She, of all the Talons of Sky Pines, would have felt his passing.

Heard-by-Gaia is away, said Speaks-for-the-Trees. *He has gone to visit the caern at Caribou Crossing.* That holy site, guarded by Red Talons and several Uktena, was many days travel further north. It was a holy place but said to have a dark past, hence the presence of a pack of Uktena Bane Tenders.

Why? This is a long journey for a great singer to take.

Heard-by-Gaia was told by the wind of a great concolation to be held in a far-off land. If it bothered Speaks-with-the-Trees that the spirits had chosen the Galliard to whisper to, she showed it not at all. *Some have said envoys should be sent and Heard-by-Gaia traveled to carry our words on the idea. We are to stand vigil at the caern until his return.*

And why, the Theurge asked at last, *have you come here?*

Part of Storm-Eye realized just how harsh the words might sound to human ears—no pretense of politeness, no false servility, just a straight question. Such was the way of wolves and such it should be for Garou. *I come to have the Dirge for the Fallen sung for my packmate Fights-the-Bear. And to have the Rite of the Last Cub howled for me.*

Listens-to-the-Night, the large white and gray Philodox who had succeeded Scents-the-Truth as the caern's main judge spoke next. *Fights-the-Bear was wolf, not Garou.* No question, just a statement. *How did he die?*

Fighting the Wyrm, Storm-Eye said in a proud howl and prouder stance. *We hunted a wolf-killer and he died killing the man.*

Wolf killed man? Speaks-for-the-Trees asked with an anxious yip, the lupus way of expressing surprise. *How? Why?*

Storm-Eye was conscious of Listens-to-the-Night looking at her, her black-tipped tail high and her paws square. No teeth were bared or hackles raised, but they didn't have to be. This was a look of judgment. She wanted to answer "Because he wanted to," but the language of wolves does not lend itself to half-truths and hidden facts. It is a language of small movements, excreted scents, rhythmic breathing and occasional barks, of eyes slightly averted. *Because I told him to*, she said.

Other Garou approached, filling the long silence that followed with their predatory shapes. Tensions rose and young werewolves paced nervously in unknowing imitation of the wolf pack's reaction to the same news.

Wolves don't kill men, Listens-to-the-Night proclaimed in a quick bark. *We do. That is one of Gaia's orders.*

The man deserved to die. He was a wolf-killer. Storm-Eye's answers came with her own raised hackles and defiant growls.

They why didn't you kill him, Two-World-Daughter? That Speaks-for-the-Trees used Storm-Eye's wisdom name, one that related the story that her damaged eye now looked inward to see the deep Umbra and in it the truth, meant the Theurge was giving her a chance.

"He deserved the glory of a warrior's death." Although she wanted to speak in the language of wolves, many of the ideas found expression only the Garou tongue. Wolves had no way to say *glory* or *warrior*, she realized. "He was alpha," she continued, stepping forward and finding the wolf-way to express her idea. *His duty it was to defend the pack's territory.*

Listens-to-the-Night did not move for several long minutes, her iron gaze boring into Storm-Eye in silent reproach. Then she turned her back and yipped, in effect saying, *This is not our way.* Such words, coming from the caern's highest judge, were no mere reproach. They were a condemnation, and the rest of the assembled Garou soon understood this.

Oh spirits, began Speaks-for-the-Trees' howl, *hear the tale of Storm-Eye Wiser-than-Gaia.* What might have been mistaken for an honorific by some cub was clearly a reproach to the assembled Garou: Only fools thought themselves wiser than Mother Gaia. The rest of the werewolves were soon howling in chorus with the elder Theurge, sending Storm-Eye's shame into the wind. *She who is blind in two worlds*, they called her. And worse still: *She who makes men of wolves*. If there was a worse condemnation for a Red Talon Philodox, Storm-Eye could not think of one.

Rage mounting in her, she took off north, aware that spirits of wind and moonlight carried her infamy far faster than she could ever run.

Chapter Ten

The spiked chain bit into Cries Havoc's neck and he let out a throaty gurgle. Crimson spittle stained the pale fur on his cheek. The Black Spiral Dancer, for his part, prattled on.

"Do you like being strung up? Fancy life without air or hope?" The thing smiled wickedly and gave the chain another yank. "I didn't think so. But that's what your kind did to him, you know. For longer than you can even conceive of, he's been like this, screaming."

Storm-Eye let him carry on, barely paying attention to the words, and moved a yard to the left. She tensed her legs and made ready to leap up, but then her enemy shifted, swinging Cries Havoc in front of her to block her leap.

"Ah, ah, ah, no jumping." The Dancer's grin stretched farther than it had any right to, series upon series of needle-like teeth shimmering in the sallow light of recessed neon. He swayed his dangling prey back and forth, pinning Storm-Eye in a corner of the stairwell. "I think you'll just watch your little friend here, just like we've watched ours for so long."

She stared right at him, making sure he was focussed on her, and began to howl. The call was a series of barks and cries, punctuated by a quick refrain drawn from the Garou Anthem of War. She just hoped the cliath Gaia had saddled her with were paying attention.

"Cry to the moon as much as you want, there's no help for your kind here."

Storm-Eye kept her gaze fixed and thanked the Incarna the Dancer seemed not to understand the details of her call. That, and for the swirls and shimmers that appeared in the air right above the Wyrm-traitor.

Carlita leapt out of the Umbra and was on the Black Spiral Dancer with a hooting Bone Gnawer war cry. Her fang dagger bit into the thing's slick fur and flesh, and it screamed. "Yeah!" Carlita howled.

The Dancer let go of the chain, and Cries Havoc came tumbling down to the ground. The tension around him finally loose, his war-form shrank to that of a thin wolf and he slipped his bonds, leaving chunks of hairy flesh on the barbs. He skipped across the tiles and was back in Crinos by the time he bounded up the stairs toward his tormentor. Storm-Eye took the more direct route, her powerful legs carrying her forty feet straight up in great leap. She landed on the very guard-rail on which the Dancer had been perched a few seconds before.

Carlita's first swipe with her dagger had bitten deeply into the Dancer's mid-section and she was trying to get a second blow to finish him off. But it wouldn't be that easy. His left arm was clenched around his wounded gut and he was backing down the hall at the top of the stairwell, but Carlita couldn't land a killing blow. He moved to and fro, dodging her blows and swiping out with the long, polished claws of his right hand. Like his teeth, they were needle-sharp and seemed to be made of steel. Carlita already had several long gashes on her left arm, but she wouldn't back down.

Storm-Eye looked to the stairs where Cries Havoc was just arriving and barked a command. They both shrank into sleek Lupus forms and headed down the corridor. Although any commuter unlucky enough to have come face-to-snout with them might not have thought so, the two wolves were small compared to the hulking Crinos battling it out down the corridor. Storm-Eye yipped again, broke into a run, and slipped to Carlita's left, while Cries Havoc took the right. One more second and they'd be past the combatants and could get to the Dancer's vulnerable back.

But Carlita, anxious to avoid a swipe from the Dancer's talons, took an ill-advised step to her right. Her muscled Crinos leg slammed right into Cries Havoc and the metis, already wounded, let out a loud yelp. The combination of tripping over the Gaian and his cry distracted Carlita, and she looked down at her leg instead of keeping her eyes on her opponent.

The Black Spiral Dancer opened up his maw and vomited forth a greenish, buzzing cloud of stinging insects. The swarm quickly enveloped Carlita and Cries Havoc who tried desperately, futilely, to shake the bugs away. Storm-Eye's chance to get at the Dancer's back was gone, unless she was willing to give him a clear shot at the young Garou he had just blinded. She shrugged on the extra mass of the Hispo dire-wolf form and leapt right at him.

He saw her coming and brought his right arm up to stop her. The quarters were too cramped to bring his talons to bear, but he was able to push on her bulging chest. For a second, her momentum kept her hanging there, pressing on his arm, just out of reach of her prey. Their maws snapped impotently at each other and then he pushed her away, against the wall. Carlita and Cries Havoc were clear of the bugs then and so he darted down the corridor, turning the first corner.

The three Garou gave chase, but the dingy corridor was empty when they got there. A rusted iron grate that clearly hadn't been opened since before the Impergium blocked further progress. Storm-Eye looked around quickly. Her own reflection stared back at her in the cracked Plexiglas covering of a dingy subway map. *The Umbra*, she barked, and stepped sideways.

The Penumbral double of the abandoned subway station was so dingy and gray that it reminded Storm-Eye of nothing more than the tales Mephi Faster-than-Death had told her of the dark land of ghosts. The walls, already dirty in the physical world, were covered in a thick layer of ephemeral ash and mold. Huge albino cockroach spirits crawled through the slime that coated the floor and dripped from the corroded Pattern Webs that laced the ceiling. The iron grate was nothing more than a thin curtain of rusted chains here, a barrier to nothing. From the corridor beyond it, Storm-Eye could see flashes of colored light, and in those flashes, the silhouette of the Dancer. She gave chase.

She arrived in the next chamber just behind the Dancer and could hear Carlita stepping sideways somewhere behind her. The Glass Walker Julia Spencer, in her sleek brown and black Crinos form, was floating cross-legged just above the Umbral ground in some sort of trance. The Wyrm-wolf was there too, but caught in a tight mass of bright, glowing Pattern Webs. More and more Weaver Spiders, each about the size of a rabbit, were appearing near Julia, each emitting a brightly colored flash as it did. They would then spin another Pattern strand, further imprisoning the Wyrm-wolf. The Dancer never broke stride. He crouched low, dragging his deadly talons just above the ground, and ran straight for Julia.

Storm-Eye let out a loud bark of warning, breaking Julia's concentration in time to save her life. The Glass Walker fell to the ground and turned toward the oncoming Dancer. Her survival instincts were thankfully strong, and she ducked quickly, raising her left arm to shield her gut and face.

The Dancer quickly changed targets—or perhaps going for Julia had been a feint all along. Either way, he sailed over the young Theurge and, with a terrible swipe, cut away most of the thin Pattern threads imprisoning the Wyrm-wolf. Without Julia egging them on, the small Pattern Spiders seemed in no rush to continue their weaving, and with a shrug the wolf-thing was free.

The two Wyrm-kin turned toward the Garou. Storm-Eye, Julia and Carlita all stood in Crinos form, teeth bared and talons extended. Carlita held her fang dagger at the ready. The Dancer took a step back toward the dingy wall and the wolf kept close to his legs. Storm-Eye tensed to strike, but was robbed of her chance. With the wet sound of flesh tearing, a great toothed maw opened in the wall behind the Dancer. It gaped wide for a second, its fangs dripping green slime, and then extended to swallow the Wyrm-kin. Its gulp was loud and deep and spoke of hungry beasts large as cities. When the mouth closed, it sealed into a raw wound where the wall had been, seeping yellow pus.

"A Wyrm-hole." Julia faced the great Umbral blister, and closed her eyes in concentration. In a second, the various Pattern Spiders were weaving a tight web over the hole. She opened her eyes and they continued unheeding. Apparently they needed no direction to seal up so blatant a Wyrm-gash in their domain, just to be told it was there.

"Right. No coming back that way." Julia turned to face her companions. "But that Dancer is long gone."

A moment later, the three Garou had headed back down the corridor and stepped sideways to rejoin Cries Havoc in the physical world. The metis was in his natural Crinos form, sitting against the wall near the stairwell. Nasty bruises, cuts and slashes from the barbed chain-fetish marred his fur and flesh. His neck was raw and bleeding. Carlita knelt by the Gaian, bravado giving in to concern, pain and fatigue. Her own left arm bore long gashes from the Dancer's talons. Julia, for her part, seemed unwounded, but as she flowed back into Homid form, Storm-Eye could see she was pale as a sheet, and smell the sheen of cold sweat that bubbled to the surface of her skin. Summoning and commanding so many spirits had taken its toll. She too slumped to the ground. Storm-Eye herself could still feel the wounds in her back and side from her first confrontation with the wolf-thing. It was a marvel, she thought, that none of them had died yet.

"What can I say?" said Cries Havoc in between wet coughs. "We kicked its ass!" He was smiling broadly, his deep hazel eyes shinning with a fire that wiped away all the blood and pain.

Soon the abandoned subway station was resounding with the four-part harmony of a great Garou victory howl.

***

Mick walked down the alley with a noticeable limp and a dark grin on his face. It appeared that these nature freaks really had some fight left in them. They didn't realize just how hopeless their cause was, he supposed. Jo'cllath'mattric was coming and no little gnats were going to stop him.

Still, they could make things more difficult. Less perfect. And the Lady demanded perfection.

He reached down to the belt of his Gucci trousers and noticed that his own blood was seeping through his burgundy shirt. A shame to ruin Yves Saint-Laurent silk like that. That little Bone Gnawer runt would have to pay for that someday. Perhaps he'd stick that repugnant fang dagger up her—

Now, now. No need to be crude, Mick chastised himself. *Back to the task at hand*.

He got out his little Nokia phone and punched in a long series of numbers. Just as it began to ring, he squeezed with all the might the Lady had given him. The phone cracked, sparked and crumbled as the little spirit trapped within it died a pitiful, but usefully loud, death. They'd be here soon.

He headed farther down the alley, noticing piles of newspapers and rags that could be humans, trash, or both. The ladder from the bottom of the fire-escape was already lowered when he got to it and he began to climb. On the third landing he paused to breathe in the stale air hanging between the tenements and the old factory behind them. *Delicious, almost as good as London.* On the last landing before the room, he kicked an errant cat over the edge and heard it hit the pavement with a satisfyingly moist thud. He was smiling when he climbed the last rungs and emerged onto the tar-covered rooftop.

"Come on out, all of you."

And they did, four of them. Mick characteristically noticed the women first. One was tall, wasp-waisted and raven-haired. She wore tight, constricting leather and a corset with iron clasps. She smelled of sex and rotten earth and called herself Mistress Gash. He hated her immediately, condemning her because of her pathetic attempts to mimic the Lady.

The other woman was distinctly more promising. Petite, she wore torn jeans, steel-tipped combat boots and a gray sweatshirt with "Property of SUNY Athletics" stenciled on it. Her face was puckered with white burn marks that contrasted with her mahogany skin and gave it a tastefully waxen quality. She was called Naz. Mick made her his second.

The man was more obviously touched by the Bane within him. He was tall, thin and sallow. Ridges of bone pushed against his flesh in a pattern distinctly reminiscent of the great spiral that the Lady had so lovingly shown Mick years ago. His hair, shockingly white, stuck up at odd angles and served as a halo for his face, which had but one feature: a great round maw like that of a lamprey. A red tongue moved about in that maw, licking up every scent in the air. He was called Eel.

And then there was the dog. Seemingly the product of generations of inbred mastiffs, it weighed over two hundred pounds and had a large, flat face. Its massive jaws were clearly visible through translucent skin. The rest of its body was covered, not with hair or fur, but with a roiling mass of white maggots. Clumps of them fell onto the black rooftop as it trotted, but more apparently grew from the dog's own body because no bare skin became exposed. That would be Boy.

Yes, these would most definitely do. "Thank you, my Lady," Mick whispered to the fouled air. "We serve you, and through you, Jo'cllath'mattric, and through him, Father Wyrm."

He was about to lead his new pack off when Eel caught a whiff of something. His tongue whipped back and forth and he emitted a beautiful cacophony of screeches. They weren't alone.

"Whaddahell?" The old derelict popped up from behind the pilings of the water tower nesting on the rooftop. Drugs, alcohol, inhaled chemical fumes, or a combination thereof, had long ago fried much of his reasoning, but he still knew enough to turn tail and run. The fomori all looked at Mick for guidance, who gave a little smile.

"Fetch, Boy."

Chapter Eleven

The holy site the Red Talons called Caribou Crossing was a good two weeks' travel north of Sky Pines. To get there, a lone wolf like Storm-Eye had to travel through the territories of a dozen or more packs, skirting them all if she wanted to avoid any contact. The spirits who carried word of her dishonor traveled far faster than she, of course, but still she ran with all her might. The Sept of Caribou Crossing would hear her tale from her own howls, not the reported reprimand of those who condemned her. And Heard-by-Gaia would listen—greatest of the Talon Galliards of the region, his call would restore her renown and carry strong and true.

But first she had to get to the caern, and the humans ahead of her were not making life any easier. She had caught scent of them a few hours ago when the wind shifted with the setting sun. Soon enough, she heard the growl of their vehicle, cutting through the territory of wolf and game with typical hubris.

Maybe she should leave them be. Maybe she should turn slightly east—take an extra day to get to Caribou Crossing and avoid any trouble. Maybe that was what Listens-to-the-Night would prefer. Instead she followed, and stalked, and closed in. And Gaia was on her side, she was sure. Why else would the tire of their damnable machine have burst as she followed? Now they were just ahead of her, trying to repair the thing. Easy prey.

She stalked forward, just as she had done with Fights-the-Bear. He had been even quieter than she, she remembered. Not a sound had come as his aging paws had picked through the snow and scrub of the northern spring. She moved like he had, keeping her nose in the wind so that her prey's scent came to her and hers was carried away. He would be proud of her, she thought.

But she also remembered odd things about that last hunt of his. The lowered tail and gaze. The subtle scent of submission, even fear. The anxious yips and hesitations she had had to quell with stares and growls. Those were not the signs of the proud alpha Fights-the-Bear had been for eight full winters. They were the signs of a cub, cowed by a feared elder.

Storm-Eye shook the memories away and tried to concentrate, an all-too-human gesture, she realized. In fact, that connection with the world of man led to others as the bleats of anxiety and frustration she heard from her prey resolved themselves into words and language. Despite herself, she understood—just as she had when Fights-the-Bear had died.

"Stop your worrying, Gene," said the one kneeling by the front of the truck she had followed. He had the damaged tire off and was placing a new one onto the rim. "The day I can't change a goddamn tire is the day I pack my bags and head back to Calgary."

"Yeah, I hear ya, but I still say we should call in." The second man was standing near the back of the truck, scanning the horizon without ever seeing Storm-Eye. He was holding a rifle. "You know what happened to Gregory Tootoosis, right?"

"No, I was asleep during the whole briefing. Those notes I took were all some sort of illusion. Jeez, Gene, you were sitting right next to me."

"Well, then? If there're wolves out here with rabies or some shit, we gotta be careful." This one was so nervous he was likely to shoot anything that moved.

"Careful don't mean stupid, Gene. A wolf killed Tootoosis—or at least that's what the Indian and Northern Affairs guy says—but that wolf's dead and it'll be tested. Maybe it had rabies or something else, but it didn't just wake up one morning and decide it was a good idea to stalk and kill Cree chiefs-to-be. Just because Old Hubert and the rest are talking about killer wolves don't mean you have to buy into it."

"I don't know, Tom. I know what you and the rest of the Ph.D.s say, but you didn't grow up in these parts. You hear stories, you know?"

"From who? Old Hubert? When I first got up here, you told me yourself he was a booze pusher and a sonovabitch, Gene." Tom stood up from his work to make his point. "If I remember correctly, your exact words were that he'd, quote, sell his mother out of the bed of his truck if it got him some more friends on the tribal council, unquote."

"Yeah, but—"

"But nothing, you big fool. He's selling this Big Bad Wolf line and organizing a hunt just to get the community behind him. It's all Little Red Riding Hood bullshit. 'Dark wolf spirits' my ass! You one of the Three Little Pigs, Gene?"

"No, but—"

"But what?"

"But I ain't against building a strong house. If that means going out with Old Hubert and calling in on the CB when we get a flat, so be it. You can always go back to Calgary. I can't."

Tom threw his arms up in frustration. "Fine!"

The moment was perfect—Storm-Eye had gotten close without either of the humans catching scent, sight or sound of her. One quick run and they were blood on the ground, food for maggots and carrion crows. Instead, she ran again, dogged by memories of dying wolves and scornful Garou howls.

Chapter Twelve

Allucious "Little Al" Henry chewed his half-smoked cigar like a bulldog with a chunk of rawhide, moving it first to one side of his wide mouth, then the other. His big, puffy lips and sagging, stubbly jowls moved rhythmically to soften the wrapped tobacco.

Little Al had been fighting his own little war against the Wyrm for decades now. His uncle and one of his sisters had the changing gift and were big with the Bone Gnawers in Queens. He was what they called kin, just a man, but one who wasn't as blind and stupid as the rest. Maybe if he'd a had kids, one of them would of had the changing gift, but there had just never been time. Anyway, Little Al had never been much good with the ladies.

Kids or no, he did his part for the cause. No one ever really noticed him, just a working stiff with his eyes on the ground, and that's the way he liked it. Back in the day, when he was a young fool and the Gnawers were all psyched about monkeywrenching, he'd done some pretty crazy stuff. Now his bones ached in the morning and his eyes weren't much good anymore, so he did other stuff. Mostly, he trawled trash from as far north as Albany, down the Hudson, out past the city to be dumped into the sea. Of course, he didn't actually do that, but the fine folks of Poughkeepsie didn't need to know just where their trash ended up. And he used his scow as part of the Gnawer underground railroad, moving things and people right under the bad guys' noses. And that's how this bunch had ended up on his pride and joy, the *May Belle*.

Al never tired of just how strange life was. Who'd ever think these folks were sacred warriors or whatever they called themselves? They were by the prow of the *May Belle*, looking down at the brackish water splitting off her and so he had a good view of all four of them. He'd heard of Big Sis, the Gnawer from Tampa who was supposed to be an up-and-comer down in those parts, but to see her now, he had to chuckle a bit. She was a kid, fer Chrissakes. A tough-as-hell kid who could kick his ass without breaking a sweat, sure, but she looked tiny in that oversized army coat of hers. The tall Limey chick next to her couldn't have been any more different: She looked like a lawyer, dressed in a suit that probably cost more than Al made in a year. Somehow that suit didn't have a speck of dirt on it. Amazing. With them was a hippie dressed in some sort a buckskin and a watch cap. Al was pretty sure he had horns under that cap.

And then there was the wild woman. She was standing a little bit back from the edge, and he had to strain to see much more than the top of her head. She had long, unkempt hair that made Al feel like a young man again. He couldn't quite forget that she's been naked as a jaybird when Big Sis had brought the bunch to him looking for a ride upstate. All she was wearing now was one of

Al's heavy raincoats, and she kept forgetting to tie it up in front.

Al sighed in the *May Belle*'s cramped little bridge. He'd never been good with ladies.

"What happened to your eye?" Cries Havoc asked the question without quite looking at Storm-Eye. His voice croaked slightly from the strain on his larynx. Although it had been a few days now since their fight in the subway station, his wounds had yet to heal completely. Apparently he was not the only one with lasting hurt, because when Storm-Eye glanced up at him, her black eyes were full of sadness unspoken. He had obviously hit a sore spot. "I'm sorry. I should not have asked."

"No," the Red Talon said in halting English. "It's all right. We live by our stories, yes?"

"Well, yes. I think so." Cries Havoc leaned against the ship's wooden rail, his back to the water. "But I was born far from here and under a gibbous moon, so my ways may not be yours."

Storm-Eye looked at the metis and wondered. His parents had willfully violated the Litany by mating. His very existence should be disgusting to her, had been not so long ago when she had joined the calls for his death at Anvil-Klaiven. And yet, he had fought hard these last few days. He had stood by her and his only moment of hesitation had come from a desire to defend his adopted home among the Fenrir. "Our ways are not so different," she said.

"I've heard a few tales of you, of course. Even at the Sept of the Dawn, there were Galliards who spoke of the Red Talon who ran with the Strider Mephi Faster-than-Death into the maw of the Wyrm." He coughed to cleared his throat. "We told the tale as one of cooperation between tribes."

"Ha, you Gaians would." She stepped forward to look at the water running by the boat. It was afternoon and the light reflected off the broken river's surface. Every once in a while, the water would be slick enough to reflect an image of the clouds above. "My story is about vengeance, Galliard. Vengeance for the dead.

"After my First Change, the elders gave me the name Judge-of-the-Trees. I ran with the Summer's Sun pack and we defended Sky Pines Sept where I was born. We were all young and full of hope. There were few humans and many wolves in the protectorate, and we felt we stood against the tide of the Apocalypse. We laughed at the Wyrm like a bunch of Ragabash and howled our victories to Sister Luna." She smiled at the water and her eyes filled with shadows. "It couldn't last."

Storm-Eye caught a glimpse of the sky in the water again. It looked beautiful, unmarred by the crimson blight that had ended her innocence. Even at night, it was not visible in the physical world. Yet.

"We should have known when Limb-Jumper turned to the devourer. He'd been our packmate and I'd even gone through passage with him, and yet we never saw it coming. It was only the elder Scents-the-Truth who uncovered his treason."

"This Limb-Jumper, he was a Black Spiral Dancer?"

"Back then…I honestly don't know." She tried to remember the details of that terrible time six winters ago. "Scents-the-Truth discovered that he'd been calling on Banes for some purpose, and passed judgment under the Litany. He renamed him Wyrm-Rutter and sentenced him to death. But the traitor escaped before we could execute him."

"This sounds like the stories we hear about Lord Arkady."

"Yes, there are some parallels. If anything, it's a lesson that we should find Arkady soon. We always said we'd go find Wyrm-Rutter, but we never did. There were always other things that drew our attention, more immediate battles to fight. That changed three summers ago, when the red star appeared." She looked at the young metis. "Are you old enough to remember that?"

"That's when I went through my Rite of Passage." Cries Havoc looked skyward for a second before returning his attention to Storm-Eye. "I can remember Anthelios shining down during my first journey into the Umbra."

"It changed many things, that star. It signaled the dawn of the Apocalypse, and there were plenty of things that answered the call. Vile things, some ancient, some young." She closed her eyes, summoning up the sights and smells of that time. "One of those things was Wyrm-Rutter."

"He attacked?"

"Yes, he and an army of Wyrm-things. He was definitely a Dancer by then. He came with his black kin, with Banes of toxic rain and with great beasts of war. He came to take the caern and we stood to defend it. We howled like fools. No traitorous Ragabash could stand before us, we thought. We were wrong."

Storm-Eye's Homid eyes watered as if against the chill of a winter gale, even though the weather was mild. "Wyrm-Rutter had one of the Banes as a pet and let it loose on us. It was a great *thing*, half-reptile, half-insect, and we never had a chance. Our alpha, Strength-of-the-Earth, was leading our attack and I saw him cut in half by a swipe of the thing's barbed tail. Its maw snapped down on Chill-Howler's head the next instant. Iron-Talons-Singing was able to get in several strong blows, and I did too, but then it swirled, moved faster than I thought possible, and cut my last packmate to ribbons."

"How did you escape?"

"I didn't, really. Wyrm-Rutter held the thing back from me and dealt with me himself. He was mad, raving about the 'truth within' and the 'truth above' and how I should see it for myself. Apparently I was special to him because we had undergone the Rite of Passage together." She raised her hand to her left eye, scarred and unseeing. "He trapped me with black lashes and then used his talons to help me with my vision.

"Wyrm-Rutter would have killed me if not for Mephi, who had been tracking the things responding to the dawn of the red star and arrived to help defend the caern. He got me out of Wyrm-Rutter's clutches, and along with the other Garou of the sept, we pushed the enemy back."

"Is that when you took the name Storm-Eye?"

"That came after Mephi and I finally killed the traitor and his beast." She let out a brief laugh, full of half-disguised sorrow. "We stalked him until the next winter and when he was weak, we struck. In the middle of a great blizzard we killed his Bane and then I gutted him. I took the name after that."

Cries Havoc looked slightly awkward, unsure what to say next. "Don't look so disappointed, Galliard," said Storm-Eye. "I am not a tale-teller. Mephi makes it all sound far more glorious. You can ask him his version when we see him next." She looked down into the water again. "If we see him again."

Then the water cleared for a second and Storm-Eye saw the Wyrm-wolf falling out of the reflected sky.

"Down!" In the same instant that she took on the Crinos form, she pushed Cries Havoc out of harm's way, her shove amplified by her extending, transforming arm. As she put on the weight of the war-form, the boat's deck moaned and the vessel pitched slightly. Hardly used to river travel, Storm-Eye froze for a split second—long enough for the Wyrm-wolf to slam into her and send the two of them overboard.

The water was cold and clinging, and the wolf-thing seemed to be made of stone, so efficiently did it drag her into the Hudson's murky depths.

Storm-Eye discovered that the Garou war-form, so well suited to ripping opponents to bloody chunks, is far less useful for swimming. The more she thrashed at the water, the farther she sank and the more cold, dark liquid found its way into her nose and throat.

She had the presence of mind to want to step sideways into the Umbra. She'd hardly have survived ten winters as a Garou if she couldn't think of that. Unfortunately, stepping sideways required staring at her own reflection and merging with it, and not only was she sorely lacking in mirrored surfaces, but she had left all of Helios's light a hundred feet above. Along with air to breathe.

Rage pounded at her heart and she gave into it. She twisted to get at the great leaden thing on her back and no longer felt its teeth tearing at her flesh or the burning of her air-starved lungs. A great war howl rose from her gut and exploded out of her open maw—and water rushed in.

Everything went black.

***

Storm-Eye woke…elsewhere.

The Wyrm-wolf was gone, but she could still feel its fresh bite on her back. When she thought of reaching back to check for blood, she realized she was back in her true form. Everything around her had a bluish, milky tint to it. Blurs of movement whipped past her from behind, careening off into the distance on some unseen current.

No, not on a current. They *were* the current. She tracked one with her eyes quickly enough to see the mercurial contours and shining inner light of an elemental river spirit. Was she in the Umbra? Surely, but it felt different from any previous journey into the Penumbra. She was deeper.

She sniffed the air and it wasn't air, but water. Not the cold, dark, choking water she had swallowed before. This was crisp and clean and carried nourishing oxygen into her lungs as well as air would. No, better than air would. The water carried scents as well. And what scents! Storm-Eye could smell the schools of fish upstream, and the frogs and the grass. And the tributaries and springs that fed the river. And the summer rain and spring thaw that fed those. She could smell what was downstream, too. Great falls into a ocean so deep it covered the world. Great whales and kraken swimming its depth as they had long before the Weaver's madness and Wyrm's rage. This was a great river indeed.

She was no Theurge, but Storm-Eye knew this was a great moment, and she marveled at it. She let the refreshing water flow in and out of her and closed her eyes. She felt at peace. She was—

A searing pain in her back broke her reflection and she turned to see a stream of red blood rising from her and drifting away on the current. The bite marks on her back burned like silver and all her muscles tensed as the agony mounted.

"Why?" she cried out to no one in particular. "Why can't I stop this Wyrm-wolf? I've slain fomori and Dancers, Banes and blight-monsters in my ten winters. Why is this wolf-thing so different?"

The voice was huge, deep and terrifyingly quiet when it answered. *The answers to your question lie within.*

And then she was rising.

***

Storm-Eye broke the river's surface and gulped at sweet air. She realized she was in Homid form when she treaded water and cleared her eyes with a hand.

"Watch out!" It was Julia Spencer in Crinos form, crying from the bow of the *May Belle*, which was bearing down on Storm-Eye at full steam. She waved and then extended a pole from her long brown arm. "Grab hold!"

Storm-Eye didn't have time even to wonder how she had ended up in front of the vessel after falling overboard. She reached up and grabbed the pole just as she was going to be swept under. Julia pulled her up with one great pull, arcing her over the railing. Storm-Eye switched to Crinos herself as soon as she landed, because it was obvious a battle was underway.

Behind the bridge of the vessel, Carlita and Cries Havoc were both in their war-forms and fighting a new Wyrm-beast. It looked like a human woman, although with far too tiny a waist and great sweeping hips. She was wearing shiny black leather and laughing hysterically. From two great seeping sores on her back extended four long, transparent insect wings.

From smaller cuts in her palms, long black tendrils extended, each tipped with a sharp stinger. Storm-Eye knew a fomor—a human who had sold what little soul it had to the Wyrm—when she saw one.

Cries Havoc made a swipe at the thing, leaping at it with his claws extended. With a terrible buzzing of its wings, it leapt high in turn and avoided the blow. Thankfully, the metis dodged its counter-attack. The stinger-tentacles missed him by mere inches. Carlita tried to take advantage of the fomor's distraction and swiped at it with her fang dagger, trying to cut into its ample hips. It flew up and away again.

Storm-Eye looked at Julia, who nodded. A moment later, the Theurge vanished into the Umbra, but Storm-Eye had already moved on to the next task. "The wings!" she growled out at her young charges. "Get the wings!"

The two Garou didn't even look her way, just acted. Carlita circled and stabbed at the thing with her fang dagger again, and again it sailed up and above her blow. But this time Cries Havoc was ready and he made a broad swipe at the air into which it flew. His claws struck into the buzzing blur just behind the fomor and tore its wings to viscous shreds. It screamed and fell to the deck.

Storm-Eye moved up to join her fellows and together they hemmed the creature in. It was wounded but still deadly, and its stinger-tipped tentacles danced in the air, readying to strike. It was about to do so when its body suddenly shook with a loud cough. Phlegm and blood shot from its mouth and nose and fear flashed in its milky eyes.

Julia. In the Umbra, attacking the Bane spirit coiled inside the fomor. Thank Gaia.

Another cough wracked the thing's body and it lifted its hands to make a last-ditch strike. Storm-Eye barked the command and she and her fellows moved in unison. She leapt high in Hispo while Cries Havoc swiped with his great Crinos claws. Carlita for her part came in low, fang dagger biting into Wyrm flesh. In a bloody blur of Garou fury, the fomor screamed and died.

The howl of victory was long and glorious, broken only by the sudden addition of a new voice.

"And I was coming to help," it said. A tall, young man—a Native American from his broad face, tan skin and long black hair—stood at the end of the deck, the air behind him still shimmering from where he had stepped sideways out of the Umbra. His bare chest showed off an impressive tattoo of a great raven. He carried a long spear and had the bearing of a warrior. "I'm John North Wind's Son. Antonine Teardrop sent me to get you."

Chapter Thirteen

The Sept of Caribou Crossing was very much awake. A bonfire burned high and true, visible from many miles away, and the chorus of wolf and human song that surrounded it was audible from farther still. As Storm-Eye crested the hill south of the caern, just past the scent marks that delineated the bawn, she could see the silhouettes of Homid, Glabro and Crinos forms dancing around the fire. Lupus Garou stood in a large pack some fifty yards away calling to beasts and spirits in a great howl. One of the wolf-howls was truer than all others, somehow catching the resonance of wind and stone just right and setting the very air vibrating. It was not the loudest song or the highest in pitch, but Storm-Eye easily recognized the voice of Heard-by-Gaia.

She loped toward the pack of signers. Her first instinct was to join in the chorus, to call out her own story to the wind and sky. *We are the warriors of Gaia, the children of Griffin and Uktena, of Caribou and Luna*, they howled. She was that as well and longed to announce it to all—but she didn't. Didn't because other songs resonated in her lowered lupine ears, songs of shame and scorn. *Storm-Eye Wiser-than-Gaia*, those songs chided from the chorus of memory. *She who makes men of wolves*. Storm-Eye lay down on the hill and watched the great song, an outsider among her own kind.

Her dark mood kept her from appreciating much of it, but the moot was apparently a grand affair. Besides Heard-by-Gaia, the group of singing lupus included a half-dozen other high-ranking Galliards, all singing of their own caerns and septs scattered across the Canadian north. Lower-ranking werewolves—mostly Red Talons or others of wolf-stock—sang back-up to these worthies. Those of homid stock seemed to be gathered around the bonfire, including several who bore the tribal markings of the Uktena, as well as a few Wendigo and Black Furies. One woman, her Crinos fur black and silver in the firelight, hefted a klaive marked with the glyphs of Uktena and Caribou. She was obviously deserving of status and deference, and even a young Wendigo Ahroun in the full grips of the fire-dance and the high, full moon above stepped aside when she strode off from the circle.

It took Storm-Eye a few minutes to realize the Uktena was headed toward her. The woman shrank down to Glabro form when she was a few steps away and knelt down to look at Storm-Eye. "The wind whispers stories of you, lost cub."

No one had called Storm-Eye a cub in many a winter and she didn't like it at all. Before she had any time to reflect she was baring her teeth in protest. The Uktena woman barely batted an eye at the challenge, just locked gazes with the great, growling wolf before her and spoke quietly. "Will you cow me as you do wolves, cub?"

Rage and shame struggled inside Storm-Eye and resolved themselves into sorrow. Her head sank to the cold ground again.

"Before you do the unthinkable, cub, remember that they once called you Two-World Daughter. That's no small blessing." The Uktena woman rose and started to walk off, adding just as she rejoined the dance near the fire, "I suggest you earn it."

The next day, after the singing and dancing were long over and many of the celebrants had rested, Storm-Eye approached the Talon Galliard she had traveled so far to see. She knew the real business of the moot—surely something grave to attract this gathering of worthies—would begin in earnest at nightfall. If she wished to have Heard-by-Gaia's attention, it would have to be today. She found the great brown and gray wolf padding near the remnants of the bonfire, sniffing the ash.

He raised his head and stared at her when she came within ten yards, a statement both that he had known she was there all along and a quick proclamation of his superior status. Storm-Eye looked away and then down in acknowledgement, and when he too looked away, approached. *Hello song-singer*, she said with quiet affection, *your voice is true and strong*.

The Galliard nuzzled Storm-Eye like a cub. *Hello to you, daughter*.

Storm-Eye hadn't seen her father for several winters, not since the days right after she and Mephi Faster-than-Death had sought vengeance on Wyrm-Rutter, not since she had returned to run with the wolves. She should submit to him as an alpha, as Fights-the-Bear's cubs had to him. Instead, her heart thrilled to his loving touch.

You are troubled, daughter.

Storm-Eye tensed, as if for attack. It would not be out of bounds for her father to pin her to the cold ground, to impose a harsh reprimand. *You have heard the wind.*

The wind has many stories, he said with a dismissive tail wag and yip. These led seamlessly to a solid stare, right at and into Storm-Eye, that said *Tell me yours.*

And she did. Without excuses or embellishment, without hesitation or defiance. How she had run with the wolf pack she had been born into and felt freer there than in any fight against Wyrm or Weaver as a Garou. How she had bonded with Fights-the-Bear and hoped to make pups with him. How she had felt sadness at his decaying health, so starkly contrasted to her own unearned vigor. How she knew he would be forgotten by wolf and werewolf alike when he failed to return from the hunt; how that was not just. How he deserved to die a hero's death, more so than any foolish cliath who perished in a foolhardy sortie in a Wyrm pit and was sung as a martyr to Gaia. She sought her wolf-brother's due, tradition be damned. Let the winds call her the fool, she was not ashamed.

Tell me, he repeated with a firm gaze.

Storm-Eye struggled for gestures and gazes that could communicate what she was feeling, the deeper truths her father demanded of her, and finally settled into the language of Garou. "Except I always remember how he defied me until I cowed him. He didn't want to go and I forced him. And now no one will sing his song and... And I don't know." The words, so human, tasted bitter in her wolf-mouth.

Heard-by-Gaia sat back on his haunches and his silver and light fur began to swim. Shoulders and arms grew as his snout retracted. His eyes shifted and his ears slipped down to the sides of his head as he changed to Homid form before his daughter's eyes. His fur slipped under his skin, and long black and gray hair cascaded down from his head. He braided it as he spoke, and shrugged on a heavy coat.

"Have you heard the story of the great standing stones, daughter?"

Storm-Eye cocked her head simply to say *No*, but couldn't hide the anxiety seeing her father in human skin caused her. He was the grandest moonsinger of these lands and he was using human voice to tell a story? It didn't seem right at all.

He closed his eyes for a second and began the tale. "In a time long before there were cities on this land, before the Impergium and the War of Rage, before the Weaver cast her webs so widely, many things were different. Among these things were the stones." He waved his arm as if to take in the whole horizon. "You have seen the great stones that stand in the northern plains."

Indeed she had. Great boulders, thirty or forty feet around, that sat far from any water or other stone in the midst of the sub-arctic plains through which the northern wolves hunted. Some said they had been carried there long ago by the glaciers, but others told other tales. Including, it seemed, her father.

"In the old days, the stones were like the wolves or the bears, great hunters. They were fearsome and mighty and whole herds of caribou were their food. They strode across the plains and the land trembled. No wolf could pierce their stone skin and they hunted as they wished. Even the Garou had to bow before their might.

"But, like many great creatures, the stones suffered from pride." Heard-by-Gaia lowered his gaze, genuinely sad. "They felt that it was beneath them to follow the caribou herds, always to be walking among mere grass-eaters. They grew tired, and looked to their grandfather mountains and said, 'They do not follow the caribou herds, and if they do not, then neither shall we.' And so they stopped.

"They all sat where they were and rested. And it felt wonderful to them. Had they not been walking with the caribou herds since Gaia called them forth? Had they not bested all other beasts and so earned their rest? And if they wished to, could they not always begin walking again? Who was to say they were doing wrong?"

He paused, as if expecting his daughter to answer, but she did not know what to say. "Exactly," he continued. "There was no one. The caribou continued on their migrations and the wolves hunted them. The stones were hungry at first, but their strength was such that they could even forget hunger. And so they sat. And sat. And sat.

"Until one day, one of the stones saw an eagle soar and wished to move again. The eagle flew fast and true and the stone realized he missed seeing new things and running across the plains. And so he tried to move again." The Galliard paused for dramatic effect. "But how did one move, he wondered. It seemed like such a complicated thing, and it had been so long since he had done it. He scoured his memory but could not remember how. He knew he had once moved, knew he was capable of it, but could not remember the way to do it. He tried for many years to remember, but he never did. Soon enough he forgot about the eagle, too, and decided he had never wanted to move in the first place.

"And so the stones sit still. Forever." Heard-by-Gaia smiled at his daughter and stood up. He walked off to tend to the moot's business and left Storm-Eye with her thoughts.

She spent the next few hours watching the moot gather. The Uktena woman who had spoken to her was obviously a high-ranking Theurge. She had a large role to play in the summonings and entreaties that accompany any gathering of the Garou. As the moon crept over the horizon and the sun dipped below it, she led the other crescent-moons in a grand Rite of the Opened Bridge, calling to the Lunes to open a shimmering gateway to another holy site. Storm-Eye was many things, but a mistress of spirit calling was not one of them. And yet, even she could recognize a great bridge when she saw one.

She concentrated, closing her one good eye and willing herself to see through the other, ruined one. Deep inside her, an awareness opened and, as she reopened her good eye, the Gauntlet parted to allow her to peek into the Umbra. This far north, Wyrm and Weaver were far off and the cold Wyld was beautiful to see in its raw form. The shining stars were brighter than even in the physical darkness, and a great glimmering moon bridge was forming in the center of the caern. Lunes, maddened by the full moon, raced across the spirit-sky, forming a great, glowing bridge. The red omen-star shone far above and Storm-Eye thought it was noticeably brighter than when she had seen it last.

Storm-Eye let the wonder of the spirit world wash over her like a refreshing wind. It had been a long time since she had traveled in the other world, and even just peeking through the Gauntlet was a wonder. Looking down from the glory of the sky, she could see that the Umbral ground was marked by thousands of hoof prints, marks of the great herds of caribou spirits who gathered at this holy site. She could see a clutch of them some distance away, but knew the tales of the staggering numbers that gathered here on the summer solstice. She stared at the glory of Gaia until the bridge was solid and she could hear the moot beginning.

"Guardians of Gaia, guests at Caribou Crossing," began the aging, white-coated Philodox Thomas Quiet-Eyes. "Welcome. We are the Garou Nation and we are undefeated!" The assembled werewolves, roughly thirty strong, cheered and howled in response, whooping to the sky.

"We are here because word has come from across the North that a concolation is being held in the

Fenrir lands. There is a dispute between the Fenrir and the Children of Gaia, and some claim that Lord Arkady Who-Knows-the-Wyrm is to blame. Some say he will be brought to task for his crimes. We have been asked to send an envoy."

"Excuse me," came a strong, young and human voice, "but why do we care?" The speaker, voicing the question on many lips, was a young man with long black hair. He sat in Homid form on the ground, wearing nothing but tattered jeans. A large tattoo of a raven, done in the style of Native tribes from parts far from here, graced his chest. Spring was heading toward summer, but this was the high north and the nights were hardly warm. Yet he seemed perfectly comfortable in the cold air and his exposed flesh was still a healthy color, probably protected by some winter spirit. Or by sheer stubbornness.

Quiet-Eyes took a moment before answering. "You have traveled here in order to learn some of the ways of your people the Wendigo, John North Wind's Son, and questions are part of learning. But so is listening." He turned to address the crowd. "There is question of a blood-price to be paid in the matter, of a Gaian cliath to die because a Fenrir fell in his tribe's care. The leader of this Fenrir caern is Karin Jarlsdottir."

Storm-Eye saw recognition among many in the crowd and Quiet-Eyes noted it too. "Some of us befriended her several winters ago when she undertook a journey across the northern lands, a journey of learning much like John's. Others may have heard of her accomplishments in taking her father's place as alpha of the Sept of the Anvil-Klaiven. All should know that she is a wise woman with the task of being judge and mother to a difficult pack."

"A bunch of cantankerous chauvinists is what you mean, old one," added the Uktena Theurge with a laugh.

"That is one way to say it, Sarah River-Walker," he answered with a smile. "But this matter is grave indeed. Garou killing Garou is nothing to be taken lightly, and neither are the charges against Lord Arkady, charges of coveting the Wyrm. Karin Jarlsdottir wishes there to be envoys at her judging so that wagging tongues and black hearts do not spread lies about her actions. This is a wise thing when dealing with the tribes of man."

Storm-Eye couldn't agree more. Rumor, scandal and lies were legacies Garou had learned from their human ancestors.

"And so Sarah River-Walker has opened a bridge to the Caern of the Anvil-Klaiven in the northland humans call Scandinavia. We need only choose an observer to watch in our name. One who can travel between our world and the world of the Get, one who can make use of the gifts of judgment and cunning. Who shall it be?"

Storm-Eye thought of the Umbral vistas she had seen and the long travels she had taken among the Garou. It had been so long, she had almost forgotten what it was like…like a stone that forgot how to walk.

She didn't realize she had volunteered until she saw her father's tail wagging.

Chapter Fourteen

The Catskills Protectorate was caught in that moment between summer and fall, when the forest is on the verge of turning into a fiery cacophony of oranges, reds and yellows, but the sun is still warm. Some trees, early to turn, already wore coats of deep red, a swath of color standing out among the lush greens of the woods.

Storm-Eye could smell that these woods were alive with wildlife. Hare, squirrel and raccoon tracks stirred the hunger in her stomach, and a whiff of deer scent only made it worse. She knew the smaller game would be out in force, gathering stores for the winter months to come. Another few turns of Luna, and these hills would be draped in icy white.

This was no pristine wilderness, however. There were scents of belching car engines on the winds as well and Storm-Eye knew a major road skirted to the east of the hills. And humans came here for their own amusement, as the occasional crushed metal can or weathered plastic bag underfoot attested. She hoped that some over-fat human would stumble through here now and see them. Seeing the terror as a two-legged sheep came face-to-face with five great wolves would be a joy indeed.

They had been on the hoof for most of the day, having left Little Al and the *May Belle* back at a small river port. From there it had been a quick run away from the human settlement and into the woods. Since then, they had been moving as wolves, cutting through woods and small farms, staying out of sight.

Storm-Eye remembered North Wind's Son from last spring at that northern sept. He was leading the way and Storm-Eye was right behind him. The others trailed a little further back, less accustomed to such a long time as wolves. *When did you leave Caribou Crossing?*

"End of spring or so." Even as a wolf, the young Garou was uncomfortable with wolf language and spoke in the Garou tongue instead. "Evan came for me and we went south."

To Teardrop?

"Not immediately. I think he was still off at Anvil-Klaiven then. No, we hung with holier-than-thou Albrecht for a while and spent some time in the Southwest too. Going from the Arctic to Arizona was a hell of a shift."

You travel a great deal. Storm-Eye thought of her own recent globe-trotting. These woods were far from her home too, but at least they smelled of Gaia. Unlike the two filth-ridden cities she'd visited in the last few days.

"Tell me about it. Evan keeps going on about how it's good for me to see the big wide world. To see all the tribes and lots of different septs To 'see what we're fighting for,' he says." He bounded over a rotted wooden fence and Storm-Eye followed. "For him, it's all about…"

Heals-the-Past. The Wendigo Evan lived up to his name, apparently, doing everything he could to bring the tribes together. *What do your alphas say of this?*

"They ain't too happy about it, I think. The Wendigo from back home ain't really the sharing kind, I think. And I guess I can understand them."

So why are you here? Why do they allow it?

"Well, I guess part of it is my Mom. She's not…she doesn't change, but she's got some juice with the elders and Evan's got some too, I think. They seem to think I'm special or something, or at least that I need to move around some more." He turned his head back, presumably to check that the others were still following. "For my part, I figure, if I can see the world, why not? I mean, I was just a kid with a grudge before and *maybe* a shot at a football scholarship with the Beavers at Oregon State. Now, well, now I got more."

This is no game, North Wind's Son.

"Yeah, I know." The Wendigo's voice carried a human ambivalence to it that perplexed Storm-Eye. No Garou reached even this cliath's young age without tasting tragedy.

They ran the rest of the way in silence.

They arrived near nightfall, the low, red, westerly sun stretching the shadows between the trees into dark pools of night. Insects buzzed about in the cooling air and Storm-Eye could feel rain coming over the hills, building in the clouds above. She also knew she was in a special place.

In the last season, she had been at a wide variety of caerns. From the simple wolf-homes of Sky Pines and Caribou Crossing, to the crowded home of the Get and the urban glade of the London Glass Walkers. And yet, it was here that she most noticed the purity of the land. Perhaps it was the contrast with the city they had left behind a few days ago, or even with the human tainted "wilderness" of the surrounding woods, but she felt as if a weight had been lifted from her back.

The wind pushed through the leaves with a melodic rustle and the air carried the fresh scent of pine and maple. Her ears perked to the far-off call of a jay and the closer gurgle of a rushing stream. The earth under her feet, rich with a summer of life and the first few falling leaves, had a delicious moistness to it. For the first time in weeks, Storm-Eye felt at peace.

"Wow," Carlita said. All the others had slowed to a trot and looked about them with undisguised wonder.

"Yeah," John North Wind's Son said, "it's pretty intense."

They found Antonine Teardrop a few minutes later, by the stream they had heard. About thirty feet wide, it had a goodly current that rushed around and over several large rocks. Teardrop was atop one of those rocks, standing in his silver-blond Crinos form. Storm-Eye hesitated to think of it as a war-form because he didn't seem to disturb the peace of the setting. Instead, he stood in all his nine-foot glory, going through a series of slow and precise movements. Water rushed over his toes, but his balance seemed sure and he pivoted with one arm extended.

Storm-Eye had heard of the Stargazers and their strange ways, of a fighting art they called Kailindo that involved quick and precise movements in combat, and a suppression of rage, some said. But she had never seen it. Stargazers had always been rare in the north and they had only become scarcer since their tribal elders had withdrawn from the Garou Nation in the wake of the red star's appearance.

"Well, hey there." Teardrop had opened his eyes, a broad grin spreading around his lupine teeth. He stepped from stone to stone, and shrank to Homid once he reached dry land. In his man-form, he didn't appear as a great warrior or sage, just a middle-aged man with a weather-beaten face. His black hair was unkempt and peppered with the beginnings of gray. He wore only a light loin-cloth and his torso showed some of the sagging and softness of age. But his movements were fluid and precise. He strode forward and hugged Cries Havoc, who took on the Homid form as well. "Thank Gaia you made it."

The Gaian seemed a little taken aback by the warm welcome. "Um, thank you. It's been a long journey."

"Anvil-Klaiven was under attack when we left, Stargazer." Storm-Eye stayed in her native Lupus form, but switched to the Garou tongue. "Do you have any news?"

"Not much. The caern hasn't fallen, but other than that I'm not sure. I've tried reaching Albrecht a few times, but haven't been able to get in touch with him. Do you know where Mari is?"

"She, uh…" Cries Havoc choked on the words slightly. "She was hurt. In Bosnia, we think. Mephi Faster-than-Death was bringing her to Albrecht."

Teardrop picked up a wad of clothing balled by a tree and pulled them on—faded jeans, a Syracuse Orangemen tee-shirt and a wool jacket. His movements lost their grace as worry built up in him.

"Albrecht would have brought her here. Or Evan would have sent word. Let's go to the cabin."

The Garou, all save Storm-Eye in Homid form, trotted after the Stargazer along the stream. At the top of the rise was a smallish cabin in a clearing and, if anything, the air smelled clearer here. Storm-Eye noticed some sort of spyglass propped up a rooftop deck. The same concern Teardrop obviously felt for this land touched his voice when next he spoke, without looking back: "What exactly happened to Mari?"

Cries Havoc began to answer. "We don't really know, she…uh…"

Storm-Eye cut to the chase. "She battles a Wyrm spirit within her. It has paralyzed her, but she returned with a Wyrm-name."

"Yes, and it's no name I've ever heard," put in Julia Spencer. "Jo'cllath'mattric."

As the last ancient syllable of the name escaped the young Theurge's lips, Storm-Eye felt the air sour in her throat. An acrid smell of rot and death made her gag and a mad cackling rang in her ears as the fomori attacked.

Eel was the first. He stepped from behind a maple the color of rust and gold, his fishy stink spoiling the air around him. He crouched slightly before Julia, who was closest to him, and seemed to stare at her. But his milky face had only one feature: a great pink pucker that slowly bloomed into row upon row of barbed teeth.

The cry that came from John North Wind's Son ripped the air like a saw through metal. It was not a formal war cry, not the ululating anthem of the Wendigo Storm-Eye knew from her days at Sky Pines. No, this was a howl of unleashed rage, of fury and disgust bubbling to the surface, overwhelming the young Garou's conscious mind and launching him into a killing frenzy. He rose to his massive Crinos form as he cried, black hair giving way to dark gray fur that obscured the tattoo on his chest. He charged straight for the monstrosity, his eyes full of rage.

Naz and Boy came next, falling from a ripple in the night sky not fifteen feet in the air above. The maggot-dog bounded straight for Teardrop, who watched it come with focussed calm. When the thing jumped for his chest and throat, the Stargazer ducked and pivoted as he assumed the bulky Glabro man-form. He pushed the dog away without making a sound.

Cries Havoc was less successful with Naz. The short woman landed near the metis, who flowed into his natural Crinos form without a moment's pause. He charged, head down to hit her with his large ram's horns, and never saw nor smelled the substance that glistened on her blistered skin. She moved like a slightly slow bullfighter and took a glancing blow, but that sent a stream of the venomous coating streaking off her and down the Gaian's side. He screamed as the corrosive poison burned his fur and flesh.

In the fight against the wasp-winged fomor on the boat, the decisive blow had come when Julia wounded the Bane within it from the Penumbra.

And that these fomori had appeared out of the spirit world—something the elders said they were rarely capable of—indicated they had help there. So Storm-Eye looked to the Glass Walker Theurge next to her. Without being asked, Spencer produced a small mirror and the two stepped into the Umbra. Carlita did the same on the other side of the clearing.

The spirit world was so sharp a contrast it took the Garou a moment to adjust. Overall, the Penumbral reflection of Teardrop's territory was a glorious symphony of colors and smells. The trees were either the brightest green Storm-Eye had ever seen or a wild bouquet of fiery shades that announced autumn like a clarion call. The stream was more of a raging river here, absolutely clear and shooting crystal spray when it hit mottled rocks. But high above, a storm was brewing. Not the kinetic fury of thunder spirits, but the dark rage of the spirit storm that had fallen on Anvil-Klaiven. Whereas that storm had been right there, though, this one seemed distant and ominous—a portent of the darkness that would envelope all. Storm-Eye had the distinct impression they were seeing the very storm that raged around Anvil-Klaiven, the Umbral vista somehow crossing the ocean.

The more immediate threat, however, was the black cloud bubbling from a point in the middle of the glade. It billowed like ink in water, forming eddies and swirls of darkness so complete it seemed to swallow the color around it.

"What the hell?" Carlita, on the other side of the cloud, moved forward, her fang dagger extended.

"The wolf!" Storm-Eye knew what was coming next and leapt to her right, putting some distance between herself and Julia to protect the Glass Walker. The cloud suddenly collapsed into the sleek, deadly Wyrm-wolf that had been stalking Storm-Eye since this all began. It was already in mid-leap when it reformed and sailed right at the Red Talon without hesitation. As she curled with the blow, Storm-Eye saw that the Dancer from New York City had appeared with the wolf. She barked a warning at Carlita and Julia, and then the wolf was on her.

It bit and clawed with the fury of a killing frenzy, but she managed to push it back before it could do more than scratch at her. The wolf leapt again, and again Storm-Eye pushed it away using her great Crinos arms. Confidence flowed through her at the small victory. She would beat this thing here and now! Then her foot hit rushing water. She realized she had not so much been pushing the wolf back as backing away from its attacks. She glanced back to confirm it had indeed hemmed her in against the river, just as an experienced wolf would with foolish prey.

As soon as she turned, she knew it was a fatal mistake. The wolf leapt with all of the control it had seemed to lack before and sank its long teeth high where her shoulder met her neck. The bulky flesh and fur of the Crinos form protected her somewhat, but she felt the daggers of darkness hook deep into her. The wolf began to thrash and Storm-Eye fell into the rushing shallows. Her blood made a scarlet ribbon through the crystal water.

The wolf had known. Had known she would look away. Known her confidence would swell and she'd become foolish. Known how she'd fight and flail. It was as if the thing knew her better than any enemy had the right to, like a friend, like a packmate. And then, as the wolf drove her into the cold mud and rocks, she remembered that first hunt as a wolf. And the bear her brother had killed. Just like this.

"Fights-the-Bear?" Her voice was a gurgle from between clenched teeth, but she felt the Wyrm-wolf tense in recognition.

In recognition of its name.

Chapter Fifteen

Storm-Eye could picture it all happening as she drowned in the spirit river. Fights-the-Bear, her littermate, her alpha male, her favorite of all wolves, selling himself to the Wyrm. Fomor wolves were not entirely unknown—the Red Talon elders said that the Black Spiral Dancers used them for breeding stock, just as they did sick and demented humans. But for Talon kin to surrender himself to the force of evil, it was unthinkable.

Yes, unthinkable.

It wasn't a voice, really. It was wolf language, the mix of movement, vocalization and scent that was the signature of the true wolf. And it was a speaker she recognized. It was Fights-the-Bear. Such communication should be impossible of course, especially if he was biting into her neck and shoulder. There was no way for Storm-Eye to see or hear him, and the spirit waters washed out all scents. But this was the Umbra, after all, a realm where the difference between thought and reality was much more fluid than in the physical world. And she had heard tales of some Garou speaking without sound, movement or smell, thorough a link of minds and spirits. If that were possible, why not this telepathy in the Umbra itself?

Unthinkable, Fights-the-Bear's "voice" said again. And Storm-Eye knew she had heard the same from another.

Sarah River-Walker. The Uktena Theurge at Caribou Crossing had used that word. She'd been talking about singing the dirge for Fights-the-Bear, no? She'd meant that true wolves, kin or no, did not act for glory. They did not think in those terms. Ever.

Ever?

The voice was mocking and bitter, and it caused the enormity of her own crimes to blossom in Storm-Eye's memory. She had made Fights-the-Bear kill the hunter of wolves. She had made him die a warrior's death even though he had no idea what a warrior was. She had shown him, in his own final minutes, the terrible world of war and cause, or the quest for glory and hate of the enemy. She had made the unthinkable thinkable. Forced on him an awareness and a burden that was her birthright, not his.

And so other thoughts must have flooded into him. Sadness, perhaps. Hurt, certainly. Hurt that his sister and alpha female had cowed him into a death that was not his own. And with sadness and hurt, had come—

Hate.

Storm-Eye felt the river sucking her down, so deep and fast in the spirit world. The Wyrm-wolf—Fights-the-Bear—bit and tore into her flesh and she knew that she had brought about his betrayal. His hatred of her had become a hatred of all, a desire to destroy everything and everyone. And that universal hate had a name. It was called the Wyrm.

A crushing sadness enveloped Storm-Eye and it too bloomed into hate and rage. She howled in the spirit waters and barely noticed that she wasn't choking. Instead, she thrashed and turned, ripping her own flesh to get at the thing she had created out of the finest wolf in her pack. She tore at the darkness her brother had become, and despaired. She despaired at his terrible end. She despaired at the death of the Summer's Sun pack two winters ago. She despaired at the missing Mephi Faster-than-Death, her only friend among the Garou. She despaired at her father, gently calling her "Two-World Daughter" even though he knew she was blind in both. Why had Gaia given her such a memory if it was only to catalog her pain? Why did the change have to come with this human hell of regret and sorrow? Why couldn't she be a true wolf and forget?

You can.

Furious that this black *thing* was privy to all her thoughts, Storm-Eye tore into it with renewed vigor. She tore black oily chunks off it and with each one, she felt a burden lift from her. The pain of her First Change vanished like mist in the morning. No more loneliness as the pack rejected her and the Garou found her. Repulsion when she first saw the Wyrm's traces in the spirit world—gone. The desire to be glorious for her father and the anger at never quite getting his full attention—gone. The maddening, bitter anxiety of betrayal when Limb-Jumper embraced the Wyrm—gone. The terrible, crushing sorrow when the rest of the Summer's Sun pack died at his hands—gone. The black, hateful need for vengeance—gone.

Even the thing she clawed into dark bits. Some part of her knew it had been important to her, but now it was just a threat to be killed. Something that wanted to stop her from feeding. Something to kill.

The spirit-water flowed past, over and through her, and for all she knew this was what the entire world was like. This was the entire world—no past, no future, just an eternal present. No pain or regret. Just instinct. No more "why?"

Within, a new voice said. *The answers lie within.*

Storm-Eye felt she had heard this other voice before, in another place like this. And when she looked toward it, she saw that the river itself had a face. Made of swirling spirit eddies and wisps of Umbral flotsam, the face was part cougar and part deer. It had the body of a great snake and eyes that saw forever.

What do you see? The question opened the river's great mouth and from it, images flooded out. The first to wash over Storm-Eye was a dark red-brown wolf, running across frozen ground after a creature twisted and black. *I see myself*, she said.

Then came other images, scenes of other people and other wolves. Like the first wolf—herself—they were in a world more solid than this one, like a hard reflection of the loose, impressionistic world that was the only one she could remember. This was a world of pain and glory that she called, with a sudden shuddering memory, "physical."

There were five of them. Five things like her, wolf-changers.

What do you see? One was huge and gray furred, a mass of muscle and fury who clutched a long spear and spat out rage. *I see a warrior.*

Another was smaller, his light fur short and scruffy and speckled with blond. He twisted and turned in graceful movements, keeping a maggot-laden monster at bay. *I see a teacher.*

Another faced off against a monster that was all tooth and tongue. His gray and brown fur was marked by scars and burns, but he fought on. Two curled horns crowned his head and gave him the look of something strange and yet wonderful. *I see a student.*

Two more fought together against a black-furred man. They were both women, but seemed polar opposites. One was sleek and deep brown, her movements dexterous and organized. Another was squat and scruffy, holding a massive curved dagger that she wielded with rage and precision. And yet they worked together to hem in the monstrosity they fought. *I see wise-women.*

All of the wolf-people stood together against their enemies, holding them back, protecting one another. She could tell their situation was dire. It was only a matter of time before one of the monsters would get through their defenses, wear them down and come in for the kill. And yet, they controlled their fear and stood their ground. *I see a pack.*

The spirit waters swirled again and she saw her reflection once more. That same dark red wolf was now in the river, with a black wolf on her, biting into her. It was herself again, but what was she? And what was the thing on her? She felt the question nagging at her, burning through her own desire to forget. If she let go of memory, then she let go of pleasure as well as pain, of honor as well as disgrace. And she could not do that. She could not betray those who fought now, or those who had fought with her in the past. Like Fights-the-Bear had.

She thought of the thing on her back and couldn't forget. It was an enemy, a monster, but she could not reject the memories of the wolf who had been her brother, her alpha, her teacher, her partner. Had he betrayed Gaia in his rage and loneliness? She couldn't know. She would fight this monster because that was her duty, but she would not forget her packmate. Never.

And the other memories flooded back. Of running with her pack and with Mephi Faster-than-Death and with Fights-the-Bear. Of victories and defeats. Of crying victory over Bane and beast alike. Memories of joy and hope. Of friends fallen but remembered. She looked at her own reflection and said, *I see a leader*.

She looked at the thing on her back and remembered other things. The Black Spiral Dancer at Anvil-Klaiven who had uttered an incantation to her dark spirits and used a chain-fetish just before the Wyrm-wolf attacked. Of how the Wyrm-wolf had always come for her, as if it came *from* her. Of how it was a repository for the hate and anger that *she* felt. Of how Fights-the-Bear had had none of those feelings even at the very end. *I see my guilt, not his*.

The image shifted and she saw its true shape: a black-winged Bane, its twisted tail wrapped around her own form. This was like the thing inside Mari Cabrah, like those Mephi had seen. This was her own memory made toxic. This was the Wyrm's corruption of her feelings for Fights-the-Bear, its violation of that great wolf's memory. She would not have it. *I see my enemy.*

***

"To the river!" Storm-Eye's call burst from her maw as soon as she broke the surface of the stream.

The other Garou responded without dropping their guard. John North Wind's Son, his great spear at the ready, circled the short female fomor Naz and pushed her toward the water that now rushed in a torrent. Julia and Carlita made a coordinated rush at the Black Spiral Dancer and he flipped back to avoid them, plunging into the water that now overflowed its banks. Cries Havoc stood his ground as Eel charged, changing to his sleek wolf-form at the last second so that the fomor misjudged his attack and was submerged. Teardrop flipped the dog-thing Boy over his shoulder and into the current.

It would be a mere moment before the monsters emerged to strike back, but none considered fleeing. Instead, as one, they leapt into the floodwaters. Storm-Eye was there and they would not abandon her. In an instant all were swept under.

Under the surface, the Gauntlet between physical and spiritual faded to nothing and spirit waters melded with the physical ones. Soon they all saw the swirling spirits that formed a great totemic face. They hung there, suspended by the impossible currents before their Wyrm-laden enemies.

"Uktena," Julia Spencer whispered. Carlita and Teardrop nodded, recognizing the great water spirit before them. Totem of an entire tribe, it was known for choosing the worthy and discarding the unworthy. It believed in subtlety and cunning, in courage in all its forms. It faced the Wyrm in an eternal dance and expected its followers to do the same. To face it thus, to float before, or more precisely, *inside* its own form, was a great honor but could also be a prelude to disaster. Only the deserving survived such an encounter.

The images came at them as they had at Storm-Eye. They saw past the three fomori and the Black Spiral Dancer who floated before them in the here and now, and saw many other enemies. The raging winged Banes sweeping in a great storm across the Penumbra. The Dancers attacking Anvil-Klaiven. The great corrupted Tisza river spirit chewing at a massive Pattern chain, spawning more and more of this new breed of Banes. And curled in the bloody soil they saw what was at the end of those chains, a Wyrm-thing so massive it could swallow the Garou Nation whole. So vile it had been forgotten by all and learned to eat memory itself. Uktena the River asked, *What do you see?*

We see the enemy we must face, the Garou said as one. *We see Jo'cllath'mattric.*

A dark cacophony screeched its way out of the Black Spiral Dancer's gullet at the sound of his unholy patron's name. Like glass being digested in a great thresher, the dark song echoed through the spirit waters, infecting all. The spirit waters roiled and seethed at the dark reverberations and freed the Dancer from their iron grip.

Storm-Eye recognized the hellish cry from Anvil-Klaiven. The female Dancer had pushed away Weaverguard's spirit protectors with the same black noise, and here it created a noxious bubble free of Uktena's essence. The totem currents rushed around the malignant sphere whipping the Garou and fomori about like bits of driftwood in a storm, but the only effect was to drag them all toward the surface, leaving the Black Spiral Dancer alone in the heart of the great spirit.

No, not alone. The Bane that had plagued Storm-Eye since Anvil-Klaiven coiled around its master's legs and settled on the silty riverbed. It was changing anew, returning to the usurped shape of a great black wolf.

No! Storm-Eye swam down, fighting the totem spirit's raging current, while the rest of her pack and their prey shot toward the surface, blinded by the waters. She couldn't let those things remain here. She had abandoned her duty too many times. Now was the time to act.

As if responding to her conviction, the currents around her shifted and she shot down toward the bubble of hate below her. She could hear the distorted song through the spirit waters and it tore at her heart. But she never wavered, riding the knife's edge of her own rage until she fell into the bubble, fell right in front of the bellowing Dancer. She tensed for his attack, but it never came.

What do they see? It was Uktena the River's voice.
Nothing, Storm-Eye realized. *They don't see a thing.*
Uktena was reputed to be a subtle totem, hiding its

charges from spirit enemies, and Storm-Eye seemed to benefit from that. The question was what to do with that stealth. She had no illusions that she could remain hidden for long, and certainly not past her first blow. And the Dancer was powerful—it had taken them all to fight him to a standstill in New York City and Storm-Eye was all alone here. She was outmatched, like a hare facing a wolf, or…or a wolf facing a bear.

She shrank to her sleek wolf-form and circled around the Dancer until she was behind it and the Bane was in front. And she jumped, just like Fights-the-Bear had so many winters ago. And like her littermate, she bit deep into her prey's shoulder and neck, causing ripples of pain and panic. The Dancer's first reaction was to try to shake her off, but all that did was rend his oily flesh even more.

The Bane wasn't immobilized though, and, still trying to assume Fights-the-Bear's form, it pounced at Storm-Eye. The Black Spiral Dancer was right on the edge of panic and seeing the big black wolf jumping toward him apparently pushed him right over. He lashed out at everything and swiped at the Wyrm-wolf with his barbed talons, drawing trails of black ichor from its flesh.

The Bane did not take kindly to the treatment. It hit the muck on the riverbed, but rose enraged. With a mighty shake it abandoned the form of the proud wolf it had stolen and devolved into the twirling winged black serpent it was damned to be. With a high-pitched screech it flew right at the Black Spiral Dancer who had dared harm it and coiled around his throat and head, cutting off his cacophonous song.

There was a terrible heartbeat of silence after the last note died and then Uktena exerted its power anew. The waters held back by the black melody rushed to fill and purify the bubble, hitting the three within like a freight train. There was no purchase to be had and they spun in the terrible current. Spirit eddies pulled at Storm-Eye, but she held on to her prey for several minutes. He was thrashing against the Bane ripping into his brain and the wolf on his back, but to no avail.

She only let go when he went slack.

Then she was rising, from the bottom and from the spirit river itself. She passed through the paper-thin Gauntlet somewhere before the surface and felt the cold water rush into her mouth. She gagged and fought for air but found instead a strong arm pulling her out of the current and onto the shore.

"Are you all right?" asked John North Wind's Son, her rescuer. She coughed and shook out her coat in reply.

"Sweet Gaia," said Cries Havoc, standing nearby. "Look!" He pointed back toward the river.

Storm-Eye turned and the other Garou did the same, and they were blessed. The sunlight came low from the western horizon and should by all rights have been a rosy amber, but instead it bounced from the water white and true. And the river, for just a few wonderful seconds, was silver.

Chapter Sixteen

"I still don't like it." Carlita picked up some the dried yellow leaves on the ground and crumpled them in her hand.

Cries Havoc was sitting cross-legged on the forest floor and looked up at the petite Bone Gnawer as she paced back and forth. "What's not to like, Sis? We were face to face with Uktena itself, remember? We defeated the fomori and Storm-Eye got rid of the Dancer and the Bane. You just need to settle down until the elders are ready."

They were all on one of the hills overlooking the gorges around the Caern of the Hand of Gaia, near Lake Seneca. They had come here after the flood waters withdrew and they all had woken up on the moist ground outside Antonine Teardrop's cabin. Teardrop himself was off getting things ready.

"I'm with Big Sis." John North Wind's Son hadn't sat still at all in the last hour, constantly going to the edge of the hill to see what the sept elders were up to. Or pacing around, shifting between man and wolf-form every few minutes. "I hate this waiting."

"Yeah, whatever." Carlita turned toward Julia Spencer, who was sitting on a stump a little away from the rest of them. Somehow she managed to look impeccably dressed. "What about you, *chica*? You like being pulled around like this?"

"I don't know about that. I still have a lot of questions. Did the river really turn to silver or was that just a trick of light? Either way, was that a good or bad omen? But that was Uktena we were with, Carlita. A totem spirit not known for its up-front and forthright nature."

"That's just it, I *hate* being manipulated, and that thing used me."

"What are you talking about?" John North Wind's Son jumped down from the branch he had perched on for a record-setting eight seconds. "Who manipulated you?"

"The Big U, for Gaia's sake! I never woulda been in NYC if it wasn't for some pissed-off river spirit waylaying our regular messenger. That can't be a coincidence." Carlita turned to make sure to address them all. "I'll bet a river or water spirit shows up in how you all ended up here too. That's how these things work."

Storm-Eye, who lay in her wolf-form, saw recognition dawn on their faces one by one. She didn't yet know each of their tales but she could imagine. How many times had rivers and waters come up in her life over the last seasons?

"Damn, we've been used," John said. "Teardrop and Evan are gonna hear about this!"

"And what will you tell them, North Wind's Son?" Storm-Eye shifted into her woman-form to accommodate her homid companions. "That you will return to your human life? Give up the changing skin?"

"Uh, I…" The young Wendigo looked around to his companions for support. "I just don't like being made a fool of!"

"The river made a fool of you by sweeping you along? Or are you the fool for refusing to swim?"

"What?"

Storm-Eye looked at them all. "Life would be much simpler if we had not changed, yes? You would live your human lives. I would run with a wolf pack far from here. We would do what others do and be content, yes?"

"I s'pose," put in Carlita. "But we have changed."

"Yes, we have, and we cannot return to the past, no matter how much we would like to. And we cannot ignore the river's current."

"But—"

"Rivers do not use, they carry. It has grabbed hold of us and we cannot turn our backs on that. It pushes us toward Jo'cllath'mattric and we can either rage against the current or use it to get us to our goal." She strode down the hill and toward the heart of the caern, where the calls of the elders were rising to a fever pitch. "In the last few days, we have stood together against vicious enemies and our own fears. I have faced a Wyrm-thing that burned me with my own guilt, and triumphed because of the courage around me. If Uktena has chosen to call me, then so be it."

She took a few more paces and rose into her great Crinos war-form. She raised her head to the night and howled in the war songs of the Garou. "I am Storm-Eye Two-World Daughter, moon-judge and Red Talon. I embrace my fate. Let this Wyrm-beast Jo'cllath'mattric tremble, for I am coming for it." She turned back toward them. "And so is my pack!"

John was the first to join in the howl, followed by Julia, Carlita and finally Cries Havoc. From down below came the voice of Antonine Teardrop and the assembled Garou of the Sept of the Hand of Gaia. Together they sang the great howls of celebration that mark the bonding of a pack. And deep below and far above that great call, Storm-Eye and the young Garou heard the liquid voice of the river. *What do you see?* it asked, and once again they answered together.

"Family."

Epilogues: Remembered & Forgotten

Heard-by-Gaia leapt high into the air and landed atop one of the great standing stones of the Canadian north. Where some saw just a large boulder, he heard the tales of once-great warriors brought low by their own pride. But tonight, with Luna barely a sliver in the night sky, the spirits of wind brought another tale. One he had to pass along. He threw his lupine head back and began a high, glorious howl.

Gaia, Mother of us all, hear me. Spirits of sky and earth, hear me. Griffin, father of our tribe, hear me. Wolves and Garou of all stripes, hear my tale and pass it on. I sing of the wisdom and glory of one of our own. I sing of Storm-Eye Two-World-Daughter, half-moon of the Red Talons, child of the Caern of Sky Pines and daughter of my own.

The rest of the Six Winters Pack, a scant hundred yards away, picked up the call, acting as a chorus to their great moon singer. Speaks-for-the-Trees recognized the joy the Galliard felt in singing the praise of his daughter, and it was her pleasure to add to that call.

Storm-Eye is blessed by Gaia's wisdom and Luna's courage. She strides toward the Wyrm with purpose and without fear, cutting at its heart. She has formed the Pack that Runs in the Silver River, under the eye of mysterious Uktena River-Man himself. She has brought Glass Walker and Wendigo together, Child of Gaia and Bone Gnawer. The spirits sing her praise to me and I sing them to all.

In the wisdom of her Mother, she has taken her errors and made them lessons. She has forged a pack from those she might once have scorned. She has shaken off the shackles of sorrow and pride and strides forth in Gaia's grace.

She is the Two-World Daughter, child of wolf and man, of spirit and stone. Let the Wyrm fear her teeth and the Garou seek her counsel!

Speaks-for-the-Trees peered deep into the world of spirits. She looked toward the great pines who were her charge and saw the spirit owls who nested there fly off. They carried the song north, toward Caribou Crossing and across the northlands. Soon Lunes and wind-dervishes would follow, and the Garou Nation, scattered and divided as it was, would hear of Storm-Eye as they had.

She only hoped Storm-Eye and her Silver Pack would survive to hear the songs themselves.

***

They hadn't changed Mick's clothes yet. In the twenty-four hours since he awoke choking on the sludge that floats on the surface of the East River in September, not a single one of the people he'd seen had done a thing to help him. His Versace shirt and Gucci pants stuck to his clammy skin. His wallet, passport and charge cards were gone.

And he had forgotten something. Something important.

He'd realized it when the copper who found him at the docks asked him his name. He'd *wanted* to answer. Really. But he couldn't. Speaking just seemed like something he hadn't done in so long.

Then, once that copper had called in other fools, he'd wanted nothing more than to tear them to shreds. But he couldn't remember how to do that, either. How could he change?

At least once the paramedics got a look at the scars on his chest, put there so lovingly by the Lady long ago, he'd been transferred to people who could help. He'd been in a Megadon lab on Long Island ever since. They should be able to help him.

Or not. Instead of being useful, all these fools in lab coats had been doing was poking and prodding him. Mick knew he should be calling the shots here, not being probed and stuck like a glorified lab rat. And he knew there was one word that would make him right again. If only he could remember it. He tried to say it, but all that came out of his throat was a croaking sound. "Ja… Jak…"

And so it went, for three full days. The men in lab coats eventually decided to strip him bare and strap him down to a large metal table. Then they started using knives. The pain was bitter and disgraceful, with none of the artfulness the Lady had shown him.

"Is this our mystery guest?" Her voice was like a dark thunderbolt in his head. He turned to see her in all her glory, standing at the lab entrance. Long raven-black hair, draping a body of muscled flesh. Tight leather binding her two-meter frame so beautifully it was painful to see. Her eyes were as dark as the abyss and zeroed in on him. Yes, she was here at last. The Lady Zhyzhak, chosen one of the Black Spiral Dancers, whose ferocity was matched only by Father Wyrm himself. She had groomed him from the time of his dark birth and she would save him now.

"Yes," said one of the scientists. "He has scarring that's slightly reminiscent of your hive, Milady, and we wondered if you might be able identify him. We're actually quite baffled."

She looked at Mick with all her vile intelligence and Mick looked back, searching for the approval that would tell him he was saved. Or the reprimand that would tell him she was condemning him as punishment for his failure. Instead, he saw no recognition at all.

"No, Doctor. I've never seen this man before."

About the Author

Philippe Boulle is a writer, a Canadian, and convinced that anything else he says about himself will be out of date by the time this hits the shelves. He dislikes talking about himself in the third person.

Tribe Novels:
Bone Gnawers
& Stargazers

THE RAGE CONTINUES...

BONE GNAWERS
Valiant Garou warriors return to Eastern Europe to eradicate the growing evil that has confounded their efforts thus far. Where the mighty and noble have failed, hope now rests with humble werewolves who make their homes in filth.

STARGAZERS
Antonine Teardrop may hold the key to Garou victory against the evil of Eastern Europe, but his tribe's withdrawal from the Garou Nation may have damaged his credibility beyond repair. Even if it has not, servants of the Wyrm want him dead.

November 2001.

White Wolf is a registered trademark of White Wolf Publishing, Inc. Werewolf the Apocalypse is a trademark of White Wolf Publishing, Inc. All rights reserved.

WEREWOLF THE APOCALYPSE

Fianna

author	eric griffin
cover artist	steve prescott
series editors	eric griffin
	john h. steele
	stewart wieck
copyeditor	anna branscome
graphic designer	jennie breeden
cover designer	jennie breeden
art director	richard thomas

More information and previews available at
white-wolf.com/clannovels

Copyright © 2001 by White Wolf, Inc.
All rights reserved.

No part of this book may be reproduced or transmitted in any form or by any means, electronic or mechanical — including photocopy, recording, Internet posting, electronic bulletin board — or any other information storage and retrieval system, except for the purpose of reviews, without permission from the publisher.

White Wolf is committed to reducing waste in publishing. For this reason, we do not permit our covers to be "stripped" for returns, but instead require that the whole book be returned, allowing us to re-sell it.

All persons, places, and organizations in this book — except those clearly in the public domain — are fictitious, and any resemblance that may seem to exist to actual persons, places, or organizations living, dead, or defunct is purely coincidental. The mention of or reference to any companies or products in these pages is not a challenge to the trademarks or copyrights concerned.

White Wolf Publishing
735 Park North Boulevard, Suite 128
Clarkston, GA 30021
www.white-wolf.com

First Edition:October 2001

The trademark White Wolf, is a registered trademark.
ISBN: 1-56504-884-9
Printed in Canada.

For James,
Against the day he finds himself, as all men do, weary and uncertain of the way home.

Once as they rested from their chase, a debate arose among the Fianna as to what was the finest sound in the world. Each of the champions told of his delight: the clash of spear on shield, the belling of a stag across water, the baying of a tuneful pack, the laughter of a carefree girl, the whisper of a moved one.

"They are good sounds all," said Fionn.

"Tell us, chief," Oisin ventured, "what do you think?"

"The music of what happens," said great Fionn, "that is the finest sound in all the world."

~The Fenian Cycle

TRIBE NOVEL:
Fianna

ERIC GRIFFIN

Chapter 1

Stuart broke from the tree line like a bellowing stag, and skidded to a halt at the edge of the road, churning up a wave of dust and gravel. He was already shifting, his keen senses scanning the periphery for any sign of witnesses or oncoming traffic, not really expecting to find either. He straightened, shedding his wolf's clothing, as he drew closer to the fold. Home.

His footfalls crunched overloud in the stillness of evening. They sounded anxious and out-of-place, as if uncertain of exactly where they stood after so long an absence. Stuart roughly shoved such concerns back down. Crossing the road, he put one hand atop the gate and vaulted it effortlessly, as he had done since he was a boy.

Colum met him halfway up the drive. His pace was unhurried, his shotgun dangled at ease from one arm. Neither his face nor voice betrayed any excitement over the boy's return. "Stuart," he acknowledged.

"Dad, I'm glad you're here. I didn't see the truck and I was afraid you had gone down into town. I…"

"Ellen's got the truck. Gone to the movies. She'll be sorry she missed you." It was clear from his tone that he did not share this sentiment.

Stuart tried to wrap his mind around the idea of Ellen driving. When he'd left she'd been no older than… He searched his memory but couldn't quite pin down the exact number. That bothered him. He hurried on to cover his embarrassment, "Dad, listen, I need your help. There's this…"

"Your mother's fine, thanks for asking." Colum's tone was hard, unforgiving. "She misses you something terrible. She's always going on about her son, the Journalist."

"Great," Stuart muttered uncomfortably. "But listen. I wish this were just a social call, but this is really important. I…"

"When a boy comes round here, he asks after his mother. Go on, now. Clear off." Colum gestured with the flat of the shotgun.

"But Dad, I…forget it. Just forget it." Stuart turned away and waved him off angrily. "I don't know why I even came back here. It's not like I need you, you know. Damn it, I knew it was going to be like this. It's always like this. Every time I try to—"

"Colum? Who's that you're talking to out there? Keeping them standing in the drive! Why is that?"

"He's just leaving, Margaret. Go on back inside, I'll handle this." There was a gleam of moonlight off gunmetal.

"Stuart!" Margaret erupted through the screen door and down the front steps in a flurry of long trailing skirts. "But why didn't you call and tell us you were coming? I would have had something ready for you, dear. Colum, why didn't you tell me Stuart was here? Well never mind, the important thing is that you're here now and this is where you belong. You just come right inside and I'll whip you up something. You're as thin as a rail. What do they feed you at that newspaper office of yours? You'll have to excuse the mess. The place is an absolute wreck what with your father tracking through with those great oversized feet of his. But, Lord, it's good to have you home! Come now, I'll just... Why, whatever's wrong, child?" She had taken him by the arm and started back toward the house, pulling him along in her wake. He instinctively fell into step and was three or four paces along before he recalled himself and managed to dig his feet in.

"Mom, Dad. There's somebody lost, probably hurt. I found the car a few miles back and it was in pretty bad shape. We've got to get—"

Colum's voice brooked no objections. "Go inside, boy. Visit with your mother. There's a Coca-Cola cake on the table. She made it special, so you're going to sit down and eat it. Damn if I can figure how she always knows when you're coming, but she does. A touch of the Sight. They say it passes through the female line. Just hope your sister doesn't come down with a case of it."

"Colum, dear, why don't you wander down to the Jennings's and see if, between you, you can't round up a few cousins to go look for this lost sheep? There's a dear."

Grumbling, he bent to kiss her cheek and, reluctantly, nodded to Stuart. "You take care of your mother. Old Man Jennings was out shooting at something night before last. Said it looked something like a bear, but it hissed and moaned like his old tractor—crazy old SOB. Back by morning."

Colum shouldered his shotgun and confidently, unhurriedly, set off across the yard. Stuart watched the retreating figure all the way to the stile.

"Why don't we sit out here, dear? It's such a beautiful night."

Stuart settled onto the front stoop. Absently, his fingers sought out and traced each of the familiar knots and cracks in the wooden steps. Routes on a map leading unvaryingly home.

Without looking up, he said, "Mom, I can't stay. I'm just here for…"

"Shhh. Hush now. It's all right. Worries for tomorrow. Tonight my boy's home." She pulled him close. He returned her embrace, awkward, out of practice. All the while he stared fixedly over her shoulder, far out over the stubble of the winter fields—pretending not to see the silver tears she hid in the hollow of his shoulder.

Chapter 2

"You sure you won't stay?" The screen door had barely whined shut behind Colum. The big man had been out all night and looked the part. Still, he had immediately taken in the situation playing itself out over the breakfast table. He'd seen it all before. Same thing, every time. You'd think she'd get used to it, but it hurt her every time.

"Colum!" Margaret scolded. "Your manners. And Stuart will stay just as long as he likes. As long as they can spare him from that newspaper office of his." She fussed about her son, fidgeting with the remains of the breakfast dishes. "He's a busy man now and has his man's work waiting for him. It's not every boy as would take the time off and haul all the way out here just to visit with his mother. And mind those great muddy boots of yours, you're tracking up the kitchen already."

Colum just snorted and shook his head. He knew how to pick his fights; he fell to unlacing his boots. "So, how long you down for then, son? Could use another set of hands along the fence line before the weather breaks. That is, assuming those hands of yours haven't forgotten what little honest work was once in them."

"Dad, I've got to go. I—"

"Don't tell me, tell your mother." He sounded even more weary than he looked. "I can find somebody to help shore up the fences. Your mother, she's not so lucky. She's just got the one son. You ever stop to think what it's like for her? What this does to her? 'Course not. You won't be here tomorrow to worry about it. She'll be up all night tonight, but she won't tell *you* that."

"Colum, that's enough. The boy has enough on his mind. He doesn't need to go worrying over some old woman who can—now that you mention it—take care of herself, thank you very much."

"Mom, I can't stay. I'm sorry. My plane leaves from Dulles on Monday morning. I'm going to be out of the country for a while. I wanted to see you before I left. I didn't want you to—"

"Out of the country! Did you hear that, Colum? Our son, the foreign correspondent. I expect you'll be rubbing elbows in London and Paris and making a name for your—" She broke off suddenly, struck by a darker thought. Her hand fluttered to her mouth. "Oh, Stuart! You're not going to be one of those war correspondents are you? I couldn't stand to think of you…"

"No! Nothing like that," he interjected hurriedly. "And nothing so romantic as London or Paris either, I'm afraid. I'm off to Norway." He finished off with a half-embarrassed shrug.

"Norway?" Colum burst in, incredulously. "What could they possibly have over there in Norway that we haven't got right here? Well, ice and snow I imagine. But we'll have that ourselves soon enough. To think a boy should have to haul himself halfway round the world just to avoid a few weeks' honest work."

Margaret glared at him. "You don't listen to a word that man says, Stuart. Dropped on his head as an infant and his dear mother never forgave herself. I am sure that Norway has plenty to recommend it to an up-and-coming young newspaperman. You'll have a wonderful time. They're not at war, Norway?"

Stuart laughed and her face lit up. She loved to listen to him laugh. "No ma'am. Least they weren't last night."

"Course they're not at war." Colum scowled. "Who'd want to fight over a great block of ice like that? So what does send you over there? Seems a strange place to just up and take a fancy to all of a sudden."

"Family trouble," he said. "Our dear cousins in the Great Frozen North. Again."

"*Fenrir*," Colum spat the word like an invective. "What is it this time? No, let me guess. They all got roaring drunk and sacked a fish hatchery or something."

"Well *that* would hardly be news," Stuart said. "No, it seems they've convened some sort of ancestral High Court of Retributions and that they are actually threatening to execute some political prisoners from other tribes. There are a lot of people up in arms about a Gaian cub who is apparently on the chopping block. And you know how everything with the Gaians swells into some great intertribal incident. But there's a rumor," Stuart said around a mouthful of bacon, "that they're going to drag Arkady before this tribunal of theirs. And if they are, I'm going to be there. *That's* the story of our generation."

"Arkady? Arkady. Now that's a name I've heard you use before," Margaret mused aloud.

"This Arkady, he's a Silver Fang, isn't he?" Colum asked. "The bluebloods aren't going to like that one bit."

"Not a Silver Fang, *the* Silver Fang," Stuart said. "The one they're always going on about, holding up as the culmination of their centuries-long pedigrees. They say the bloodline bred truer in him than it has in a score of generations—that he's got a pelt as pure as moonlight on sea foam. And there are those who have insisted, ever since he was a cub, that he's the *one*— the one who will lead the tribes in the Last Battle."

"That's gonna be tough if the Get hand him his head first," Colum said.

Stuart seemed alight with a restless energy. "I've got to be there."

"Well, you can't very well print that sort of thing in that newspaper of yours," Colum prompted.

"No," Stuart admitted grudgingly. "I…I'm taking some time off."

"Oh, Stuart," Margaret turned away. She knew when he was lying, had always known.

"I quit the job at the paper," he admitted. "They said the Richmond *Times* didn't really need a correspondent on the ground in Norway just now. Go figure. Hey, it's no big deal. I can always talk my way back in when I get back. It's not like they're gonna forget who I am or anything." He crossed the room and put his arm around his mother's back.

Her voice, when it came was soft, subdued. "'Course you can dear. Gift of gab. You get that from your father's side of the—" She broke off abruptly and threw a worried glance toward her husband.

Colum had gone red. They didn't talk about Stuart's paternity under his roof. Time was when the very mention of the subject would have sent him into volatile rage. But that was years gone by now, back when Colum thought that the only thing that could keep the indignity that had been forced on them in check was to submerge it in bourbon, holding its head under the thick sweet syrup until it quit squirming.

Things were different now. The fire of resentment still roiled within his gut, but now he kept it banked with hard work instead of hard liquor. It was easier now that the boy was grown, out of the house, out from underfoot.

Colum said nothing, just glared at the boy.

A long, uncomfortable moment passed. At last Colum stirred and spoke, "Well, as I don't imagine anyone's gotten round to the morning's chores yet, and since they aren't likely to do themselves, you all will have to excuse me. Ellen will give you a ride back into town. And don't even think about sneaking off before she gets up. She may forgive you after a while—she gets that from your mother. I won't. Nice seeing you, Stuart."

Colum tromped back out onto the back porch, without either the sleep or the breakfast he had come in for. He left without ever telling Stuart that they had found the bodies of that young couple. They couldn't have been dragged more than a quarter mile from the wreck.

The scavengers had not yet gotten to the corpses and that was a small blessing, as Old Man Jennings was quick to point out. Colum wasn't so sure. He'd far rather have found himself faced with some large predator staring him down across the kill than be left with the certainty of knowing it was no animal that had dragged these bodies this far, and through rough terrain. Not even so much as a cloud of stinging insects marked the place where the young couple had at last come to rest. And that, too, was wrong.

As they had drawn closer, Colum's vague sense of unease only became more focused. The bodies had been laid out precisely, formally. They looked almost peaceful, lying there in the center of the secluded moonlit clearing, their pale white hands steepled neatly upon their chests. Slight smiles played at the corner of bloodless lips, as if the pair shared some final secret. Only one jarring note gave the lie to the impression of a tranquil passing—each of the sleepers bore a gaping wound in the center of the forehead. A single perfect, piercing blow to the center of each creaseless, unworried brow. The force of each of those blows had crumpled brow ridge as if it were as insubstantial as eggshell, leaving in its wake a jagged hole, gaping like a single unblinking red eye.

Not that the boy cares, Devil take him. Colum scuffed angrily at the dirt of the path. His bootlaces, still untied, lashed out at random as he walked. *The boy never so much as asked if we'd found the bodies.*

Chapter 3

Not that the boy cares, Devil take him.

If Colum had known just how close he stood at that moment to a very ancient, a very brooding evil, he would have held his peace. In fact, it's doubtful he would have left his family alone in the house at all that morning. No, he would have turned right back around and barricaded the door behind him, for all the good that would do them.

But Colum really had no way of knowing what was within earshot, and one could hardly fault him for his anger. As he stormed down toward the coop, he did note the darkening of the sky, the gathering thunderheads looming low on the horizon, swelling, marshalling their forces. He needed to get the animals in quickly. He really could have used a hand, but he would be damned if he would go back and ask that layabout boy for help a second time. He had his pride. And he had work to do. And that was enough.

Not far from Colum's path, across the yard and just on the far side of the stile, something dark came seeping, seething, bubbling up out of a hoary old crack in the rock. The moss-heavy lightning-split boulder had been called the Touchstone for as long as Colum could remember. The boundary stone had served the family for generations, marking the farthest reach of the ancestral plot long before Colum's ambitious and systematic fencing projects had rendered the old marker stones nothing more than a quaint reminder of a bygone age. His father might have remembered a time, some fifty years past, when last the Touchstone had spoken.

The dark essence that now seeped forth from the broken grin of the Touchstone took little notice of the bull-necked man hurrying toward the chicken coops, hunched low against the impending downpour. It heard him mutter something beneath his breath, and it seemed to swell. A tentative black tendril tested the air like a serpent's tongue. Then an oily appendage, dark as the forgotten places that lie beneath mountains, snaked out of the cleft. The inky blackness stretched obscenely. There seemed no end to it. Soon the sinuous ebon flow was the mocking trickle of a brook, and then a surging stream pouring from the Touchstone.

Colum was no longer anywhere in sight when, at last—with a wet, viscous slurp—the Touchstone disgorged the tail end of the monstrous afterbirth. It writhed, flopping from side to side in the thorny undergrowth that encroached from the edge of the surrounding woods. Then the darkness seemed to curl in upon itself, a first awkward coiling. But whether it was nursing the wounds of its passage through the stony birth canal or already gathering itself, tensing to strike, it was impossible to say. The thick mucousy coils grated and slipped across one another as they wound ever tighter.

There, at the very heart of the dark spiral, something was taking form. A slight, dark, fragile, man-like form. It opened its mouth, gasping, choking down ragged gulps of the chill mountain air. At the sound of its birth-wail—or more precisely, its rebirth-wail—all the dogs across the farmyard threw back their heads and began to bay.

Hearing them, Father-of-Serpents shivered and fell silent, drawing the coils of his bunting closer about him.

He tugged at it, kicked it, stretched it, but it refused to cover him. Already he was the size of a boy of seven—old enough to leave behind the child's-work of the farmyard to learn the man's-work of the fields. He shrugged the blanket from his shoulders like an ill-fitting skin and stood erect in the uncertain light of the stormy morning. He was a young man of sixteen years now, with his full man-height already upon him, and still the constricting coils of the years fell away from him on all sides, sloughed wetly to the ground.

He kicked disdainfully at the shed skin and then stepped free of it, a single step carrying him free of the spreading puddle of ichor. He wore the skin of a man with a full forty years to his credit—a hard, lined, sun-ripened face. A balding pate.

Today, he had his man's-work ahead of him. That work brought him far afield. It had been years, decades maybe, since he had taken it into his head to stretch long-forgotten legs. To have a wander down pasture, to take in a bit of air, a drop of drink, and just overlook his holdings. The sight of the scrabbling man-things that eked out a living in the shadow of his mountain brought a smile to his face.

It had been too long, he thought, drinking deeply of the mountain air. He savored the warm animal smells—sheep and goats, pigs and chickens. He tasted the first moist hint of the looming thunderstorm. He rolled around on his tongue the delicate bouquet of human toil, of sweat, anxiety, poverty, sacrifice and silent suffering. It was sublime.

It was not that he took pleasure in the misfortune of others. That would be ungracious. But he had his work to do and he was good at it. None better, if the truth were known and he was not too shy to admit to it. And if taking pride in a job well done was a sin, well, then, you could just add that to the list of his faults. He had something of a running tab at this point.

He was close now. Although it had been many years since he had come this way, it was all starting to come back to him. There would be that blasted crag just to the right as he rounded the next bend, and beyond it, the first graceful hint of the valley. There.

For their part, the locals generally shunned this inaccessible stretch of the Appalachians. The old women, who ought to know, called the place the Devil's Back Forty. But it wasn't old women and dirt farmers that had brought him all this way. Before his eyes hung a vivid image of a young slip of a girl, skin paler than moonlight, hair deeper than midnight. A familiar tune began to pick at the corner of his mind.

***

Dierdre heard the whistling coming from far off across the field. The tune she knew, although it had been nigh fifty years since she'd last heard it. She sat very still for a long while, just listening, knowing what must come next. And then finally, she shook herself as if waking from a long dream.

"There now, Eileen," she said, turning loose the black ewe. She gathering up the shears and fallen fleece, making a pocket of her apron. "No fretting now. It's only the master of the house, I should imagine, returned home again after these many years. Let us go down to the hedge gate and see what the Old Man is after."

He was waiting for her there. Leaning against the gate, a ridiculously long piece of straw sticking from his teeth. Testing the breeze like a serpent's tongue. He removed a floppy hat and held it over his heart. He smiled.

Lord, she hated that smile.

She was everything he had remembered. She stood there, radiant in the half-light of dusk, both darker and brighter than everything around her. All moonlight and midnight. *How long had it been?* he found himself wondering.

"Fifty year or more since last you darked my door," she replied to his all-too-audible thought. "And I might have done with another fifty, thank you kindly for asking."

"You haven't aged a day," he said, a breathless hiss. It was a simple statement of fact. No hint of flattery clung about his words.

"Small fear of that, as well you know. Now tell me, Old Wyrm, what brings you tramping across my field, raising racket enough to put the sheep to flight? It's well I didn't take you for a pack of hoodlums and set the dogs on you."

She knew he had a sore spot for dogs.

He ignored the dig. "I've come, my dearest," he said, his smile drawing thinner, "to whistle myself up a witch."

She turned her back on him then and pounded angrily back up the path, her shoulders set as if daring him to stop her.

He gazed after the retreating figure until she was nothing more than a dark mote in the cloud of dust she kicked up.

Of course, he was waiting for her there, back at the house, leaning against the porch rail. Same stupid piece of straw. Same stupid grin.

"I've got a special job for you," he said as she approached. "Delicate. Requires a woman's touch."

Dierdre kept coming, head lowered slightly, eyes unwavering. She was a mere ten paces away now and closing. She showed no sign of either stopping or slowing. She was a force of nature, a storm cresting the mountain. Given half a chance, she would break over him and trample his remains underfoot. Five paces.

"And I've brought you something," he said.

That put a hitch in her step. She recovered quickly, so quickly that most men would never have noted her hesitation. He was not most men. Angrily, she stalked up the three steps of the front stoop, each footfall thundering on the hewn planking.

She stomped straight up to him and leaned in close so that their faces were nearly touching. She smelled of warm wool and fresh milk, of living and growing things. Father-of-Serpents drank her in, his eyes falling half closed.

"I want nothing from you," she said, her tone sharp as shears. "Nothing save what's rightfully mine. What you took from me!"

He sighed, having a hard time maintaining his half-dreaming adoration in the face of her obvious scorn. "What you gave freely," he countered patiently. "It is a gift I treasure. I keep it always next to my heart."

He neatly sidestepped her wild lunge, a movement as sudden and fluid as the strike of an asp. "Except of course," he said as she plowed past, "when I'm planning on paying a visit. There's just no knowing what lengths a resourceful girl like yourself might go to in order to reclaim such a treasure. Why, even a cunning old serpent might find himself sorely pressed."

She recovered her composure as best she could, straightening regally, smoothing down the wrinkles in her dress. A wayward strand of hair tickled the corner of her mouth and she blew at it irritably without noticeable effect. Frowning, she smoothed it back behind one ear.

"Whatever it is that's brought you," she said coolly, "I want no part of it."

"Come now," he said with an ingratiating grin. "Be a sensible girl and hear at least what I have to offer."

"I've had quite enough of your gifts, thank you. Enough to—"

"To last a lifetime?" he interrupted. She choked back the reply that was on her lips and fumed.

"Come, let us not quarrel," he coaxed. "It is such a little thing I have to ask, and I have come fully prepared for you to shame me in the bargaining. I know you do so enjoy our little negotiations. Yes? There's a clever girl. Reminds me at times of my own dear daughter."

"I'm listening," she said. "You've got five minutes. Then I set the dogs on you." She crossed her arms over her chest.

"It's almost embarrassing, really, it's such a trifle…" he began.

She rolled her eyes.

"I would see to it myself if my time were my own. But you know how things are. I'm weeks behind now and you know how hard it is to find reliable help in this business. I mean, if these folks were trustworthy, they wouldn't be showing up at my office in the first place, now would they?"

"Four minutes," she said.

He extracted a gorgeous red-gold pocket watch, flipped its face open and regarded the dial skeptically. "I put it at four and a half," he said.

"You're rambling. And you're a poor liar. I charged you thirty seconds for that."

He looked hurt as he replaced the watch. "There are some that would say I am the very Prince of…oh, never mind. You'll only tell me that I'm a poor boaster as well. And that would, likely as not, cost me a full minute. Look, the job is very simple. Even a mere slip of girl could do it."

She shrugged. "Then get yourself a mere slip of a girl. I have other things to tend to. Thanks ever so much for stopping by. We'll have to do this again real soon. Maybe in another fifty years or so." She put two fingers to her lips to whistle for the dogs.

"Ah, ah," he caught her hand and, stroking it gently as if it were a ruffled bird, smoothed it back down to her side. "I was promised three more minutes of your delightful company."

"One minute," she said. "And counting."

"I will come to the point. All I need," he said turning up his hands imploringly, "is someone to keep a little story for me. There, is that so much to ask?"

"What's the catch?"

He clutched at his heart as if mortally wounded. "Catch? There's no catch. A story has been entrusted into my keeping. These things happen. In my role as Patron of Serpents, I have certain duties. Most of them are not unpleasant—the occasional garden party, that sort of thing. But my people spend a lot of time with an ear to the ground. They hear things. I can't help that. Occasionally, they hear something they probably should not, something that shouldn't get out. You're a discreet girl, you know the kind of thing I mean…."

She tapped one delicate foot. He hurried on.

"I would like to be sure that this story does not fall into the wrong hands. Naturally my thoughts—as they so often do—immediately flew to you. You are such a resourceful girl and this is really such a small favor…"

"Tell me the story, then we'll see," she said.

He smiled. "Promise me first. That you'll keep it safe for me."

"No promises. Once I've heard your story, I'll know who's likely to try to kill me for it."

"What kind of fiend do you take me for?" he cried indignantly. "I would never knowingly put you in peril. Why, I would rather die first!"

"Well, we both know that's not going to happen, now don't we? So how about you stop with the long face and just tell me the story."

"I can't tell you the story," he said.

"Then I can't help you," she said. "And I'm afraid your minute is up."

"I can't tell you," he interjected hurriedly, "because I haven't committed the tale to memory." He shrugged apologetically. "It's a very long story."

"I don't believe this. You know, sometimes I wonder how you manage to get anything done. Do you have the story written down?"

"Yes," he said, shifting uncomfortably from one foot to the other.

"Yes, *but…*" she prompted.

"Yes, but it's not here."

"Okay, I'll play along. I'm going to ask, but only because I have the sneaking suspicion that you're going to stand around on my porch day and night, grinning that idiot grin until you've told me. So, where is it?"

"It is written under a mountain," he said.

"I see," she said, but didn't. "And have you actually seen this story?"

"Not so much me, personally. It's like I told you, a little serpent told me."

"A little serpent? No, never mind. I don't want to know. So this little serpent, he told you the story, only you can't remember the whole thing."

"He didn't actually tell me the story so much as tell me *of* the story."

"You've got no idea what this story is about," she accused. It was not a question. Her growing exasperation was beginning to peek through.

"This Wyrm…" he began, and then checked himself, "this little serpent, he made it quite clear that this story was of some importance to my people. And that it was of utmost importance that it be kept safe. If it were to fall into the wrong hands…"

"Yes? What if it were to fall into the wrong hands?" she asked pointedly.

"Well then, the story could be used to hurt my children. Among others," he said with a smile. "I should not like for anyone to threaten my children."

"You mean the serpents?"

"Of course," said Father-of-Serpents. "Then you'll do it?"

His voice was eager. "Hardly," she replied. "I can't say I much fancy the idea of crawling around on my belly under some mountain to help protect a few serpents who would just as likely poison me as look at me."

"They would cherish you as I do," he protested. "They would make of you their queen!"

"You have never 'made of me your queen,'" she retorted.

"You are more precious to me than any queen."

"That's not at all the same thing, and well you know it. And I do not see why I should want to be some Queen of Serpents. I suppose next you will be offering me the honor of becoming Queen of Vermin."

But he knew now he had her. "You will go to that far place, in the shadow of the mountain, on whose heart the story is graven. You will wear your name openly. Men will know you for what you are and they will despair before your terrible beauty."

"Perhaps," said she. "And perhaps I will carry away with me the wages I have earned tending your estate this fifty year: Mastery of Growing Things, a Serpent's Casting, Youth Without End."

"Done," he said quickly. "And I will set you on an onyx throne and give to you the key to a great kingdom. And I will send to you the most shining prince to be born in a score of generations, but you will suckle serpents at your breast."

Well, that took her aback, but to her credit, the witch just squinted up at him hard then and drove home her bargain. "And when I have kept your story for a year and a day, then you will return to me what you have stolen. My little locket and the prize you have imprisoned there."

"It is an awkward and embarrassing thing to have, a soul," he said reflectively. "I, frankly, cannot understand what everyone sees in them. I have drawers-full of the damned things cluttering up the place, but I've yet to find any use for them."

"I think I will take my chances," she said bitterly.

"And a soul is a such a fickle thing. You realize of course, that it would never abide any of the other little presents I have brought for you over the years—Mastery of Growing Things, a Serpent's Casting, Youth Without End…"

"Then I will renounce them."

He raised an eyebrow. "You would go back to being what you were before? An ambitious girl like you? I find it hard to credit."

"Is it a bargain or not?" she snapped.

Father-of-Serpents just smiled. "Could I ever refuse you? It will be as you say."

Without so much as asking leave, he turned and strolled through the front door and into the house. She stood there, hands on hips, open-mouthed at his audacity.

The house was full of the smell of a good wood fire, of roasting meat, of biscuits baking. Smells the like of which he had not savored these fifty years.

"Be a good girl now," he called over his shoulder, "and fetch me that fine black wool you sheared today. Card it well and spin me a coarse yarn. And do not tarry, for you must be on your way this very night."

Dierdre bristled. She did not know how he knew about her morning's shearing, but did as she was bidden. She *was* an ambitious girl. She forced herself to focus upon the priceless treasure that awaited her in only a brief year's time. She could put up with even his unwelcome visits for so short a span. She was whistling softly to herself as she went to fetch the carding combs.

Chapter 4

The moonbridges sang atop the Hill of Lamentations. It was a living, vibrant sound. The music did not arise from the bridges themselves; they were its conduit. The song thrummed along them, carrying the multiform and wondrous sounds of distant lands to the Sept of the Anvil-Klaiven.

Stuart listened, enrapt, trying to pick out the individual strains. He wondered when last the ice-hearted caern had heard the twilling of cicadas, the patter of scaled claws over desert sands, the laughter of falling water over sunbaked stones, the rustle of gentle rains settling through the canopy of the rainforest.

And now the night was alive with all these far-flung sounds at once, woven seamlessly into the more familiar background music—the thrashings of the ice-choked Hammerfell, the mournful wail of the shifting ice floe, the rustling of a dark wind through the pines.

Stuart's very bones seemed to hum with the all-pervasive music. The sound of things happening.

The sky glowed with the light of a dozen moons. Sharp shafts of moonlight crisscrossed the heavens. Each gleaming lunar pathway seemed to leap from the apex of the Hill, as if it might catch one of those dozen moonglobes within its jaws. A fanfare of lights that would shame the aurora borealis streaked outward into the night sky, sounding its triumphant howl in denial of the vast impersonal interstellar distances. Calling the people together, calling them home.

But it was not the play of lights that captivated the attention, but rather the song. The moonbridges sang, not to the ears, but to something more primal within each of the Garou. The music echoed within the secret chambers of the heart; it piped through the hollow of the bones; it snatched at the spirit like a strong wind catches an autumn leaf, sending it tumbling back skyward.

The song called to mystical side of the Garou, courted it, coaxed it out. It was a summons, a call to run, to leap, to dance. Those abandoning themselves to the communion of that song literally danced between the worlds. They chased over Umbral pathways, crossing the vast distances between the septs in a single evening.

Stuart stepped from the moonbridge, down onto the crest of the Hill of Lamentations. He thought that he could still vaguely make out the outline of the proud longship of the Old Jarl that lay buried beneath the Hill. He closed his eyes and drew a long deep breath, savoring it. Yes, it was not hard to imagine that he could still feel its gentle rocking underfoot.

Seeing him, the old troll beneath the bridges shuffled forward, closing on him, grinning a saw-toothed grin. Stuart stood his ground, glancing nervously at the four hulking lupine forms that ringed the twisted man. Gratefully, they did not break ranks nor so much as look his way. Each of them wore the lumbering dire-wolf form. Their heads were thrown back in the attitude of a great soul-rending howl, but the only sound that escaped their throats was the multiform song of the moonbridges.

The twisted man jabbed Stuart ungently in the shoulder with a stick even more crooked than himself.

"Youth is wasted on the young," he croaked. "You've barely an hour's moonlight left to you and there's not a patch of roof left to lie under in all the sept. Leastways not one where they're not already piled three deep like pups."

"Thank you, Rite-master," Stuart said. "It was a glorious trip. And the song along the bridges tonight! It was worth coming all this way even if I have to spend the rest of the night in a snowbank."

The crooked man ground his teeth together, a sound like knives sharpening. Stuart took this as a sign of approval, but he was often given to wishful thinking.

"If it comes to that," said the Rite-master, "there's always dry ground among the pine needles. Treeline's well within the bawn and safe and dry as any hall."

"Again, my thanks. It does look like quite a crowd." Stuart took in the firelight and raised voices streaming from the halls below. And the scuffle of hulking forms contending in the central square. And the restless shifting of countless shadows through the tree line. "Where to start?" he mused aloud.

The stick rapped him twice sharply upon the shoulder and then shot out and down, sighting toward the hall at the center of the maelstrom of activity. "House of the Spearsreach," the Rite-master said. "You'll find the Jarlsdottir there. But keep your wits about you and your tongue civil. The warband is at its cups." As if that explained everything.

"That I will," Stuart said. "Thanks for the warning. Can I have them send you up anything?"

The Rite-master spread his arms in a gesture that seemed to encompass the entire Hill of Lamentations, the moonlight on the ice floe, the dazzling spectacle of the moonbridges, the fullness of the swelling song, the immensity of the night sky.

It was a gesture that clearly said, "What more could I want?" Or, perhaps more precisely, "What more is there?"

Stuart smiled and bowed his head in leave-taking. Then, the song of the world at his back, he set his steps toward the House of the Spearsreach.

Chapter 5

Stuart shouldered open the door to the House of the Spearsreach. It resisted his efforts, as if the sheer weight of the riot of sensations beyond the door pushed against him. As the door gave way, his senses were immediately bombarded with the blaze of the roaring fire, the press of hulking figures, the animal tang of sweat, the aroma of roasting pork, the reek of spilled ale. There was a commotion of pigs and chickens underfoot and all around him voices were raised in boast and contention. He thought he heard the musical thunk of a war axe biting heartwood.

It was too much to take in at once. A lesser man might have hovered in the doorway until the maelstrom of flesh and sinew had resolved itself into some semblance of comprehensibility. Until the shifting tides of light, shadow and clamor had resumed their individual and clearly defined forms. Stuart was no wallflower. He liked a crowd, liked its pulse, its shove, its intimacy, its anonymity. He smiled and pressed blindly forward into the mass of bodies.

There was something about a crowd, its shifting layers of veils, its raw potential. A face swimming toward him through the fray could be anyone—a kinsman, a lover, a rival, a prophet, a mark, a corpse. Or perhaps all of these. It was really just a matter of perspective and of time. Given long enough, everyone would eventually get a chance to try on all the masks. Anything was possible here. It was the place where the boundaries between people came crashing down.

Stuart moved with the surging of the tide of bodies and after a time he found himself tossed ashore upon a long rough-hewn wooden bench. The mountain of food and drink heaped upon the adjoining table recommended it highly to Stuart's mind. The vantage point had the additional advantage of giving him a clearer view of an altercation that was heating up in the vicinity of the high table.

A huge Fenrir warrior, shoulders as broad as a hillside, stood before the board, head thrown back, eyes blazing. In one hand he clutched a freshly bloodied battle standard. His sudden appearance had caused quite a commotion in the hall. The crowd instinctively shrank back before him, not so much from his obvious air of authority as from the dangerous fire that roiled just beneath the skin.

Stuart jogged his neighbor's elbow to get his attention and nearly succeeded in overturning the cup that was already halfway to his lips. "Who's that?"

"Hey, watch it! Damned fool." He banged the cup down and tried to rise to his feet but there wasn't really room enough to maneuver without overturning the entire bench.

Stuart shoved the nearest ewer toward him and repeated his question more loudly. "Sorry. I said, 'Who is that?' At the high table. With the bloody flag?"

His neighbor followed the line of Stuart's gaze, then grunted and settled back into his seat. He glowered at Stuart a moment more, but finally accepted the proffered pitcher. "S'the Warder. Brand Garmson. You know the Warder," he insisted.

Stuart looked blank.

"The other fellow, the one he's got by the scruff of the neck, that's his packmate, Jorn Gnaws-Steel. I'd say it looks like there's been some sort of scuffle out on the perimeter."

Stuart thanked him, but the words were drowned out beneath the Warder's bellowed command: "You tell them what you told me." Garmson shoved the younger Garou forward.

Jorn recovered as gracefully as possible, dropping to one knee before the High Siege. "A party arrived at the perimeter shortly before sunset, Jarlsdottir," he began uncertainly. "Under a flag of truce. They claimed to be a delegation from Lord Arkady."

At that name a murmuring swept through the hall.

Stuart studied the young woman perched in the High Siege. The one Jorn had identified as the Jarlsdottir. His first impression was that she seemed very young to have risen to a position of such authority over these grizzled veterans. She was in her mid-twenties at most. But as Stuart watched her step forward and raise Jorn to his feet with both hands, he could see the gratitude and unguarded admiration in the young warrior's eyes. He would obey the gruff commands of the Warder without hesitation, leaping claws-first to certain death; but he would give his life for this Jarlsdottir without ever being bidden.

Karin's voice cut through the clamor. There was no hint of softness about it. "A flag of truce? We are not at war with the House of the Crescent Moon. Here is Arkady's own kinsman, Victor Svorenko, seated at table with us." Then the Jarlsdottir's look became suspicious. "Where is this delegation, Jorn Gnaws-Steel, and why have you not brought them before us?"

Jorn shifted uneasily under her scrutiny. "The three were not of House Crescent Moon, Jarlsdottir. They were Black Spiral Dancers."

The hall erupted with cries and accusations.

"Wyrm-taint! A black stain upon all his House."

"What further proof is needed?"

"Did he not command the Knockerwyrm? His own kinsman has admitted as much."

"Even the Spirals run his errands for him!"

The Jarlsdottir struck the butt of her great silver hammer thrice upon the ground to restore some semblance of order. Still there were isolated outbursts.

Stuart watched the unfolding pandemonium with an air of patient aloofness. He had watched similar scenes play themselves out among his own people time and time again. He had even—on occasion—taken a hand in encouraging some of those uproars. His kinsmen, the Fianna, had acquired something of a reputation for their fiery passions, for their love of strong words and stronger drink, and for the scuffles and challenges that invariably resulted from that volatile combination.

In a way, Stuart found this unfortunate reputation understandable. Certainly this boisterous minority was colorful and tended to make a lasting impression upon bystanders, innocent or otherwise. But for every hard-fighting, hard-drinking, Irish nationalist among them, there were at least a dozen others whose passions ran just as deep, but tended to follow a less obvious course. For every tale of a fearless young cattle-raider sung by the tribe's Galliards—the finest storytellers to be found anywhere among the Garou—there were a myriad of other stories. Stories of more reflective passions. Of a doomed love from afar; of dwelling upon a haunting failure or glory from the past; of the cherishing of family and kinfolk, even to one's own undoing.

The lore of the Fianna was filled with tales of lawcases and dreamquests, of poets and devils, of card games and pillow talk, of mission bells and bloody idols, of men with wits lighter than air and children strapped to the lodestone of having to grow a second tongue. Of princes and exiles; warriors and holy hermits; and of exiled-warrior-princes-cum-holy-hermits. And yes, even of the proud, sea-coursing raiders who pressed Stuart so sorely on every side this very night, reminding him of the labyrinthine passions of his own people.

"What is called for here is clear thinking." The Jarlsdottir's voice broke in upon his introspection. "Did this delegation offer any proof that they came from Lord Arkady? There is often a chasm between what a Spiral says and what is, in fact, truth."

Jorn considered a moment. "No," he admitted. "Although the spokesman did claim to be a kinsman of Lord Arkady. He said his name was Knife-between-Bones."

A short way down Stuart's table, Victor Svorenko surged to his feet, his hands slamming down upon the board hard enough to rattle the crockery. "I will not have my House slandered in my presence. I came here in good faith, to speak the truth as I have witnessed it. Those of you who last night heard me tell of the fall of Arne Wyrmsbane know that I am not one to shirk the truth—even if this truth would seem damning to one of my kinsmen. House Crescent Moon is the truest of all the Silver Fang noble lines.

This point is uncontested and excruciatingly documented. To assert that Lord Arkady is kinsman to such—it is unthinkable. Retract your claim, or defend it with the strength of your arm!"

Jorn bowed slightly in the direction of the incensed Silver Fang. "You mistake me, cousin. I was only reporting the words of the Spiral as I was ordered. I do not myself press this accusation. And it may please you to learn that the Warder has already avenged you this insult."

The bared neck seemed to mollify Victor more than the carefully chosen words. "I accept your retraction. But have a care to tell us only the exact words of this Knife-between-Bones that we can avoid such confusions."

"I will give them to you as nearly as I can remember them," Jorn replied and proceeded to give a fairly accurate rendering of the peculiar conversation. When he got to the part about Arkady being "detained," the clamor rose up again, drowning him out.

"This is a foul business," Victor called out. "Arkady has obviously fallen into the clutches of the Spirals. Why else would he not be here by now?"

"Because he is afraid to face us!"

"Who says such?" Victor challenged, reddening. "We must mount a party to track these Wyrm-spawn back to their lair. If Arkady has been taken captive…"

Karin again brought her silver hammer down. "I am sure the Warder already has our best trackers out on the trail," she said. As she scanned the room, however, she saw that Thijs and the other hunters were still among them. The Warder had not been at all himself these last weeks, she reflected. The shadow of death rode him mercilessly, goading him on with the lash of vengeance.

Before anyone else could remark on this oversight, she pressed on. "If Arkady fails to present himself, however, we will be forced to pronounce judgment in his absence. We have heard the testimony of Victor Svorenko—Arkady's own kinsman—telling how Arkady commanded the Knockerwyrm and it obeyed him as its master. We have heard the tale of the Silver Crown and how Arkady conspired with the servitors of the Wyrm to capture the throne of the Silver Fangs for himself. We know that he was forced to flee the States under suspicious circumstances and that the cloud of suspicions followed him all the way home to Russia. And thus far, not one voice—from any of the twelve tribes—has come forward to speak in his defense."

There was a long silence in the hall. Stuart gazed around at the sea of downcast faces. No one so much as looked toward the Jarlsdottir, much less rose to meet her challenge. Had the proud Silver Fang lord fallen so low that there was no one among this vast company who would speak up for him?

The silence stretched and Stuart could feel anger and indignation rising up within him. This was *Arkady* they were talking about. The hero who had been proclaimed the best hope of the Garou Nation. The king who would unite the fractious tribes under a single banner and carry the battle into the very teeth of the Wyrm!

Before he even realized he had moved, Stuart was on his feet. As eyes turned toward him, he self-consciously smoothed at the front of his rumpled suit. It was too late to back down now. The golden wolf-headed torc at his throat seemed suddenly too tight, as if it were choking him, sinking its teeth into his neck.

He cleared his throat loudly and began to speak. His voice was not loud, but his words carried to the far corners of the hall and beyond. They streamed like firelight out through the cracks beneath windows and doors. They spilled out among the tipsy revelers staggering across the Aeld Baile. They slipped like shadows through the tree line and skidded out over the ice floe. The slight, but unmistakable Appalachian drawl sounded alien, almost exotic, here in the domain of the north wind.

"Not one of you, eh? Not a one. Well, it's not hard to tell which way the wind blows through this room. I came a long way hoping to find some answers, but I see nobody here's even asking the questions. Still, I can't very well sit by and see a man condemned without a word spoken to his credit. My given name's Stuart; they call me Stalks-the-Truth.

"Now, I don't personally even know Arkady, but I do know the stories. I know what's in them and I know what's not. And when I hear about Arkady quelling the Knockerwyrm with only his voice, I am put in mind of an old saying, 'A house divided against itself cannot stand.' You don't cast out devils by the power of the Devil and you don't subdue the minions of the Wyrm by the power of the Wyrm. That's in a book somewhere, or near enough. And if I remember the story right,

Arkady was not banished after the affair of the Silver Crown. In fact, if he were already under formal censure for his part in that tale, there would be no need for us to sit around passing judgment on him now. No, if Albrecht had had it in mind to judge Arkady, he would have done so. There, on the spot. All in all, a few stories is pretty thin evidence on which to convict a man without even giving him his say."

There was a silence in the hall, broken only by the scrape of the Jarlsdottir's silver hammer as she rose to her feet. The note of sadness and disappointment in her voice was plain. These were her people. And they had failed her far more than they had wronged Stuart, with their hard hearts, their blood prices. "Our stories are our past, Stuart Stalks-the-Truth. As a law-speaker, I put my trust in the songs and stories of our people. As Arkady has not presented himself, he will be judged by what is said and sung of him—not only by us, but by all who come after. His reputation and his renown must be his defense. It does you credit that you are willing to speak up for him, a stranger to you. I can only wish that there were more voices raised in his praise and fewer in his condemnation."

There were mutters of agreement from around the room. Karin cleared her throat and pitched her voice to carry the length of the hall. "I speak for the Fenrir. It is the judgment of the tribe that Lord Arkady of the House of the Crescent Moon has willingly consorted with the Wyrm and is further complicit in the death of our shield-brother Arne Wyrmsbane. He is from this night declared outcast. No longer shall our halls be open to him, nor shall any of our kinsmen give him aid or succor. His blood is declared already fallen; there shall be no question of wergild or any other repercussion against one who is found to have harmed, maimed, or even killed him. We mourn our cousin, fallen in private battle with the Wyrm. Sergiy Dawntreader, how say the Children of Gaia?"

Stuart did not have the heart to hear the rest. Silently, he slipped from the hall. He had had about as much as he could stomach of Fenrir justice. Outside, in the crisp night air, beneath the ice-sharp stars, hulking silhouettes—each towering over nine feet tall, bristling with fur and knotted sinew—vied to throw one another to the frozen earth.

He picked his way carefully through the combatants. It was not the object of their games that eluded him, it was their purpose. At the end of their desperate grapplings, one contender lies flat upon the earth; one raises a clawed fist heavenwards. But what is gained, what is lost? At the end of a game of chess, the vanquished overturns his king, capitulating. The toppled monarch lies stretched out insensate upon an unadorned square of white snow or black ice. But what dynasty falls with him? What kingdom is despoiled? What army, relieved of its head, is broken and scattered?

Somewhere behind him, within the riot of the Hall of the Spearsreach, in the wake of the elaborate and raucous game of intertribal justice, a king-that-might-have-been had just been toppled. The *duc bellorum* that they had been promised had been taken from them. And without a single blow being struck.

Who could say what doleful price would yet be exacted for this presumption? And who, of all of them, would be left to pay it?

Chapter 6

Upon Dierdre's return, she found Father-of-Serpents still hunched over the hearth as she had left him. He was staring intently into the dance of flames as if trying to wrest from it some secret. His shadow swayed hypnotically in time to the flickering of the flames. If he had stirred at all since early morning, however, he gave no sign of it.

She took some smug satisfaction in that. If she had managed to keep him from his usual mischief, even for the space of a single morning, the world would be a better place for her trouble.

Hearing her footfalls creaking on the uncarpeted wooden stair, he turned toward her, smiling broadly. *Lord, she hated that smile.* "There's a clever girl," he purred, extending one blackened claw toward her.

For a moment, a wave of cold panic swept over her, fear that he intended to take her by the hand, to draw her close to him. She stiffened and involuntarily retreated a half step, before she caught herself, forced herself to hold her ground before him. There were some adversaries you did not turn your back upon.

His smile didn't waver.

Then, flustered, she realized his true intent. Embarrassed, she thrust the skein of yarn—the fruit of her morning's shearing and carding and spinning—into his outstretched hand. This had the desired effect. That terrible appendage withdrew.

He teased loose one end of the skein and played out a handsbreadth of ebon yarn. He rolled it between thumb and forefinger appraisingly. It was finer than human hair and strong as a rope.

"It's beautiful work," he said at last. "Your talents are wasted here, among the dirt farmers—a golden lamp hidden under a bushel basket. If you can do this with mere lamb's wool, imagine what you might do with the finest silk of all between your fingers, the dream-fine thread of human misery. Perhaps when your year and a day is up, I might entice you to—"

"No, thank you," she said curtly.

"I would reward you in queenly fashion for your trouble," he pressed. "And it would be so little trouble for a clever girl such as yourself. Here, I will make you a gift. As both a token of my affection and as a pledge to seal the bargain…"

Her hesitation could not have amounted to even a fraction of a second, but it was enough. He knew he had her. And after so long and intimate an association, perhaps it was no longer even a fair contest. He knew exactly where the chinks in her armor lay.

"I said I want nothing more to do with you or your presents," she said.

"But you do not even know what it is yet," he coaxed. "How can you say you want nothing to do with it?"

She started to retort and broke off abruptly as he turned his free hand palm up. The motion revealed two long, gleaming knitting needles. Delicate scrollwork, or perhaps a flowing script, coiled lovingly about them, covering their entire surface. The firelight did not so much reflect off them as become trapped in the flowing engraving, following its curves like water following a channel.

"Spinnerets of purest silver," he said. "And there's not another set to match them in all the breadth of the earth. With such needles as these in your hands, your efforts would be nothing less than the stuff of legend. Why, one might even weave the ethereal threads of dream and nightmare, desire and fear, hope and—"

"Put them away," she said, unable to take her eyes from them.

He watched their reflection glittering deep within her eyes. "But they are yours," he said. "For the asking."

"I said, put them away." Her voice had a note of desperation to it now. And still she could not wrest her eyes away.

He rose from his chair, but she was aware only of the dazzling needles. They drew closer, almost within reach.

"Very well," he said. "Tell me where you would like them, and I will put them away for you." He surveyed the room a moment and then reached up toward the mantle. "Here, perhaps?"

She felt their moving away like a hole opening up within her. She yearned toward them.

"No," she said, shaking her head stubbornly. "Take them away. Far away. Before I cannot…" From somewhere within, she seemed to draw on a hidden reserve of strength, of steel and firelight. Her tone became hard and sure. "Before I am forced to take you up on your unwise offer and tell you, with most unladylike exactitude, where I should like you to keep your needles."

A look of anger settled low on his brow like a storm cloud. It passed just as quickly, evaporating before she could even be sure that she had really seen it. But that infuriating smile vanished, and that was a victory in itself.

Even if it that disappearing act was followed a moment later by the peerless needles. Gone.

"As you wish," he said, shrugging with feigned indifference. Then, without so much as looking at her, he cast the skein of ebon yarn—her entire day's labor—directly into the heart of the flames.

A cry of protest escaped her lips as she lunged forward. She brushed roughly past him, trying to ignore the way her skin seemed to creep beneath the caress of thousands of skittering legs at the contact. Seizing the poker, she caught at the smoldering ball of yarn and, with a deft twisting motion, she snared it. But when she drew it forth from the flames, she found she had hooked, not a ball of yarn, but a finely woven shawl.

She turned, a look of incomprehension on her face. And he laughed then, genuine laughter. Not just that stupid, maddening grin. And he drew her close to him and she could not resist him.

He took her by the hand and led her back out through the door of the farmhouse. She could not so much as manage to draw the door closed behind her, although she knew she would not return. She thought of all the lovely things within that she had accumulated these fifty years. And of going away, just leaving the front door gaping wide. Where anyone might walk in.

And that Father-of-Serpents marched her right back up the lane to the gate. And that too she could only leave standing open behind them, swinging lazily in the wind. Then, with a flourish, he wrapped her in the long black shawl, encompassing her above and below. And lifting her up, he set her adrift upon the night wind. The coming storm caught at the hem of the shawl and billowed it out like a sail.

Chapter 7

The sound of footsteps crunching through the thin crust of snow brought Stuart around sharply. His own feet had carried him, as if of their own accord, far from the press of reveling Garou—down to the silence and serenity of the Hammerfell. The river, choked with ice, creaked and groaned like a ship. Straining toward the open sea. Anxious to be free.

A solitary figure was picking its way toward him from the direction of the Aeld Baile. After a moment, its features resolved themselves into the face of Victor Svorenko.

"I hope I do not intrude," Victor called, hesitating a dozen yards away. "I...I would thank you before I go. For what you have done for my kinsman."

Stuart scowled. "I have done nothing," he said. "I am sorry."

Sorry I could not have done more. Sorry my words carried no conviction. Sorry they fell only upon deaf ears.

He turned back toward the river.

After a moment, the footfalls drew closer. "You have nothing to be sorry for, Stuart Stalks-the-Truth. You spoke up for my kinsman, and at a time when I could not. For that I am in your debt."

"Forget it," Stuart said. "I meant I was sorry about what they did. To Arkady. To you and your kin. To all of us for that matter. I really thought he might be the one.... Forget it. You don't owe me anything."

Victor was beside him now. He spoke in a choked whisper. "All of these proud warriors," he said, gesturing disdainfully back toward the House of the Spearsreach, "they are cowards. All of them! They judge my kinsman without having the courage to face him. Without one of them having even the strength to speak in his defense! Better that I should never have spoken. Better that I should have let the things I have seen fester within me, turning like the Wyrm in my belly. Better that I should have cut out my own tongue than I should have brought this indignity upon my house."

"It's not your fault," Stuart said. But Victor was having none of these platitudes. He scoffed and shook his head, pretending to study the complex patterns of moonlight on the frozen river.

Stuart could sense that the Fang had taken the first steps of a solitary path that only spiraled down into disillusionment and despair. He could not follow Victor along that path, but he could accompany him in spirit, by pouring a steady flow of bolstering words, like strong drink, into him.

"Look, if you had not spoken out," Stuart persisted, "that doubt would have gnawed away at you. Chewed you up from the inside until it found your heart. All it takes is a tiny opening, even a well-intentioned one, and the Wyrm has you. I've seen it happen. A lie to save a kinsman and the Wyrm slips in. It wraps its coils around the deception, encysts it. Soon you're scrambling to conceal not only your kinsman's failing but your own part in the cover-up. Then the Wyrm takes its tail in its mouth and draws the noose tighter. Something leaks out, you don't know how, and now it's blackmail. A stranger contacts you with a simple request, a favor. And who would it hurt, really? Before long your kinsman's stumble has dragged you down with him. Another champion lost to us. This is the way the Wyrm works."

"This is the way the world ends," Victor replied flatly, his eyes fixed on some distant point amidst the ice-sharp stars. Stuart could feel the Fang fosterling slipping away from him.

"Let me tell you something about the way the world ends," Stuart said hastily. "You know what I think? Sometimes I think the Apocalypse is not some Final Battle waiting for us at the end of time. Where the assembled champions of Gaia all line up on one side and the minions of the Wyrm all line up on the other. And then Luna, knowing what must surely come, opens her throat in a banshee wail for her lost children. And the armies take that keening note as the eagerly awaited signal and set upon one another in earnest. And they kill and kill and kill again until that wailing stops. Until they have drowned it in a sea of spilling lifeblood and the moon's face vanishes under a film of blood."

"Gaia forfend! Do not speak of such things," Victor made a sign against the Eye of the Wyrm. "By giving voice to such misfortune you only invite it upon yourself. It is better not to think of such things at all."

"But I do not think that this is the end that we are speeding toward," Stuart said. "If I did, I do not know how I would find the strength to rise and face another day. No, I think the Apocalypse is something quite different."

Eric Griffin

He leaned closer, confiding a secret. "I think the Apocalypse is already upon us. I do. I think that we are the children of the Apocalypse. It's the battle we all fight, every day. It's a battle, not against doing 'evil,' but against doing what is convenient, what is comfortable, what is expected. Let's face it, the Wyrm doesn't have to put on some great martial display to carry the field. He only has to keep whispering and churning. Telling us that we are doing all that can be done. That we are already fighting the good fight. Telling us there's no harm in taking little 'shortcuts' for the greater good. A silence, a complacency, a deception—that's all it takes. Good men, strong warriors, fall in this battle each and every day. And we go on as before, listening to the whispers in the dark, pretending the Final Battle is still years off. Pretending that all is well."

Victor was silent a long while. At last, he turned to Stuart and met his eyes. "I have grown tired of pretendings," Victor said. "I have no further time for childish things—for the posturings of our cousins, for their playing at the games of justice and of conquest. I must go and find my kinsman. Even if he has fallen into the clutches of the Black Spirals, I must go to him. I was a fool to have ever left his side. I saw him command the Wyrm-spawn and I was afraid. No, do not interrupt. I was afraid; I will not put a more flattering face upon it. Arkady may have been in the midst of his greatest need, of his own Final Battle with the Wyrm, and I turned my back upon him. Out of fear."

"You are no coward, Victor Svorenko," Stuart said. "Few would have the courage to do what you have done. To speak out when silence was in your best interest. It could not have been an easy decision."

"It was the only decision. But did I speak from courage or from fear? I would not be so fast to judge. I was afraid, Stuart Stalks-the-Truth. Afraid of what Arkady had become. And afraid because, if the Wyrm could do that to Lord Arkady, to that one who was the best and purest of us all, then the Wyrm could do that to any of us. To you. To me. No, it was not bravery that drove me, but desperation. Despair."

"You had hoped that the concolation would prove you wrong," Stuart said. "That the elders would vindicate your kinsman."

"I had hoped that they would drag him here. In chains, if need be," Victor answered with sudden vehemence. "I wanted them to make him answer. To prove to me, with his own acts and his own deeds that I was wrong. That what I had seen, with my own eyes, was a lie. A trick of the Wyrm, nothing more.

"I wanted him to show them—to show them all!—that he was better they were. Larger than life, more than merely Garou. That he could crush a thunderwyrm with a mere word. I wanted him to make them follow him. To love him," he trailed off weakly. Victor's anger seemed to drain from him. "I wanted him to make *me* follow him. To believe in him again. As if nothing had…"

Victor broke off and turned away. There were tears at the corners of his eyes.

Stuart left him to his private thoughts and recriminations. But he stood beside him, within easy reach. If

Victor should find himself overmatched in his own Final Battle, he would at least know that someone was there. He would not fall alone and unmourned.

The moon settled gingerly toward the horizon, as if reluctant to dip her toe into the icy waters.

At last Victor stirred, stepping from the field of battle back onto the icy shores of the Hammerfell. As he became aware of his surroundings once more, he cleared his throat and shifted uncomfortably, obviously embarrassed. "You have been too indulgent of a very foolish man this night, Stuart Stalks-the-Truth. And now the moon is already low in the sky and I have little chance of catching up with the hunters and picking up the trail of the Black Spirals. I only wanted to thank you."

Stuart shook his head. "You are welcome, Victor. I am glad we had the chance to speak. And it helped me as well, gave me a chance to get some stuff straight in my head. Now I find myself wondering if I can ask you a favor."

"Ah, and then a stranger asks you for a favor." Smiling, Victor parroted back Stuart's earlier words.

Stuart, in turn, laughed aloud. "No, nothing like that. Your secrets are safe with me. But it occurs to me that I would very much like to find Lord Arkady myself. To ask some questions. To find some answers. I know it is a great imposition, but do you think you could take me to the place where you last saw him—the site of the battle with the Knockerwyrm at the tin mine? I would consider it a personal favor."

"I am in your debt," Victor said, waving aside Stuart's protests to the contrary. "I would be honored if you would join me in the search for my kinsman. I should be glad for your assistance and your company."

He clasped Stuart by the forearm. Stuart returned the gesture, sealing the bargain. "You are a good man, Stuart Stalks-the-Truth," Victor said. "And a brave one. We will meet again tomorrow night and travel back to the Sept of the Dawn. But tonight I must learn what I can from these Fenrir hunters. Good night."

Stuart nodded and let Victor take all of three steps along the ice floe. Then, silently, he fell into step beside the Silver Fang.

Victor turned to him with a look of puzzlement and slight annoyance.

"If the hunters have turned up anything," Stuart explained, "I don't want you rushing off into some nest of Black Spirals without me." He slapped Victor on the back and the two set their steps toward the perimeter.

Chapter 8

In three shakes of a serpent's tail, that wind washed Dierdre ashore upon a high mountaintop half a world away. It was a desolate place, a blackened stump jutting up out of a range of forbidding crags. A crooked finger pointed accusingly heavenward.

The retreating winds tugged at Dierdre's skirts as if repenting their cruelty in depositing her here in such a place. She could almost hear them whispering one to the other, "Enough. Not here. Come away now." But she held her ground. This was the place. She could feel it in the pulse of the mountain reaching up for her, rising through the layered granite, piercing the soles of her feet. Rooting her to the spot.

She breathed deeply, eyes half closed, savoring the night air, attuning herself to the slow, steady pulse of the mountain. Yes, there was something buried here, a story, a word of power graven upon the very heart of the mountain. The low, patient murmuring through the rock whispered of its existence, even as it shielded the story itself from prying eyes.

Peering down into the hollow, Dierdre could see that its floor was split with a gaping crack, the remains of an abandoned mineshaft. In some decade past, a conscientious soul had gone to great trouble to board up the fissure, although Dierdre could not imagine that there had ever been much danger of any passersby who might take a tragic misstep in the dark. Surely visitors to this remote and unwholesome spot were few and far between—an impression that was only strengthened by the state of disrepair into which the site had fallen. The boards that had not rotted away altogether had splintered as if someone had rolled a great boulder down upon the orifice. It now gaped like a maw full of broken teeth.

But even as this thought crossed her mind, she became aware that the site had not been altogether abandoned. There were figures below, tiny man-like figures, scurrying around that crack. No, upon further scrutiny she became convinced that it was not the mineshaft itself that was the object of their attentions, but something at the very brink of the precipice. The moonlight glinted off something there. A pool of water, perhaps a spring.

It was no matter. She would shoo them away soon enough.

She lingered there upon the summit a while longer before setting about her appointed task. She took her time, drinking in each and every one of the mountain's scents and sounds.

And beneath her touch, the landscape began to take on recognizable form. The mountainside spread out below her like a well-loved patchwork quilt. With an artist's scrutiny, she began to tease out the name of each wrinkle in the rockface. Soon a pattern began to emerge, as clear to her as if she had stitched it into the mountainface with her own hands. Each irregular square of fabric, a promontory; each stitch, a looping path.

The seam of the highest lane was dotted with a flock of scraggly mountain goats that kept twisting free like frayed threads. Each bounding dirty white flank was a living fiber in the tapestry she wove.

And once she had done, once she was certain that she knew that mountain's name and that it was now her place, she began to unpack her things. A place for everything, and everything in its place.

She took her black shawl—the one that Father-of-Serpents had wrapped around her shoulders with his own hands—and she spread it out below her until it covered the entire mountainside. It settled in like a dark and low-lying fog. It seeped down into each and every crevasse of the ascent. Where it touched the tiny man-beasts below, it clouded their thoughts and cast them into a shifting labyrinth of fog. They wandered aimlessly, ranting, not recognizing their fellows even when they came upon them suddenly in the mists. The shawl also softened and blurred the boundaries between worlds until it was hard to tell where one reality ended and the next began.

And Dierdre saw that this was good. And again she reached into her apron and drew out her carding combs and cast them down the mountainside, where they took root and burst with new life. Each tine of the combs sprang up into a forest of thorns, blocking all hope of progress up or down the slope. Cutting off the hollow from the outside world. Walling out even the moonlight from the rocky path.

And she saw that that too was good. Finally, she knelt down and carefully unfolded her kerchief, spreading it before her on the ground. Inside its folds was a single midnight-black seed. It shone like polished onyx in the moonlight.

Leaning far out over the abyss, she let the seed fall. It dropped straight down to the floor of the hollow, straight into the gaping maw of the old mineshaft and straight down to the very heart of the mountain. She craned forward, straining to catch the sound of the distant impact. She wished the writhing man-things below would be still, if only for a moment. There.

The distant echo swelled to the roar of a freight train and then something dark and terrible erupted from the gaping mineshaft, gleaming like a tower of onyx and writhing like the old Wyrm itself.

Yes, she thought, gazing down with satisfaction. She would have this place feeling like home in no time.

Chapter 9

"Well, the good news is that you don't have a nest of Spirals in your backyard," Stuart said.

The old troll smiled his saw-toothed grin. "That much I know," he said. "But you can do better. Now, attend." He rapped his gnarled stick sharply atop the nearest marker stone.

The Hill of Lamentations was quieter tonight. The moon was but newly risen and the Rite-master had not yet called the first of the moonbridges which had so dominated the night sky above the sept yesterday evening.

"You crossed over last night," the old troll accused. "My eyes are rheumy but they are not blind. The remembrance of the spirit world still clings to you like the morning dew."

"We meant neither slight nor deception, Grandfather," Victor said. "We were following the trail of the Black Spiral delegation. We managed to track them all the way back into the mountains to the north—no mean feat—to the spot where they stepped across. We had to follow."

The Rite-master nodded, mollified. "And what did you find? I am many years your senior and have never known a man to step across from this caern without bringing back some sign for the defenders of the sept. The land here has grown accustomed to our touch. It whispers to us—to those who have ears to hear—mumbling warnings, portents, omens."

"They came through at the source of the Hammerfell," Victor said. "Not the physical source, the icy spring high in the mountains your kinsmen call the Fist, but at the Umbral source."

"I know the place," the old man replied. "And you are right, it is warrior-work to win through to it. Even in more charitable weather."

"Which brings us to the bad news," Stuart said. "There's a contagion marking the spot where they came through. But it's dug in deep, under the surface of the frozen river. We could see it throbbing down there, seeping, gangrenous. But we couldn't break through to it. Someone's got to root it out before the thaw, or you're going to have a serious problem when that water starts flowing again."

"I knew you would not disappoint me," the old troll said, slapping his hands together sharply. "In every coming and going there is a new learning. You should stay here among us for a time. There are strong backs and willing hands enough here; you could lead a party to the river's source. Carve out this corruption. The Fenrir would drink to your courage and feast in your honor."

"I think we've had our fill of the hospitality of the Fenrir warband for the present," Stuart said, his words sounding jarring and bitter even to his own ear. He quickly continued to cover up the discordant note. "And besides, we have an appointment to keep with one of Victor Svorenko's kinsmen. I only hope we are not already too late."

"I think you are perhaps a bit uncharitable to my kinsmen. But you may yet have the opportunity to make amends. And if your appointment is with the Lord Arkady," the Rite-master said shrewdly, "then I think you are not yet too late for that either."

"You have news of my kinsman?" Victor demanded, pressing closer. "What have you seen, old man?"

The Rite-master planted the end of his stick firmly in Victor's sternum, bringing him up sharply. "It's not what I've seen, young lordling. It is what I have not seen. If the great Arkady had fallen in battle, do you think we would not yet have seen his flayed pelt—as blazing white as First-snow, they say—paraded before us? The Wyrm would not waste such an opportunity to crush our spirit."

Still, somehow Victor did not seem reassured. Perhaps he was thinking of the grisly battle standard of Knife-between-Bones and his delegation. "And if he has fallen in another kind of battle?" Victor asked. "A more personal, private conflict?"

The old man lowered his stick and leaned closer until a mere fingersbreadth separated his eyes from Victor's. "Then, child, we would have heard from Arkady himself. Standing atop the ruins of some despoiled caern. Spitting defiance in the face of the Twelve Tribes. Rallying the forces of the enemy about him for the Final Battle."

Victor looked away. "We must go."

Stuart cleared his throat. "Can you open a path for us, Gatekeeper? We have to get to the Sept of the Dawn, back to the last place we know Arkady was seen. Maybe we can pick up his trail from that end."

"No great feat, that," he replied, smiling. "But let us give Luna a chance to climb out of bed at least, before we start making demands of her."

Chapter 10

"Something is not right here," Victor's voice was taut. He raised muzzle to the wind, a distinctly lupine gesture that looked slightly ridiculous in his human form. Stuart did not call this fact to Victor's attention.

"It is something on the wind. Do you scent it?" the Fang asked.

The steep rocky trail was little more than a hint of footpath at this point, a way more suited for the scraggly mountain goats that haunted this desolate height than for either man or wolf. Stuart had shifted form experimentally several times, but each time returned in frustration to his accustomed human proportions.

They were already well within the fog-riddled Carpathians. Overhead the moon was bright, gibbous. And that was some small comfort. But Luna's gaze did not so much illuminate their way as infuse the low-lying mists with an eerie phosphorescence. Wispy serpents coiled intimately around their calves. Stuart felt as if he were wading ankle-deep through chill water.

It also meant that he could only intermittently see his feet, much less his footing. Now, Stuart was no stranger to a mountainside at midnight. He had spent the better part of his growing-up clambering over and through the Appalachians and the Blue Ridge. But even he had already given up on trying to avoid a misstep in the dark tonight, stumbling about one step in every dozen. Resigned to proceeding at a snail's pace, he tested each step gingerly before he put his weight down upon it. A twisted or sprained ankle he could ignore, block out the pain and press on. A broken one—or an incautious step out over the edge of a precipice—would be another story.

Victor seemed to be bearing up pretty well for his part. The physical rigors of the climb didn't seem to faze him so much. He had fallen flat several times already without so much as a curse or a grumble. But this blind groping through the luminous fog was starting to work on him in other ways. He had grown silent, absorbed in his own thoughts. Perhaps he was retracing some treacherous trail of memory and regret from his previous fateful visit to this desolate height, when he had walked beside Lord Arkady. Already he was jumping at shadows.

"I don't smell anything," Stuart replied. "Just pine. And mud, of course. And…rotting wood? And the damned goat droppings."

"Shh," Victor cut him off with a sharp wave of his hand. "We must be close. We should be able to hear it by now. I fear something has gone terribly wrong."

Stuart drew to a halt, letting the currents of mist drift languidly past him. He didn't hear anything out of the ordinary. "Hear what? You said we're looking for a mineshaft. What's there to hear, an echo?"

Victor waved at him angrily to keep silent. At last he gave up listening in frustration. "Maybe we have gone past it in the dark. It should be right here somewhere. Off to the right of the path."

"I haven't seen any turnings since you pointed out that old signpost about a half mile back. What am I supposed to be listening for?"

"Gaia's Tears," Victor replied.

"I don't think I'm following you," Stuart said distractedly. "But I'm pretty sure I can make out something just ahead. There, do you see it?" He slapped his companion's arm and pointed off to the left of the trail.

Victor squinted. There was something there. A vague shape, as tall as a man, just standing there. Waiting, watching, sizing them up.

"Hello!" Victor called. "We're from the Sept of the Dawn. Can you take us to Speaks-Thunder?"

"Who's Speaks-Thunder?" Stuart asked in a whisper and again Victor gestured him to silence. Stuart thought that this habit was getting old very quickly.

"We've brought supplies," Victor called again. He began moving forward slowly, his arms spread wide to show that he bore no weapons.

Still no answer. Stuart didn't like the look of this. If the watcher were a friend, why didn't he answer? Slowly, Stuart began to circle around wide to one side. If this were a trap, it wouldn't do for both of them to waltz straight into it.

Victor cursed. Stuart instantly pitched his senses into full lupine alertness and dropped into a fighting crouch. His companion's hulking form seemed to deflate. Victor scuffed angrily with one foot, sending a scree of loose rocks clattering down the treacherous mountainside. Stuart was not too pleased to discover the sheer drop mere paces from where he stood.

Victor turned his back upon the shadowy stranger and plopped himself down onto a rock that barely jutted up above the ever-present layer of fog.

"It's that damned signpost again," he said. "We've been wandering around in circles."

Stuart let out a long breath. "You sure?" He warily approached the shadowy figure until it resolved itself into the half-rotted wooden signpost. He swiped another notch out of the upright, just to vent his frustration. "Well, at least we know where we are now," he offered.

Victor didn't reply.

"Look," Stuart said, "it's obvious we're not going to make any further progress tonight. Why don't we just settle in for the night? The fog is likely to be even worse first thing in the morning, but given a few hours to work at it, the sunlight will burn away even the worst of fogs. And this climb has got to be easier in the daylight."

"You're probably right," Victor admitted grudgingly. "With the moon this bright, I didn't expect we'd have any trouble. I've come this way twice before, but it wasn't like this either time. This damned fog…"

"Not your fault," Stuart said. "Don't worry about it. I'd venture that this tin mine of yours will still be there in the morning."

Victor grunted. "I hope you can say the same for us. I'll take the first watch, just to be sure. Just give me a chance to gather some wood for a fire."

"Do you think that's a good idea? A fire, I mean."

"If it helps keep this fog off, it's a good idea," Victor said.

Stuart shrugged. "I guess anything else that might be abroad tonight is going to be more surprised at finding us then we'll be at meeting it. But stay within hollering distance. I'd hate to think of you falling off the mountain without me."

Victor gave him a curious look as if trying (not for the first time) to determine exactly how serious Stuart was being. "Don't worry," he said at last, "It is my intention that we should go down the mountain together."

He struck off through the mists and within moments was lost to sight. Stuart busied himself with clearing a place for the fire. Every few minutes, he would sing out, "Victor, you fallen off this mountain yet?" And Victor would yell back, "Not yet. Be patient."

Soon the Fang returned, grinning. His dark mood seemed to have lifted with having accomplished something—even if that something was as simple as gathering firewood. Stuart's own jokes and good-natured ribbing didn't hurt either. Victor was dragging what seemed to be the upper reaches of a fallen pine tree behind him.

"It's all soaked through," he said, depositing his burden. "It will be a minor miracle if we ever get it alight. Damned fog."

"Fortunately, I just happen to know that particular miracle," Stuart confided. And before long they had a roaring blaze going. One that kept the worst of the fog at bay.

Victor nodded approvingly. "It may be that the others will see the light of the fire, even through this fog. If we cannot win through to the mountaintop, perhaps the mountaintop will come to us."

The dance of flames made Stuart drowsy. He stifled a yawn and tried to concentrate on what Victor was saying. "What others? That's the second time tonight you've mentioned others. I haven't seen sign of anyone else since we left the Sept of the Dawn."

"That is one of the things that has been bothering me," Victor admitted. "Surely we should have seen some sign of them by now. The path to the old mine cannot be more than a half a mile from this crossroads. Even if no one had sighted us for the fog, still they should have heard us. Someone should have come to investigate."

Now Stuart was really lost, and he was tired and starting to get annoyed. "Okay, I give. What the hell are you talking about? Who should have heard us? And what were we listening for back there?"

"Gaia's Tears," Victor repeated stubbornly. Then realization dawned upon him. "Ah, now I see. I am sorry, my friend. I thought that you understood. That you had heard the tale at the concolation—the story of what happened when we returned to the tin mine. They all wanted to see for themselves, of course. I could hardly deny them. That is how I came to be leading Sergiy Dawntreader and the others back to the place where Arkady had commanded the…where we had fought the Knockerwyrm," he finished awkwardly.

Stuart found his eyes straying away from the welcome glow of the fire to where he thought the trail ahead must lie. He was suddenly aware that there were certain glaring holes in his knowledge. Certain questions that had gone unasked. And that wasn't like him.

What, for example, had become of the wyrm *after* Arkady had quelled it? Victor had never mentioned anyone actually dispatching the beast. For all he knew, Arkady might simply have left it there, brooding in its dark hole. Suddenly the prospect of spending the night on the exposed mountainside seemed even less appealing.

"You told me that you returned home with the body of Arne Wyrmsbane," Stuart accused. "You didn't mention anything more about what had become of Arkady. Or, say, this towering Wyrm-beast, for that matter. And what the hell has any of this got to do with Gaia's Tears, whatever they are?"

Victor nodded, which only served to irritate Stuart further. What he wanted was some answers. But Victor only poked at the coals with a snapped pine bough. "There is more you should know," he said.

"I should say there is," Stuart said. His thoughts were still clouded with fatigue, but his journalistic instincts were kicking in now and, given their head, they could carry him on autopilot for hours—even through an appalling haze of alcohol or even stronger brain-damping substances. "We should have had this talk last night."

"Last night we were out hunting Spirals all night," Victor said. "Which may explain why you can't seem to keep your eyes open."

"All right, you've got my attention now. How about you start me out slow." Step by step, Stuart painted the scene, taking Victor back across the intervening span of time to revisit the battle at the mineshaft. "Arkady. The wyrm. You're carrying the broken body of your friend, Arne, in your arms. And you just walk away. You turn your back on your kinsman. You just leave him there, alone with that thing. Why?"

"The battle was over," Victor said, perhaps too abruptly. "The wyrm, it could no longer harm Arkady. Perhaps it never could have hurt him. That was how it seemed to me, at least."

"You never found out what happened. You were afraid," Stuart accused. "You ran."

"No! I was not afraid. I would not be afraid were it three wyrms bearing down on me. I…"

"No, not of the wyrm," Stuart interrupted. He leaned closer, purposefully crowding Victor, trying to rattle him. "Of your kinsman. Of Arkady. Or rather, of what he had become."

"My battle was not with Arkady. And if you had been there, if you had stood beside him when he *commanded* the Wyrm-spawn, then you would not be so quick to judge others."

"All right," Stuart said. "So you weren't afraid. You just freaked out. You took off with Arne's body. But you never stopped to wonder, just once, what happened? To Arkady? To the Wyrm? Hell, for all we know they could still be up there. Waiting for us to come stumbling along."

"Of course I wondered! Do you think me without feeling? But my duty was to my fallen friend. My kinsman, well, he could obviously fend for himself. Oh yes, he had demonstrated that."

"So that's it. You never even looked back? Just closed the book on him. And then this concolation thing comes up and you go all the way to freaking Norway to give evidence against your kinsman. Damn, Victor! I hope you'll forgive me saying so, but you are a hard man. I hope I never do anything to freak you out."

"Ah, now I see," Victor said. "You are having a joke at my expense. I am not such a hard man as you suppose, Stuart, called Stalks-the-Truth. As soon as I had fulfilled my duty toward my fallen friend, as soon as he was safely back at the Sept of the Dawn, then the questions began to nag at me. And then the doubts. Had I really seen what I remembered? Was Arkady all right? I had seen him command the Knockerwyrm with little more than his voice and his stare, but I did not know whether or not he could break that contact without the wyrm rising up and turning upon him. Perhaps he was trapped there, held in thrall as surely as he himself held the wyrm."

"So you went back?" Stuart prompted.

"Of course. I had to go back. How else could I be sure? I convinced Dawntreader himself to accompany me. He must have thought me half mad with grief. And others came as well, I could not have kept them away—Speaks-Thunder and his pack among them."

"And that is the second time tonight I have heard you mention that name—Speaks-Thunder."

"He was always kind to me. From the time when I first came here from my home, it must be more than three years now. Speaks-Thunder treated me like a man and not like a frightened cub. Even when the evidence would have tended to suggest the contrary. *Especially* those times, when my temper got the best of me, or the frustration of having to relearn everything I thought I knew already, or stigma of being different from everyone else."

Stuart nodded. "I understand. So you take this Speaks-Thunder and Dawntreader and a handful of others back here. Back to the scene of the crime. But when you get here…"

"When we got here," Victor said, "we could find no sign of either Arkady or the wyrm. Oh, the signs of the battle were clear enough, but the combatants were gone."

"Of course you searched the area?" Stuart prompted.

"Certainly. And when we could find no proof of what had become of them, Dawntreader set about the Cleansing."

Stuart shot him a questioning look over the intervening fire.

"To clear the site of the Wyrm-taint," Victor explained. "For three days and three nights, Dawntreader sat there, unmoving, perched upon the very brink of the mineshaft. We could not prevail upon him either to sleep or take a bite of food. Not a word would he speak to us, nor even acknowledge our presence. I began to fear for his safety. On the third day I took to pressing a rag soaked in creek water to his mouth, thinking that if I could not get him to drink, I might at least force a trickle of life past his lips. The water only streamed from the corners of his mouth, but I told myself that his lips and tongue did not look as parched and cracked as they once had. What else could I have done? We waited. We kept vigil."

Caught up in Victor's peculiar tale, Stuart could only gesture for him to continue.

"I did not sleep at all that night. I stood watch over Dawntreader. He was too weak, I could see it in his face. He wore each of the three nights he had spent upon the brink as if it had been a full year. I tried to coax him back to us. I pleaded with him."

Victor paused, as if unwilling to tell more. At last, he steeled his resolve and pressed on. "In the end—and I admit it freely—I resolved to drag him bodily back from the edge. I am not proud of it, but I had already lost a kinsman here. I was not about to lose my liege as well.

"But when I took him beneath the arms, he weighed no more than an armful of dried autumn leaves. I feared to move him lest he crumble in my hands. If the spirits had come for him then, they would have taken him easily. He could not have resisted them. They could have swept him up bodily into the heavens, or buffeted him over the edge of the precipice.

"As the moon set, we heard a great rumbling from deep within the earth, from the heart of the abandoned mineshaft. An oily black cloud belched forth from the depths and spread across the heavens, blotting out the light of the stars. Where the vapors touched the skin, flesh blistered and peeled away. We fell back before it, smarting, howling with rage and indignation at the foe we could bring neither claw nor fang to bear against.

"Only Dawntreader and I held our ground at the edge of the pit—he because his eyes no longer focused upon things of this world; I because I refused to abandon him there. Choking, I tried a second time to drag him back from the brink, but my arms passed right through him as if he were of less substance than the viscous fumes that clung to my seared flesh.

"I think I may have cried out then, for I knew that he was lost to us, and that he had been the best of us. And that for the second time, this hellish abyss had robbed me of my lord, and of my best remaining hope.

"I do not know for how long I held that mournful howl. It was as if something had broken inside me. I could not make it stop. Others, brothers and sisters that I was aware of only as raw nerves at the periphery of my pain, took up the cry. The sound swelled to brim-fill the mountaintop, to ring out over the foothills and the plateau, to drown the valleys and to swallow the night sky. Time itself had ceased to have any meaning for me. I was adrift, devoid of any point of reference. Deprived of the stately age-old procession of sun, moon and stars, we had only the cadence of that song, the rising and falling of the howl, to mark out time. Our grief remade the passing of time in its own image.

"And then it happened. Another voice, a voice I had longed to hear these three nights, joined in our communion, our desperate plea. Dawntreader stirred, threw back his head, and opened his throat to the unseen stars.

"His voice was strong and true, but he sang not with the breath of his life—for if the truth were known, there was barely a whisper of life left within him—but with his very lifesblood. A fine red mist funneled out before him, spiraling out into the night, seeping into the impersonal void between the distant stars—a darkness more silent and ravenous than any mineshaft.

"Where that fine red mist met the inky blackness, the darkness gave way before it. Soon it had streaked the eastern sky and puddled into a ruddy pool at the horizon. With infinite patience, the spilling life resolved itself into the radiant face of Brother Sun, cresting the rim of the world.

"The first hint of dawn broke the morbid paralysis that had crept into my heart and I rushed to Dawntreader's side. He was slumped forward precariously over the brink. His breath came only in shallow, rasping sobs—the effect of breathing deeply of the vitriolic cloud. The exposed flesh of his face and arms had all but blistered away. A steady trickle of blood ran down his forearms, over the hump of his wrists, and trailed between his fingers to fall down into the murky abyss below.

"For a third and final time, I set to pull him back from the edge. And this time he did not resist me. Even as I began to lift him, however, to carry him to safety, the inexplicable happened. The miraculous. Even now, I hesitate to tell of it, as if my very words, leaden and impure, might somehow pollute the memory of it. But there was no denying what I saw.

"From the very spot where Dawntreader's blood had run into the pit, water bubbled up. Clear, sparkling water. The earth cracked asunder, revealing a natural basin that had lain hidden there, a still pool, a font. Speaks-Thunder said that it was Gaia Herself who wept for Dawntreader's pain."

Victor fell silent, overwhelmed at the memory.

"Gaia's Tears," Stuart put in gently. "The gurgling of a spring. That's what we should be hearing."

Victor only nodded. "I do not know if you have ever been present when a lost caern is reclaimed from the enemy, Stuart Stalks-the-Truth. It is the most...consuming elation I had ever hoped to experience. I..." Victor's eyes glazed over with tears.

"It must have been glorious," Stuart whispered.

Victor angrily wiped at his eyes with the back of one hand. "I have seen the miracle of Gaia consecrating a new caern to Her glory. Words are messengers too clumsy to carry the gift I am trying to place before you. I have seen the Great Mother Herself stretch out Her hand! Watched as She moved a finger through time, and eternity danced like a flame on Her fingertip.

"In that instant I knew—knew with searing clarity—that even our worst fears were for naught. Even the Old Wyrm itself could not hope to stand before the majesty of that simple gesture. It is no wonder to me that it must go about on its belly before Her, scratching in the dirt all the days of its torment. Trying to bury itself from the very sight of Her."

"You have been blessed beyond the lot of man or wolf, Victor Svorenko," Stuart said. "I envy you your certainties."

They sat in silence for a long while, neither one aware of the fact that the fire had grown dim and that the mists had crept closer as if craning to overhear them.

"Your words make me all the more anxious to reach our destination," Stuart said at last.

"Yes, but you should rest now. I will watch," Victor said. "I will wake you at first light."

"Many have tried, but few have lived to tell the tale," Stuart said ominously. But his eyes were full of laughter. "In any event, we can't go anywhere until the sun has burned off the worst of this fog. Good night, Victor. See you in the morning. In the *late* morning."

After a long night of wandering around in circles, Stuart was more than ready for sleep. He curled up before the fire, pulled the blanket of his wolf-form over him, and was soon sound asleep.

He awoke some time later to the sound of muffled cries. The moon had long set, but the sun had not yet put in its appearance. With the fire having burned down to a dim glow of coals, the only real illumination seemed to come from the creeping tendrils of fog. Emboldened by the dying of the fire, the wisps of mist had stolen closer and coiled all about his sleeping form. For a moment, Stuart had the distinct and unsettling impression that he was drowning. He flailed wildly and lurched to an upright position. Not upright enough—Stuart realized that he was wearing his lupine form. The fog still pooled about his chest, his muzzle barely staying above the damp caress.

He shifted. In human form, he found himself soaked to the skin, his clothing clinging wetly to his body. "Victor!" he cried out, choking and sputtering.

The only answer was a moan from the far side of the ring of stones circumscribing the dying fire. He could barely pick out his companion's form, slumped, back against a tree. Victor seemed to be struggling with something. Some unseen assailant? Stuart lurched toward him, stumbled over a stone, and barely managed to avoid plunging to his knees amidst the coals. The stone he had tripped over shot into the fire, sending up a shower of sparks. In the brief flare of light, Stuart could see that Victor was totally entangled in thick coils of mist, the Fang struggling fiercely, but to no avail. The coils were slowly crushing the life from his body.

With a cry, Stuart leapt forward. Angrily he slashed down at the thick tendrils binding Victor's arms. He aimed his blow carefully, hoping to avoid biting into the flesh beneath. But his claws passed through the coils without meeting any resistance. Victor stiffened as the swipe drew blood, but he remained as securely bound as before. Sheathing his claws, Stuart grabbed at the tendrils trying to tear them free with only the strength of his arms. The bonds did not so much as budge. Then Stuart felt a sharp tug at his ankle and he went down, falling face first to the rocky path. The fog closed over him.

The ground grated against the flesh of his stomach, face and forearms. He was being dragged rapidly backwards, away from his companion. It was not enough to strangle him on the spot, it seemed. The mists needed to separate the two of them, to ensure that he could not help free Victor. As if they wanted to rob him of even any shred of hope of either rescue or release.

And with most victims, this strategy would have worked superbly. But Stuart was nobody's victim. Most men, faced with his predicament, would have brought their arms up to shield their faces, would have waited out the ungentle ride across the rocky path, would have bided their time until the motion of the ground had stopped and that threat had passed. Not Stuart.

Realizing that he was being dragged backwards by his feet, he immediately threw his arms out wide, opening himself up to the worst ravages of the rough terrain. His extended left arm found its target, dragging directly through the heart of the smoldering fire. Stuart screamed and thrust his fist in deeper.

Stirring the coals, freeing the flame.

As the fire surged to life, he could feel the misty tendrils shrinking back from it. He felt the grip on his ankle loosen, unravel. And then he was at rest.

He wasted no time. Cradling his burned hand to his chest, he rolled toward the fire, curling around it. He rose to his knees, feeling the bite of the stones at the fire's edge. His good hand groped blindly until it found the discarded pine bough that Victor had used to poke at the fire earlier. Stuart churned the coals with it, and fed the slumbering flames.

The mists shrank back from him. As the circle of firelight expanded and the domain of the mists receded, more fuel came within his reach and all of it went immediately into the blaze. Soon he had a roaring bonfire burning and a clear path to where Victor still struggled in the grip of the deadly fog. The enemy might have braced itself for the slash of claw, the tug of grappling hands. It was surely not prepared for what Stuart did next. With a great heave, he rolled the rigid form of Victor Svorenko closer to the fire.

The entwining mists twisted and writhed. Stuart rolled his friend another turn closer. Then another.

The mists broke and scattered before the assault of their most ancient enemy. Victor's chest heaved, free at last of the constricting pressure, and he sucked ragged gasps of the mountain air. Stuart pounded him on the back until Victor coughed up the last tenacious strands of watery death that had crept down his throat and into his lungs.

"Thank you, my friend. I don't know how I could ever…" Victor managed to force the words past another fit of coughing.

"Save your breath. You can thank me, at length, later. Assuming there is a later. Right now we've got to concentrate on keeping that fire lit until morning."

As Victor got his breath back, he was quick to grasp their dilemma. The only fuel they had to feed their fire was whatever wood currently lay within the circle of firelight. As the night wore on and fire burned lower, the area from which they might gather more wood rapidly dwindled. It was a losing proposition.

At the outskirts of their protective circle, the mists seemed to gather, piling higher upon themselves. Soon the encircling wall had risen to the height of a wolf. It would not be long before it stood taller than a man. As unsettling as it was watching the fog pile higher—swallowing the rocks, the undergrowth, the signpost, the trees—Stuart was suddenly struck by an even more disturbing thought. If things continued at this pace, it would not be long (certainly not so far removed as morning) before the walls would be high enough that the mists would close *over* them and their little fire. Blotting out even the stars and walling them up in a sealed tomb of shifting vapors.

"If you've got any ideas," Stuart said, a bit louder than was necessary, "this would be the time to get them off your chest."

"Don't know about you," Victor said, "but I'm all for making a break for it. You can't fight what you can't hit. And you can't throttle what you can't get a grip on. And if this fire goes out again—sorry, *when* this fire goes out again—we're both dead. Just plain old dead. And I'm not ready to be dead yet. Not here. And not like this. I was always taught to pick my fights better."

"I'm with you so far," Stuart said. "What do you have in mind?"

"Stepping sideways. Even the uncertainties of the spirit realm have got to be better than what's awaiting us here. Worst comes to worst, we could just sit tight there until about noon when most of this thrice-damned mist has burned away. Or if that's not good enough for you, we could even try to flag down a passing—"

"Normally, I'd say that's a great plan," Stuart interrupted. "Except for one thing. There isn't any 'elsewhere' here. No other side. There hasn't been all evening, ever since we set foot in this fogbank."

"That can't be," Victor said stubbornly. He tried unsuccessfully to reach out across the barrier into the spirit realm. Nothing. Confusion gave way to anger. "There has got to be an elsewhere. Everywhere's got a damned elsewhere. Otherwise it would be…"

"Nowhere?" Stuart asked. "That's all a bit metaphysical for me. But I do know there's nowhere to step across to here. It's as if we were already there."

"Damn it, I'm not dying here."

There was a flickering of light overhead. It took Stuart a moment to realize what it was—the stars, one by one, being swallowed by the canopy of fog.

"We'll make a break for it," Victor said. "We'll each take a brand from the fire. We'll strike out until we find more wood or until the torches start to burn down. Then we'll just come back here…"

"We'll never find it again," Stuart said. "Take a look at that wall of fog. It's solid. As soon as we're out of the circle of firelight, the mists will tighten around us again, walling everything else out. We could be within ten feet of the fire and never see it again. And meanwhile, the vapors would crowd around us even more closely, held back by only the thickness of a torch flame instead of that of a campfire."

"Well, we've got to do something." Victor lurched to his feet and, snatching up a burning branch from the fire, launched himself at the nearest section of wall. He shredded it with brutal swipes of his torch, rending and tearing it until he was short of breath. All around him, his victims piled higher, wriggling serpentine strips of fog carved drizzling from the smooth, unbroken wall. They flopped and squirmed at his feet, coiled about his ankles, vying for his attention.

Watching from the fireside, Stuart had the unsettling impression that the wisps of fog were actually a clutch of serpents, each as black as onyx. A moment later, Victor swiped angrily downward with his torch, shattering the image and burning away the last of the mist clinging about his feet.

But in the end, his efforts were to no avail. Despite his struggles, the wall stood as smooth and towering as before. Exhausted, Victor fell back toward his place by the fire.

"No good," he panted. "Can't make any headway."

"We've just got to hold out here a while longer," Stuart said. "Until sunup. The dawn might not be enough to burn away the mists entirely, but surely they can't maintain fortifications of this scope in the face of the new day."

"I hope you are right," Victor agreed. "How long until daybreak?"

"I don't know," Stuart said. The stars were completely hidden now, offering no help. And even at his most responsible, Stuart had never managed to bring himself to wear a watch. "But it can't be long now."

So they sat and they talked and they waited, until the circle of firelight had shrunk to little more than the thickness of their own bodies, and their voices fell to hushed whispers.

"I am sorry to have brought you here, Stuart Stalks-the-Truth. It is bad enough I go to my death without a foe to sink my claws into and drag with me. But I fear that I have brought your death down upon you as well. And I had accounted you my friend."

"It's not your fault," Stuart said. "I chose to come. To find my own answers." He chuckled quietly. "It's just this damned waiting! I'm afraid I'm much better at seeking than hiding. Here, let's try something.

What do you say to me taking a shot at that wall and you sitting back for a moment and telling me what you see? All right? Good."

Stooping, Stuart retrieved a makeshift torch from the fire and hurled himself at the nearest fog bank. Frayed wisps of fog fell all about him as he wielded his brand two-handed, like an axe.

"I think you are making progress," Victor called encouragingly. But Stuart knew better.

"But what is that there?" Victor wondered aloud. "Watch out! By your foot." He was on his feet, and rushing to Stuart's side. Glancing down, Stuart again had the impression of a writhing black serpent rearing to strike. Then Victor's claws came down and slashed it in two.

Out of breath, Stuart fell back toward the fire. "What did you see?" he demanded, not bothering to thank Victor.

The Fang took the omission in stride. "I don't know. It seemed like a twist of rope at first, darker than the fog around it. Black like pitch. Then it rose up and I thought it must be some Wyrmling coming at you through the fog. Just because we cannot see a thing in this blasted haze does not mean that others are similarly handicapped."

Stuart smiled and clapped Victor on the shoulder. "Excellent. One more time, then. I'll try the wall again. But this time, if you see your Wyrmling, you don't cut it, you *grab* it. Follow me?"

Puzzlement was clear on Victor's face, but he nodded. He would do what was needful.

Stuart grabbed an additional torch from the fire and laid into the wall two-handed. The fog seemed to fall back a pace before the intensity of his onslaught. He advanced, wading through the writhing bodies of his victims. Another step. A third. Through the shredding layers of fog, Stuart saw a dark silhouette looming up ahead of him—the bole of the tree against which Victor had fallen asleep at his post earlier that evening.

"There!" Victor shouted and lunged. His hand shot out toward a mere wisp of fog fallen in Stuart's wake, but one that looked somehow darker, more solid than its fellows. He grabbed for it and howled triumph as he felt the thing twist in his grasp. Something solid at last.

"Now, don't let it go, whatever you do!" Stuart called. "Have you got a good grip on it? With both hands, then, pull!"

Victor set his shoulders and heaved. It was a proud effort, one that might have uprooted a young tree. Victor stumbled under an unexpected give, braced himself anew, and pulled again.

Even Stuart could see it now. The thing in Victor's grasp looked like a length of strong black cord, no more than the length of his arm. But it twisted like a living thing in his hands and it was all Victor could do to maintain his grip.

Throwing down both torches at their feet, Stuart latched onto the rope. "On three," he called. "One… two…"

On three the fog bank surrendered another length of the living ebon rope and the battle was joined in earnest. Within ten minutes both Garou were bathed in sweat. But they had won a good ten feet of the slippery shifting "cord" to show for their efforts. And they had tugged and fought their way back to the fireside.

"This is no Wyrmling!" Victor gasped, fighting for breath. "What *is* this thing?"

"Don't know," Stuart replied with some effort. "But whatever it is, it seems to be unraveling. We seem to have worked loose a frayed end."

"Yes, but what will we find at the other end? This one's not so bad, if you can keep it from coiling about your legs and tripping you up. But the other…"

"Better tie it off then," Stuart said, casting about. "We could try to fight our way back to that tree. You could loop the end around that."

This time it seemed to take only half as long to recross the distance. "Progress," Stuart said, and Victor wrapped the twitching end around the bole of the tree three times before lashing it off.

"The knot will hold," he said appraisingly, examining his own handiwork. "If the rope does not break…"

"If this thing is alive somehow," Stuart said, "it's not going to pull so hard it tears itself to pieces. I'll hold on here for a minute. I want you to get some sticks from the fire and give us a little working space here. I want to try something."

Victor hesitated only a moment to see what Stuart was about. Then, nodding his approval, he went to fetch fire.

Stuart held the rope at arms length in front of him with both hands, and began slowly, methodically, circling the tree. The rope began to wind about it as if it were a spindle.

"I think the fog is lifting a bit," Victor said, returning. "I could see your outline even from the fire. The dawn must be close." He began arranging several smaller fires in a circle about the tree, where they would not interfere with Stuart's circuit.

Looking up, Stuart noted that he could again see the dim twinkle of starlight above them. He almost cried aloud. "Not the dawn, look! It's still well dark, but the fog is definitely thinning."

Soon Victor took his place beside Stuart and the work began to gain momentum. "It is as if the fog itself were unraveling," Victor said after a long while. "I can see the ground now, and the way upslope." Stuart looked in the direction the Fang had indicated with his nod, and he could make out the telltale path of the winding black thread, zigzagging upwards toward the summit. It was as clear as any blazed trail.

"Tie it off again, I'll brace it," Stuart said with a crow of triumph. "I think we might yet make some progress tonight."

Chapter 11

"Can't be far now," Stuart said. The sun was a clumsy red smudge on the horizon, a child's fingerpainting. The fog would be unraveling on its own soon, retreating to wait out the heat of the day. Stuart felt better already. He took a deep breath of the clear mountain air and then quickly abandoned the effort, a sour look on his face. "You smell like a wet sheep," he accused.

Victor sniffed himself and grunted. "Yes," he said, nodding. "As do you, I'm afraid. Wet wool. But that will also pass, as the sun climbs."

"You'd think they'd be able to see us now. From the summit, I mean," Stuart said. "Shouldn't there be watchers, at this spring? If it is truly a site of power, Dawntreader would not leave it undefended."

"That also worries me," Victor admitted grudgingly. "I called once when we started our ascent, and again when we saw the first hint of the sun. I haven't heard any response, nor seen any sign of another abroad this morning. But you are right, we must be close now, we should try again." So saying, he threw back his head and howled. The thinning mist seemed to drink down the sound almost before it escaped his throat, just as it leached the heat from their bodies.

"I hear nothing," Victor said after a patient interval. Resignedly, he started upwards again. Stuart fell into step behind him.

"Perhaps they've got a good reason to keep silent," Stuart said. "If they're not expecting visitors from the Sept of the Dawn, they may be wary of leading other uninvited guests to the site. If there are Spirals in this region—"

Victor hushed him sharply. "Do not speak such things aloud!" he said, making the sign against the Eye of the Wyrm. "And even if the Fallen Ones are nearby, there are even darker things in these mountains. Ancient evils that sleep only fitfully, with one eye open."

"What kind of 'ancient evils'?" Stuart asked. But just then Victor stumbled again and fell heavily to the ground. There was a cascade of loose scree and then a muffled cry of alarm.

"You okay?" Stuart called, pressing forward through the hail of small stones to give him a hand. Then he too stopped abruptly. He cursed quietly as he saw what it was that Victor had stumbled over.

The hump of rock swathed in the remains of the low-lying fog resolved itself into the unmistakable outline of a body.

Victor knelt over it, batting impatiently at the tendrils of mist which obscured the dead boy's features. The body had been arranged precisely, formally. It lay on its back, legs together, arms tucked close in at its sides. Someone had gone to the effort of aligning the corpse along the *axis mundi*—its feet pointing due east, its head west.

As the mist scattered before Victor's flailings, it revealed an almost serene face, uncontorted by rage or pain or suffering. The cub looked as if he had just lain down to rest and died peacefully in his sleep. There was even a slight smile on his lips. Then the misty veil drew aside fully and Stuart drew a sharp breath.

There was a gaping wound in the boy's forehead. It looked as if he had been struck a piercing blow in the exact center of the brow. The force of that blow had crumpled the brow ridge like an eggshell, leaving a jagged hole like a single red eye.

This was certainly not the work of fang and claw. Stuart's imaginings, already primed perhaps by storybook notions about abandoned mines, leapt to the thought of a pickaxe.

"It is Gennady," Victor said, his voice choked with emotion. "The cub was one of Speaks-Thunder's pack. Speaks-Thunder was the first to give voice to the miracle that Gaia had worked here; Dawntreader had entrusted him with the warding of this site."

Stuart hesitatingly laid a hand upon the youth's throat. He shook his head sadly. "His flesh has grown cold," he said, "and there is no pool of blood here that I would expect from such a wound. He's been here a day and a night at least. How…how many others?"

Victor looked up sharply, as if realizing for the first time what they must find here. This was no murder; it was the prelude to a massacre.

Chapter 12

They left the boy's body where it lay, staring with its single unblinking red eye toward the west of west. Toward the place where even the sun must soon stumble and sink beneath the benighted waters.

A dark forboding settled upon them and they knew speed might well be of the essence. Turning his back upon the treacherous ascent, Victor picked his way to the right of the path, following the point of the corpse's feet. With such a clear signpost, there was no mistaking the mouth of a narrow dirt track winding away toward a hollow.

Thick undergrowth encroached upon the path from either side, but the signs were plain: Something heavy had been dragged this way recently. Stuart found his steps quickening, hurrying toward an engagement he was already dreading. As the pair rounded the corner of the trail, the reek of decay rushed up to meet them. The way forward was choked off by an impenetrable canopy of thorns. The wall of vegetation towered above them, as thick as a jungle, as bristly as a phalanx.

They had no choice but to try to force their way through. Donning the thick pelt of his warrior form like a shield, Stuart forged ahead, laying waste to all before him with great swipes of his claws.

The thorns could not stand before him. They tore at him and clung to his fur. They batted mercilessly at his face and eyes. They turned him aside from the true path time and time again, leading him into deadends and deadfalls. But they could not gainsay him.

Covered head to toe in angry red weals, choking on the stifling air that hung heavy beneath the low ceiling of nettles, Stuart plunged forward and down, oblivious to all opposition.

Victor crashed along in his wake, his passing made easier by the Garou-sized rent Stuart left in his wake. "Would you like me to take the lead for a while?" he called up to Stuart. "I'm certainly not—" He stopped cold, staring in alarm and disgust at something in the undergrowth just off to his right.

"You're not what?" Stuart growled, turning back toward his companion. "Jeez! What the hell is that?"

There, draped languidly over a thorny bough, was a grisly spectacle—the dry, cracked skin of a man. The branch seemed to droop slightly beneath its burden. The paper-thin deathmask stared back at them, unblinking, its features a distorted mirror of their own horror.

Victor took an unsteady step toward it, reaching out a shaky hand. He brushed against the skin and then jerked his hand back as if stung, his own skin crawling from the unsettling texture of the sun-baked flesh. "What could do something like this?" he voice rang with disbelief and indignation. "To skin a man whole and then to hang his skin upon a tree? It is inhuman! It is—"

"It is not something we want to run into," Stuart interrupted, his voice pitched low. He gestured for Victor to follow his example. "I don't like this any better than you do, but there's no sense in calling attention to ourselves. At least not until we figure out what we're up against here."

Victor dropped his voice to a whisper, but it rang with menace. "Whoever has done this," he raged quietly, "will pay dearly."

"Oh, we'll get him, all right," Stuart assured his companion, backing away slowly. "No fear of that. But you've got to keep your eyes open. I can't see six inches in front of my face when I'm carving through that curtain of nettles."

"My turn. You keep watch," Victor growled. Stuart did not argue the point.

After the discovery of the third such desiccated corpse, Stuart simply stopped pointing them out to Victor. The exercise no longer served any purpose except to eat away at his companion's thin veneer of self-control.

Soon it seemed to Stuart that everywhere his eye traveled, it was met by the same macabre sight. His head swam and he had to keep blinking against the heat and dripping sweat to force his vision to focus. He could not seem to wrest his gaze free from the steady procession of the dead, from the unbroken line of morbid scarecrows, From these victims who had shed their skins.

In vain, he found himself wondering what fate could have befallen them, forced them to trade their familiar bones for new frameworks of briar. He could almost hear the sap trickling through channels that had once carried the noble blood of the warriors of Gaia.

After a while, Stuart simply stopped counting. He couldn't seem to wrap his mind around the sheer magnitude of this atrocity. It must be over a dozen deathmasks now, adorning the thicket. Stuart could no longer bring himself to meet the ragged, gaping stares. Unspoken reproaches assailed him from every side.

It is a blessing of youth to fail to find familiar faces among the dead. Perhaps Victor was fortunate to catch sight of only one, but that one nearly undid him entirely. Upon finding the remains of his friend Speaks-Thunder hung upon a tree, Victor's resolve left him and he sank to his knees. Speaks-Thunder's skin was stretched taut and rustled like dry leaves. His limbs swayed gently in the breeze. Victor threw his arms around the shattered husk that had once been his friend, and embraced him tightly. There was no resistance. The skin parted like old parchment and slumped to the ground all around him.

Victor knelt there, his fists knotted in the tattered shreds for a long while and Stuart left him to his private mourning. He watched as Victor's visage slowly hardened. Until that moment Stuart might have fooled himself into believing that their quest might yet end simply by winning their way through to the tin mine. Now something essential had changed. Victor's features took on a hard, fixed expression that was mirrored back to him from the deathmasks hung from every thicket. Blood called to blood.

"Victor," Stuart said gently, laying a hand upon the young Fang's shoulder, "your friend is no longer here. He is safe now. His spirit has departed this empty husk."

"I know," Victor said, without looking up. "We must go on." He peered up through the twisted brambles as if he had caught some hint of the dark tower rising beyond the thorns.

Stuart took the lead. It was growing hard upon midday, and the stifling heat under the low canopy of thorns seemed to squeeze life and will from his body. Exhausted, he fell back from the wall of brambles and shrugged off the thick pelt of his warrior form.

"My turn now," Victor said, pushing past him, but Stuart waved him back.

"Can't even lift my feet at this point," he panted. "Let's just rest a bit. Catch my breath."

Victor frowned. The thought of stopping, or even slowing, clearly rankled. He was focused solely on finding whoever was responsible for this atrocity—for this garden of shed skins—and then crushing the life out of him with his bare hands.

But, seeing the weariness on his companion's face, Victor relented. The Fang was clearly beyond caring for his own well-being at this point, but this did not give him the right to push his friend beyond his limits.

"Rest," he said. "When the sun has passed its apex, then we continue."

Stuart sank onto a nearby stump and tried not to watch Victor's restless pacing. It was as he turned away that he caught his first glimpse of the thing that had been trailing them since they had entered the thorns.

At first Stuart thought it was a reflection of the sunlight piercing the canopy overhead. His mind leapt immediately to thoughts of water—perhaps a small pool!—concealed within the undergrowth. But just as he opened his mouth to call this discovery to Victor's attention, the reflection glittered once and vanished. A moment later, it winked again, a short way off.

Stuart listened for the sound of running water, although he knew he would surely have noticed such a welcome sound before now. Nothing.

But there was definitely movement through the heart of the thicket. He could pick out the rustle of its slow shifting. Something large, slipping through the clinging nettles.

Stuart cleared his throat to call this presence to Victor's attention, but the words died on his tongue. It was then that Stuart saw the face.

Stuart had already seen a dozen agonized faces hanging in the thicket. He had almost convinced himself that he had grown numb to them. This face, however, shattered his conviction. It broke in upon him and shook him to the core. This was no familiar visage left as a parched monument to an old friend. This was the death mask's complement—not the fleshy outer wrappings, but the face beneath, the true face. A face that had shed its skin.

What unholy transformation must have taken place to birth such a monstrosity, Stuart did not know, nor did he ever hope to learn. The thing's features were porcelain smooth and pink all over. Every line of bone was clearly visible on the hairless head. Its eyes protruded in a most horrifying manner and moist flaps of membrane over its nostrils fluttered at each hideous breath.

For this thing drew breath. It was alive, as surely as Stuart himself was. Only it was as if someone had painstakingly peeled back its skin and cast it aside, perhaps leaving it draped over a branch to dry in the sun.

The image hung before his eyes only an instant, but in later years, Stuart would see that face again, in the dark of night, peering back at him from the insides of his own eyelids. Reproachful. Loathing.

Then the creature twisted away and was gone as suddenly as it had appeared. Stuart listened for the rustle of its withdrawal. *Skinned one!* its body hissed accusingly as it dragged itself, pink and vulnerable, through the cruel briars. The thorns bit and sank deep into the vulnerable exposed tissues. At the creature's slightest motion, the jagged spikes tore away long bloody strips of it. And still it struggled on, dragging itself along on its belly.

Stuart silently prayed that Victor had been spared the sight of it. Or that at least, if he had seen it, he had failed to recognize in its features those of his friend, Speaks-Thunder. Hairless, yes. Skinless, yes. But recognizable even to one who had never seen the man in life, knowing him only by the dry and shriveled husk hung high in a tree.

Knowing only the mask, never the man, Stuart thought.

The wretched creature was gone as quickly as it had come. Stuart was more than half surprised that he had not cried aloud. He realized this only distantly, feeling a strange dislocation. It was as if he were somehow outside himself, looking down with mild curiosity upon the bedraggled and travel-worn journalist whose curiosity had again gotten the better of him. Who had again been caught peering into places he was never meant to.

How strange, he thought, that the other Stuart there did not even scream. Didn't really even flinch. He just sat there stupidly, peering into the heart of the thicket, while that angry red streak broke from the undergrowth and rushed—with great loathing and single-mindedness of purpose—toward the young Silver Fang.

The realization broke through the haze of shock that had settled like a layer of thick dark wool over his mind.

"Victor!" The word broke from Stuart's lips as he lurched to his feet.

Victor spun, his warrior-senses instantly alert. Quicker than thought, he took in the import of both Stuart's cry and the crashing through the undergrowth behind him. His body instinctively triangulated and his claws split the difference.

The vicious upward slash would have disemboweled any man foolish enough to stand before it. But the oncoming assailant was not standing upright before it— it came low, on its belly. And its charge slipped cleanly below the flashing claws and crashed into Victor's legs. There was a sharp crack and a cry of pain and then, suddenly, Victor's feet were cartwheeling above him. He landed heavily, his wind knocked from him.

Fortunately, for all the creature's speed, it was slow in bringing itself back around. The turns exacted a heavy price from his exposed underside, as cruel thorns dug mercilessly into skinless flesh. Yet come around it did. It took its bearing and charged again, oblivious to the shiny red trail it left in its wake.

Stuart launched himself toward the beast, trying to throw himself between his fallen comrade and the doom descending upon him. But already he could see that he would be too late. In desperation, he shouted, "Speaks-Thunder, no!"

Stuart winced before he words had escaped his lips. The shout did little to slow the approach of the creature, but it had a remarkable effect on young Victor. Stuart saw the Fang's lips mouth the name as his guard dropped.

Then the beast crashed over him.

Stuart might have cried out. The damning certainty of what he had just done hit him like hammer. One thought kept racing through his head, over and over again: He had just killed his friend. Killed him as surely as if he had stabbed Victor in his sleep.

In desperation, Stuart grabbed the only thing ready to hand. Not surprisingly, it was a length of vine covered in wickedly sharp thorns. He wrapped it tightly around both his hands, ignoring the sharp pain as the briars pierced his flesh. He deserved no better.

The flesh is incidental here, he thought, *disposable*.

Stuart saw the skinless monstrosity—slick with not only its own blood but with that of Victor as well—wheel toward him. It held his eyes for a moment and then lowered its head and charged.

Stuart could only watch it come. He had killed his friend. He counted off his few remaining moments as the distance between the two antagonists shrank rapidly, trying to gauge exactly how long he had. The timing surely was important. But he could not seem to concentrate.

The time actually passed much more quickly than he had feared. The reek of spilled blood and decaying flesh crashed over him first, but the full weight of the creature could only be a moment behind. With a cry of abandon, Stuart leapt to one side. The creature barreled past, barely clipping him. It knocked his feet cleanly out from under him, but that no longer mattered. He had snared the foul creature as it rushed past, wrapping the lacerating vine tightly around what had once been its throat.

Stuart clung desperately as he too was dragged through the thorns in the beast's wake. He bore down more tightly, feeling his knuckles slip between the fatty layers at the back of the creature's neck. He saw the pink sheath part as the bramble vine cut clean through to the spine.

Stuart gave a great wrench. With a crack, the creature's head bent backward at an improbable angle, staring into Stuart's eyes as the light behind its own went dim, lost focus, glazed over.

Stuart lay there on top of it, panting, until his arms stopped shaking. Then he set about the grisly business of extracting his shredded hands from the makeshift double-edged garrote. The work was slow, messy, and excruciatingly painful. His eyes and thoughts repeatedly strayed to the broken body of his friend. He had to go to him, to help him. But he forced himself to focus on the task at hand. Until he had extricated himself, he could not hope to help Victor.

At last, he managed to tear free the last barbed strip of vine. He slid from the creature's back and lurched to his feet. Staggering half-blind across the clearing, he at last reached the spot where the body of his friend lay.

A sobbing gasp revealed what he had not dared to hope. Victor was alive! As Stuart crouched over his fallen comrade, however, he knew that 'alive' was all he could hope for. Victor's wounds were deep, severe. And very probably mortal. Broken in body and spirit, it was unlikely that Victor would ever move again.

His chest was crumpled in an alarming manner. Blood poured from the wounds where the creature's jaws had torn at his face and throat. His hair was a matted mess from where his head had impacted the ground.

And already the thorns were growing up around him—through him!—barbed tongues testing the air, lapping eagerly at the spilling lifesblood.

Stuart slashed angrily at the tangle of nettles, but for every shoot he tore away, three more crept up to replace it. Soon Victor was covered in a thick carpet of creeping life.

All around him, Stuart could hear them, closing in, the rustlings of new life craning toward the wreckage of the old. He knew they came for him and that their caress meant certain death. But he was beyond caring for anything but freeing Victor's body. For anything except carrying it back to his kin.

Perhaps it was better this way, he thought. Just to let the thorns take them both. Better, by far, than the grisly alternative—that they should end up like Speaks-Thunder, skinned alive and cursed with a monstrous half-life.

Stuart was only vaguely aware of the thorny coil—as thick around as a strong man's arm—curling lovingly, almost protectively, around his waist. Then he felt the sudden sharp flaming rush of air from his lungs. And then the cool caress of darkness, of welcome oblivion.

Chapter 13

Stuart awoke with a curse on his lips, so he knew he could not be in Heaven. But he wasn't sure he liked the alternative. He lay on his back staring up at a gibbous moon rising above a retreating canopy of thorns. The pearl on black velvet seemed to swim closer for a moment, stooping over him. Then, with a flicker of disapproval, it resumed its distance.

The throbbing behind his eyes and the piercing pain in his chest vied for Stuart's attention. He did not want to think about either of them, but as he pressed the awareness of these two greater pains from his mind, a slew of lesser affronts rushed in to fill their place.

Stuart groaned aloud before he had the chance to think better of it. If he were still alive, it was a glaring oversight. And one which he was in no hurry to bring to the attention of those who might be around him, still lurking nearby, watching him from the cover of the thicket.

His breath came in whistling gasps, struggling its way up past what were certainly cracked ribs. His chest ached as if he'd been holding his breath for a few days. Over the hammering of his heart, Stuart could hear something moving through the thorns nearby. He could see the thick vines, even now, snaking away from his prone form. He tried to lever one cheek up from the crushed undergrowth and look about him. After a long pause, a second attempt proved more successful.

As his surroundings swam into focus, he managed to pinpoint the movement nearby. That streaked red and white patch that lay a short distance away was certainly the body of his friend Victor Svorenko. It wasn't moving. The figure that crouched over him, however, was. It batted distractedly at the last creepers still clinging to the fallen Fang. All the vines in the immediate vicinity—including, it seemed, the ones that had bound Stuart—seemed to trip over themselves in their hurry to withdraw.

That can't be good, Stuart thought. He tried to silence his lungs' ragged gasping as the figure took Victor's body by the ankles and began to drag it away through the thorns. At this latest indignity, Stuart felt the first stirrings of rage within him. It jerked him stumbling to his feet and sent him shambling off in the pair's wake.

Fortunately, the trail was none too difficult to follow. Victor's new assailant was making good time as the thorns seemed to shrink back before the two of them. Stuart found that, by dropping into his lupine form, he could keep pace while still keeping out of sight. This proved important as the brambles seemed to regroup quickly at the pair's passing, choking off the tenuous trail once more.

Before long, Stuart became aware of a reek of decay and corruption that soon grew to overwhelming proportions. The smell seemed to originate from ahead. Downslope, he realized.

He was startled to find the pervasive canopy of thorns giving way suddenly before him. The transition was as sudden as the throwing of a light switch. One moment, he was dragging himself through the towering wall of thorns; the next, he was gazing down into a hollow.

There was no mistaking his whereabouts. His eye followed the slope of the ground down to where it disappeared into a foreboding darkness—the first hint of the funnel of an abandoned mineshaft.

In the moonlight, Stuart had the vague impression of a squat structure at the very brink of the abyss. An abandoned shack, perhaps a toolshed that had once served some function in the operation of the old mine.

His head swam with the noxious scent of decay that reached up for him from the depths. But Stuart knew he had to press forward. He couldn't afford to lose his prey now. No longer caring if his movements were observed, he strode boldly out of the cover of the canopy of thorns.

So far, so good, he thought. There was no sign of Victor, or of the ghoulish figure that had taken such an interest in his dead body. Stuart picked his way forward across the broken ground. Ahead, he could make out the lip of a natural basin. It was no farther across than he was tall. The jagged stones thrusting skyward all around its rim gave the impression that the earth itself had been rent asunder here, revealing some hidden wonder that had lain long buried within. A gift from the heart of Gaia Herself.

Gaia's Tears, he realized. Victor had spoken of the pure mountain spring—a sign of the Mother's perpetual sorrow, of Her compassion for Her children and all they must endure in Her name. But there was no aspect of the pure crystal spring about the benighted tarn that met Stuart's gaze. It was the puddle of a darker mystery, filled not with tears but with a miserable trickle of far less savory secretions.

A monstrous appendage lay mired in the muck, half-buried. Even in the dark, Stuart's eye could pick out the oily body segments of the great wyrm, each chitinous arc bristling with coarse tendrils like spears. The wyrm was almost too vast to take in with a single glance. Stuart found himself involuntarily craning backwards to try to take the full measure of the beast.

He could not tell with certainty whether the appendage mired in the tarn was the beast's head or its tail or some other abortive stump of its massive bulk. With growing apprehension, Stuart traced the ebon line of glistening body segments back toward the wreckage of the mineshaft. He immediately realized that what he had first taken for a building at the edge of the abyss was only a single coiling of the blasphemous creature. The beast rose like a great tower of onyx straight from the bowels of the earth.

Stuart approached warily. He could clearly see the feeler tendrils along the roll of its nearest side twitch in the slight breeze. But otherwise, the atrocity did not stir.

Please let it be dead. Let it be dead. Stuart whispered a silent prayer to whatever spirits might still be tenaciously clinging to the desecrated shrine. He found himself wondering if this was the thing that Victor, Arne and Arkady had fought. The Knockerwyrm.

But no, Victor had told him of returning to the mine with Dawntreader. There was never any mention of anything like this. And it would be difficult to overlook.

A slight sound, a soft plish of water, wrenched Stuart out of his musings. It came from the direction of the befouled tarn. With growing horror, Stuart watched the ripples spreading out across the murky water. His keen eye followed the concentric circles back to their center, to the source of the disturbance. The viscous appendage of the Wyrm-beast twitched, once, twice, straining against the pull of the mud.

Stuart leapt. Four powerful legs pushed off the earth as he bounded—a high, powerful arc that carried him three-quarters of the way up the wyrm's flank. Claws scrabbled frantically for purchase, chewing up great rents in the shining onyx armor and the mealy white flesh beneath. Then Stuart was atop the great beast, sighting along its length to its very tip. Any moment now, the questing tendril would tear itself free of the sucking mud and lash out.

But the monstrous appendage did not pull free. Instead it seemed to sigh and collapse in an exhalation of fetid vapors. Stuart found himself choking, even as he crept closer along the slick body segments. In vain he squinted through the miasma, but it seemed in no hurry to disperse.

By the time his sight cleared, the wyrm lay still once more. But there was another movement from below.

Where the wyrm's body spilled over the edge of the defiled pool, a sphincter-like opening gaped. The dark hole, ringed with dripping cilia, was certainly the source of the stench of decay.

It was not the opening, however, that captured Stuart's attention but the tiny figure that emerged from it. A slip of a girl, radiant in the half-light of dusk, both darker and brighter than everything around her. All moonlight and midnight. She had taken a half dozen brisk strides away from him before Stuart remembered to breathe. There was a terrible beauty about her. Stuart felt it like a weight upon his chest.

In the girl's arms she carried a woven basket. It must have been brimming full, for it took all the strength of both her arms just to keep it upright. She found a level patch of ground within a stone's throw of the old mineshaft and set her burden down with a thump.

Fascinated, Stuart peered closer. The girl unwrapped a shawl from her shoulders and spread it out before her on the ground. The act itself was not so unusual as the fact that Stuart could have sworn she had not been wearing a shawl a moment before. He held the mental image of his first glance of her still. It was seared upon his mind's eye, like the burning afterimage from staring overlong at the sun. No shawl. He would have sworn to it.

But it was there before her now, a square of midnight-black wool, woven finer than any silk. Even from this distance, however, Stuart could see that the piece was worn, frayed about its edge. One trailing onyx thread had worked its way loose and writhed in the slight breeze.

Stuart found himself suddenly put in mind of another trailing end of black thread, from their struggle in the fog. At least the damned fog seemed to have lifted tonight. Or perhaps it never reached quite reached this summit. At any rate, he took its absence as a blessing.

The girl set about unpacking her hamper, her hands quick and clever. As she worked, however, her eye lit upon the place where Stuart crouched, high on the back of the wyrm. He had unconsciously slipped back into his accustomed human form as he clung there, the curve of the wyrm's flank concealing all but his head and shoulders from view.

"Well the worst of the work's over," she called, brushing a wayward strand of ebon hair back from her eyes. "I've managed to retrieve the body from the thorns. I'd say you're probably safe to come down now."

Stuart scrambled to his feet uncertainly on the slick scales. He couldn't say anything. He could hardly breathe. He tried, in vain, to remember the last time he'd found himself at a loss for words. *The gift of gab*, his mother had always said. *You get that from your father's side of the family.*

If Stuart hadn't been aware of it before, he knew now. He was lost. Completely and utterly lost. He knew something was very wrong here. *Hadn't he just seen this girl actually emerge from the gullet of the Wyrm-beast?* But before he could properly form the thought, he was already sliding down toward her. Feet first, then backside, and finally elbows. With a splash, he landed shin-deep in the murky secretions of the tarn. He hardly noticed them.

She shook her head and smiled at him then, and he felt a hole open up within him. A hole the exact shape of that smile. It was an emptiness that he knew would start aching just as soon as that smile turned away from him. He had the presence of mind to smile sheepishly back, a crooked, idiot grin.

"I suppose they gave you a name," she prompted, replacing something in her hamper and closing the lid upon it. "Parents are funny that way."

"Stuart," he said. "That's my given name. But my people call me Stalks-the-Truth. That's my found name."

She accepted this odd pronouncement without question. What could this girl know of the Garou ways? he wondered. And what was she doing in such a dangerous and desolate place?

"All right, Stuart Stalks-the-Truth. From your accent, I'm guessing that your people aren't from anywhere around here. But this mountain has let you make your way this close to its heart, so it would seem that it's taken a fondness to you. Couldn't say why from looking at you. But you're no stranger to mountaintops and mountainways, so perhaps that's something. All I know is that the mountain is not resisting you in earnest. And that's a problem."

"Not resisting?!" Stuart sputtered. "This place has tried to strangle me in my sleep. It's tried to tear me into pieces with thorns. It even tried to crush me in its coils. I really don't see what more resistance, it could…"

The girl raised an eyebrow and glanced sideways toward where her delicate black shawl lay spread out upon the ground as if awaiting a picnic. Stuart followed her gaze and then started, his blood going cold. There was now unmistakably something beneath the woven black shroud—a something that bore a startling resemblance to the body of a large, well-built man.

"Victor?" Stuart muttered, uncomprehendingly. "But how did…" He moved toward the body, but she laid a restraining hand on his arm.

"Easy now," she said. "He's beyond harm, and soon we'll properly speed him on his journey. Now, if had been you that the mountain resisted in earnest…"

Eric Griffin

Stuart shook his head as if trying to clear it. "All right, point taken," he muttered. "But you're not trying to tell me that the mountain is somehow responsible for all this? For what happened to Victor and to Speaks-Thunder and all the others? A mountain doesn't skin people alive. A mountain doesn't hit people in the forehead with a pickaxe…"

Her nose wrinkled. "A pickaxe? Oh, I see. You have a colorful imagination. That will get you into trouble. Look, Stuart. I've been entrusted with protecting this mountain, with seeing that no one comes nosing about. This is a dangerous place. Why, the last time a bunch of folks came traipsing up here, it led to no end of trouble."

"Tell me about it," he said, thinking of Arne Wyrmsbane and Victor and Arkady—all three victims of this desolate place—and of the war that had nearly erupted in consequence of that first, ill-conceived expedition.

"So it's important that we make sure that no one else gets hurt," she said pointedly. "Do you understand?"

He nodded and offered no resistance as she took him by the elbow and led him to Victor's side. Stuart sank down on his haunches and reached out a tentative hand to lift the corner of the winding sheet, to peer once more at the face beneath. Distractedly, he noted a frayed back thread trailing from it. He angrily jerked it free.

The girl came to ground beside him gently amidst a cascade of skirts and smoothed his hand away.

"I'll tell you what, Stuart. I have a bargain for you," she said, regarding him over the body of his fallen friend. "You're mountain-born and bred, there's no concealing that, so you know the value of protecting your own and of keeping your word. Now, I can see to it that you get back down this mountain without further mishap. You take the body of your friend and you see that he gets a proper burial. That's the right thing to do."

"That's very kind," Stuart said. "And I intend to do just that as soon as I've found the answers to a few questions. But that hardly sounds like a 'bargain.' There is some way I can be of service to you in return?"

"You can warn the others. So no one else comes bumbling up here and gets himself killed. I would take it as a personal favor. I'd do it myself, but those folk down there don't know me from Adam—or rather, from Eve—and they've no earthly reason to heed my words. But you could make them understand the danger. I know you could. Will you do that for me, Stuart?"

Stuart looked into her eyes and knew he could deny her nothing. "I will do as you ask," he said quietly, "if only you would tell me that I might come to you again. Tell me that and I will gladly do battle with mountains to return to you."

"That remains to be seen," she replied, neatly sidestepping his entreaty. "But go now, and quickly. Before the moon sets."

"You doubt me?" Stuart exclaimed. "Why I would—"

"I offer you a chance to prove your devotion," she corrected gently, "with actions rather than pretty words. Now then, I have lulled the mountain into a fitful slumber so that we might speak. But it will awaken soon and shrug off this stony complacency. You must be away before then. You are strong enough now to face the return trip, if only you go quickly. But do not forget your promise to me, Stuart Stalks-the-Truth."

She raised a hand in parting, already knowing she had won. He would carry the fanciful story she had sown to the people down-mountain. The story of a vengeful mountain spirit who frowned upon trespassers in his domain. And who marked them all with a single, unblinking red eye and took from them their skins. Yes, guarding the secret graven on the mountain's heart would be easier once word spread and she no longer had to take such a direct role in removing uninvited guests.

She smiled at him, her most devastating smile.

And that was her only mistake. He could not, of his own will, turn his back on that smile. He shuffled his feet; he cleared his throat. He opened his mouth and said the first thing that came to mind, just to prolong the dalliance a few moments longer.

"We came here, my friend and I, looking for one of his kinsmen," he said. "Perhaps you know of him or have seen him. His name is Arkady and he is a noble Silver...I mean, he is a great lord among our people. And they say his coat gleams like moonlight on new-fallen snow."

"His coat?" she replied, perhaps a bit testily. "That's the best you have to say for him, that people talk about his coat? You must admit it's not much of a description."

"They will talk about your shawl, my lady," Stuart replied evenly. At that, she looked a bit flustered.

"Well, I've not seen any foppish lords in fashionable coats trooping up this mountain," she retorted.

"And I hope you can find something more flattering to say of me than 'she had a black shawl!'"

"Brighter than the faces of stars," Stuart murmured admiringly, holding those peerless eyes. "And darker than the unguessed voids behind them."

She crossed her arms and turned away from him, but he could see that she was not displeased.

"They say he fought a great battle with a Knockerwyrm here," Stuart blurted, again taking up the thread of the only topic that seemed to keep looping through his thoughts. He gestured to the monstrous onyx wyrm. "A big one. Something like that, I imagine. And they say he quelled it with nothing more than his voice. Victor and I, that's my friend, we came back here. What else could we do? It was the last place anybody had seen Arkady alive."

"Yes, yes. An interesting tale. But I'm afraid we've no time for that right now. I can feel the mountain stirring. If it finds you here, it will kill you. Take your friend and go. Now." She took him by the arm to raise him to his feet.

As much as it cost him to break that contact, he disengaged his arm. "But I cannot depart leaving you with your conviction that I am some idle layabout. You have been kind to me. You will at least let me help you with your basket—"

"There is no time for that," she said firmly. "He comes, even now. You must be away before…"

It was too late. As soon as Stuart took hold of the hamper, his eye lit upon a still-fresh droplet of blood clinging to its lid. With growing apprehension, he flipped it open. The basket was filled with grisly tools whose purpose there was no mistaking. Stuart saw the array of wicked flaying knives, jars of preserving balms and even less savory substances. And, jutting defiantly from the tangle of ceramic and cutlery, a gleaming stainless-steel awl and blood-stained wooden mallet.

Dierdre saw him stiffen and backed away slowly. One pace. Two.

A great howl rose up within him. Rage and betrayal echoed out of the hollow and rang out over the mountainside. Even miles away, at the Sept of the Dawn, a patrolling Garou along the bawn cocked his head at the sound of a distant thunderhead cresting the mountains.

Then, emptied of all but his hurt and a promise of vengeance to his dead comrade, a most startling change came over Stuart. His face screwed up in hideous rage. One eye squinted closed and it seemed to be swallowed up in his head. The other bulged out and hung loosely. The scowl on his mouth split his visage clear around to the back of his head and his skull flapped open and closed with the sound of gnashing teeth. All of his hair stood on end, each strand as straight and sharp as a dagger. A warrior's halo rose black and gold above him. Blood welled up and oozed from the pores of his face and his whole frame shook with a wrath that threatened to rend sinew from bone. He let out a bellow that shook loose stones from the walls. He beat his breast. He stamped his feet. The hollow trembled beneath him. His warrior strength was full upon him, and he was a terrifying sight to behold.

And standing directly in the path of this ravening tower of contorting fur and sinew was Dierdre. She looked very small indeed, but she showed no fear in the face of Stuart's warrior rage. As his claws drew back and loomed over her like a thunderhead, she simply seemed to flow out from beneath the blow. Stuart's claws struck sparks from the rocky ground. He ripped his hand free and howled in frustration.

The blood forcing its way out through his every pore was now a steady flow. Catching the slightest hint of movement in the moonlight, he quickly pivoted and launched himself at her a second time, his entire frame shaking as if it would tear itself into pieces.

And again he came up empty-handed. His eyes filmed over with rage. The trickle of blood was now a torrent and it seemed he must surely fall. One wouldn't think that there was that much blood was in a body. But a third time he came at her, and a third time she eluded him, seeming to coil around the path of the oncoming blow, neatly avoiding even a scratch.

Stuart spun, pawing the blood-streaked fur out of his eyes with the back of one mammoth claw. But just as he caught sight of her again, he stopped short.

Dierdre's entire form seemed to tremble under the force of the dark thing that was forcing its way up through her. It scooped her up and shook her out sharply like a laundry sheet. Then it pulled and prodded her out to a length of about ten feet and set about rolling her—none too gently—between its palms.

It was her Serpent's Casting—the dark and hard-won gift of Father-of-Serpents. The shedding of her human skin. When she had completed her unholy transformation, no trace of human form clung about her. The tremendous serpentine form reared back—higher than a tall man's reach—and crashed like a wave over the battle-mad warrior.

He took the brunt of the blow on his upraised forearm, feeling flesh part and bone splinter beneath the force of her strike. Stuart sank to one knee, howling agony and defiance into the teeth of the storm.

The next attack fell on him with all the speed and subtlety of a lightning strike. He only narrowly rolled out of the path of the lethal fangs. The impact churned up the ground behind him, hurling him into the befouled tarn. He pushed himself up to his hands and knees in the muck and saw the third and final blow already descending.

Stuart knew this third attack must surely finish him. So he did the only thing he could do: He leapt straight into the jaws of the great serpent.

The couple crashed together with force enough that the mountain itself trembled. They fell heavily to the ground, rolling, grappling desperately like young lovers. Stuart felt lithe arms coil around the back of his neck and passionately draw him closer. He drove against her and bore her gently over backwards. Her back arched at his touch. She drew in a breath sharply as his hand traced a delicate line along her breast.

Their coupling was brief but passionate, as intense as the last fleeting moment of life. He penetrated her like fire; she collapsed gasping for breath against him. There was a slight trickle of blood that turned quickly into wave after wave of oceanic warmth. And finally the blissful cradling caress of oblivion.

In the grips of the Little Death, the witch resumed her human form. She lay heavily against him, his arm around her. The slight telltale hint of claw could be seen protruding, ever so timidly, from her peerless breast.

With excruciating care, Stuart drew his clawed fist back from where it had lodged within her and lowered her tenderly to the ground again. Then he surrendered to the fit of wracking contortions as he shuddered back into his true form.

Chapter 15

Numb and alone, Stuart stared down the gullet of the wyrm. The sphincter-like opening from which the girl had emerged was ringed with jagged tooth-like shards and wriggling cilia. But if she could navigate the way, emerging from the belly of the beast, then he could retrace her path. And if there were any answers to be found here, this was the path that would lead to them.

Muttering a silent entreaty to whatever saint might be within earshot, Stuart ducked low and placed his head within the maw of the wyrm.

He tensed, but the anticipated blow did not fall. Tentatively, he tested the ground before him with one foot. It squelched in a most unsettling manner. The weight of his footstep set up an reverberation that rippled along the corridor of soft tissue ahead of him. Satisfied that the mucousy secretions lining the tunnel were not actively devouring the soles of his shoes, Stuart took a deep breath and stepped forward with the other foot. Totally committing himself.

His first impression was of the weight of the air in the confined space. It hung heavily upon him, warm and moist. The reek was nearly overpowering—a smell of rotting flesh and something more. Something acidic, vaguely vinegary. Stuart had a moment to be grateful that he was not wearing his lupine form with its heightened senses. There were some environs in which the prison of the limited human senses was a blessing. Still, he found his eyes watering and his throat stinging in the pungent, humid air.

He had to bend nearly double to advance, brushing past questing cilia that dangled like Spanish moss. Their touch left angry weals upon his shirt, staining it a gangrenous green-black that seemed slightly phosphorescent. It was difficult to keep his footing on the soft, yielding tissues. Stuart did not relish the thought of losing his balance and finding himself sprawled out face-down in the fetid muck and secretions that trickled past underfoot.

The tunnel seemed to constrict as he pressed his way forward. Twice he went rigidly still, anxious about a reverberation conducted along the fleshy wall of the passage. Peering ahead, he could not see anything else in the darkness, nor identify the source of the thrumming.

After what seemed an eternity, the channel began to slope noticeably downward. Stuart's first thought was that he must be making some progress. This momentary sense of victory was quickly replaced by the realization that the footing had suddenly become even more treacherous. After a few wild flailing tumbles, Stuart had to resign himself to the fact that he would not make any more forward progress on two legs.

He shifted to his lupine form, hoping that four legs might prove surefooted where two had failed him, but he immediately regretted it. His keen lupine senses screamed danger and abhorrence. There was something fundamentally unnatural about traversing the gullet of another beast. His senses howled wrongness at him, tugged his body around, fought for the freedom of the outside air. Stuart shook his head sharply to clear it, fearing he might have blacked out for a moment. He found himself desperately scrambling back up the passage, reversing what progress he had made.

Resignedly, he shifted back to his clumsier human form. Surefooted as his wolf-skin was, still he could not force his lupine senses and instincts to make any sense of these surroundings.

After fighting to regain the ground he had lost, Stuart found himself forced to submit to the indignity of having to scoot forward on his backside, feet before him to slow his slipping descent. Every once in a while, his heels found some more substantive purchase, some cartilaginous ridge, perhaps, a buried strut of the wyrm's pseudo-spine. These outcroppings allowed Stuart to catch a small rest. To wipe the acidic slime from raw hands onto his already ruined pants legs.

It was on the third such pause that Stuart noticed the change. It was in the soft flesh underfoot, or rather in the ridge against which he had come abruptly and jarringly to a halt. The hard rib-like strut had been laid bare of all concealing flesh. It jutted up defiantly, piercing the floor of the tunnel.

Stuart ran his hands over the smooth surface. It seemed the flesh here had been purposefully carved away. Judging from the carnage, it looked as if the work had been done with a heavy chopping blade. A machete, or perhaps an axe.

Stuart shivered. Although he knew intellectually that he was not the first to traverse this unholy tunnel—had he not seen the girl emerge from this very passage?—still, there was an intimacy to the moist, dark confines of this passage. An intimacy that made him believe that its trial and indignities were his alone. An intimacy that balked at the proof that others had come here before him.

There were some sort of markings carved into the exposed rib, again with a blade, but Stuart could not make out their significance. Were these trail signs, meant to mark the path deeper within the beast? Stuart could hardly credit the hypothesis. If what Victor had told him had been correct, the body of the wyrm could not have been here for longer than a few nights at most. Surely there would not have been either opportunity or reason to blaze such a trail in so short period of time. Perhaps with months of comings and goings along this blasphemous route…

Stuart pressed on, but soon the tenor of the path changed again. The way grew continually more steep, the exposed ribs more frequent and more pronounced. Some of them now seemed to have been excavated entirely. More than once Stuart found himself with a wrist or ankle painfully lodged beneath such an outcropping of bone.

The sloping descent was soon a climb, clambering hand over hand down a rough ladder of notched and carved ribs. And then even these handholds were gone. The descent suddenly transformed into a slide and then, perhaps inevitably, an unchecked fall.

Chapter 16

When Stuart at last came to rest, he did so rather abruptly and with bone-jarring force. He seemed to have found the "floor" of the tower. There was no sign of cushioning fleshy membranes here. He was in a natural cavern, deep within the heart of the mountain. There was some slight illumination that he was reasonably sure did not come from the flashfires of pain inside his skull.

At least he had managed to keep his feet pointing downward for most of his slipping, sliding plunge. He had come down heavily on one ankle. It hurt like hell, but didn't seem to be broken. The momentum had sent the rest of him sprawling out across the hard floor, but a little blood was not going to deter him at this point. He had come for some answers. Legendary obstacles had lain between him and his quarry. He damned well wasn't about to turn back now—even if he could figure out how to accomplish that trick.

As his eyes adjusted to the gloom, he saw that the cave bore signs of recent habitation. And not just by the blind white Wyrmlings that gnawed away at the tower of flesh from its insides. There was a banked cookfire in the center of the cavern with a large copper pot hung over it by means of a four-legged construct. On closer examination, perhaps the term "four-legged" was a bit too literally true for Stuart's tastes. Each of the four supports seemed to be a long, gnawed femur bone, lashed together at the apex with a fine woolen thread.

There were other signs of grisly goings-on here as well. Against one wall was a kind of shrine where the decomposing head of a white wolf had been propped up on a natural outcropping of stone. The creature's bones had been carefully arranged in complex patterns around the base of the pedestal, as if someone had been enacting some rite or perhaps reading omens in the fall of the bones. A pair of long, blackened iron boarspears were crossed behind the trophy, but there was no sign of the rest of the beast's body or pelt.

The girl's personal effects were few, and functional rather than decorative. There was a silver looking glass and an antique steamer trunk in one corner, wedged between the wall and a foul tangle of more bones, brambles, pine boughs and unwound bolts of fabric. He gave the whole area a wide berth. It gave him the unsettling impression of being some sort of nest and he was none too eager to probe the secrets of that dark bower.

Instead he turned his attention to the source of the dim illumination. The sickly gray-green light originated from a recess in the farthest wall of the cave. Some phosphorescent lichen or fungus, Stuart thought. The unwholesome light certainly did not look in any way natural.

What Stuart found there was surely not the work of nature. As he turned the corner, he could see clearly that the light arose from three runes carved into the wall of the cave. Each of the sigils simmered with the leprous glow of balefire.

Stuart whistled low and took out his notebook from back pocket. He wiped away the worst of the slime from its cover, more than half surprised he hadn't lost the book during his descent. The pencil had not weathered the trip as well and was broken in no fewer than three pieces.

He turned to the wall at his left hand and ran the knuckle-length pencil stub rapidly back and forth, giving it some semblance of a point. He was careful to avoid any contact with the wall on which the blasphemous runes were etched.

Satisfied with his efforts, he set to work slowly and carefully, copying down the complex sigils. He saw immediately that two of the three symbols had been defaced. They bore the sign of vicious gouging, claw marks that rent deep furrows into the rock itself. The sickly balefire had run from the patterns, dripping down the wall's surface and scoring it with ugly burned streaks.

Stuart felt the outrage of that act of vandalism like a hole in the pit of his stomach. These runes might have been lost lore captured by the Black Spirals on one of their all-too-frequent raids upon the lorekeepers' lodges. Now there was no use even trying to reconstruct the stories that had once been contained here—perhaps the last surviving record of some ancient legend now lost to the Garou.

But the third rune was still intact, and it was here that Stuart concentrated his attentions. The pattern was not one that was familiar to him. Although he was no lorekeeper, all of his tribe had a soft spot for the old stories. Even a cub among them had more than a passing familiarity with the legends of Garou contained in the rune symbols of the Silver Record.

But this story he did not know. He was not sure he even understood it in its entirety. He recognized some of the familiar twistings of the complex pattern glyph. That powerful downstroke was the surely the mark of an ancient hero—and a Silver Fang, if Stuart read the supporting flourishes correctly. They certainly were meant to elaborate on the hero's lineage, but Stuart did not have the genealogical background to put a name to the signatory marking.

He recognized the telltale curve of the Eater-of-Souls in the story, one of the three mightiest incarnations of the Wyrm. But he could not identify the pattern of the Wyrm-spawn that arose from it—the antagonist pitted against the ancient Fang hero. Its sign seemed to arc sharply back upon itself, devouring its own tail, erasing all sign of its passage.

There had been a great battle, that much was obvious, one from which the Fang hero had emerged victorious, but at a great cost. The serifs on the sign of triumph trailed like spilled lifesblood. Stuart could read a great sacrifice in those strokes, but the details of the cataclysmic battle and its consequences he could not unravel.

This did not dishearten him. There were others among his people who would succeed where his own clumsy efforts had fallen short of the mark, kinsmen trained since birth in the deciphering and the keeping of the Record. If this was a lost tale that had fallen into the hands of the enemy, the lorekeepers would know.

And they would also honor the one who succeeded in recovering such a treasure for them—a story written on the heart of a mountain.

The silence under the mountain was broken only by the agonized scratchings of the pencil stub. When Stuart was through, he went over the entire pattern again to make sure he had it exactly.

With a smile he flipped the notebook shut and replaced it in his pocket.

The scratchings did not stop.

Unsettled, Stuart strained to catch the slight, telltale sound. There it was again. It seemed to be coming from just beyond the wall. He cast about, but could not see any sign of an opening or any way to reach the space beyond. He needed to get a better vantage point. Using the story rune as an anchor, he stepped sideways into the spirit realm.

There was no longer any barrier of fog to impede his crossing. Stuart found himself in another cavern, nearly a twin to the first. But he did not have much time for detailed comparisons. He was not alone.

The scratching sound stopped suddenly as Stuart stepped through. There was a figure here, seated crosslegged on the cave floor, his back to Stuart. The stranger half turned at the sound of Stuart's entrance and regarded him curiously.

Despite the uncertain light, Stuart could make out the other's features clearly. The stranger seemed to radiate his own light. His pelt was the gleaming white of moonlight on new-fallen snow. Stuart could name a half-dozen Silver Fang nobles that would give a dozen years off their lives for such a coat as that— the crown of a proud and refined lineage. Stuart had never seen its equal. Already he had a pretty good idea that his search had not been in vain.

Even crouched forward, the Fang's bearing was regal. There was a certain unconsidered nobility to his simplest gesture, a curious but aloof cock of his head as he sized up the newcomer, the unconscious straightening of his shoulders as he swallowed a sigh of disappointment.

Stuart spread his hands to show that he was unarmed, his claws sheathed. The Silver Fang studied Stuart for a moment, staring in a manner that would have been considered rude in a more formal setting. Stuart returned his stare levelly, but held his ground. He made no move to advance that might be interpreted as threat or challenge. He had not come this far only to leave his questions unanswered in some rash challenge, in some senseless catharsis of blood.

It was something about the Silver Fang's stare that brought Stuart up short, held him there. There was a look of resignation in those ice-blue eyes and something more—a vast and slow-moving sadness. Stuart thought he could recognize the first tentative touch of Harano, the deep and all-consuming river of sorrow. It was an ancient foe and one that had claimed the lives of countless proud Garou warriors. It was an adversary against which all the weapons of the Wyrm paled by comparison.

Then, as if reaching a decision, the Fang gave a slight shrug and turned away again. The meaning behind the gesture was plain—Stuart not only posed no threat, but did not measure up. He recoiled as if struck. The Fang was making it painfully clear that he considered Stuart to be of no account whatsoever. He barely registered on this stranger's consciousness.

Maddeningly, the scratching sound resumed.

Now the sound grated directly on Stuart's nerves. He fought to keep his rising anger and indignation in check. When he was sure he had mastered himself, he cleared his throat and stepped forward.

"I am sorry to intrude," he said. "But I have come an awfully long way—and at no small personal risk…" Stuart started to add "my Lord Arkady," but choked back the honorific. He realized that, although he had his anger well under control, there was still a lingering resentment there. He would be damned if he was going to pay deference to someone who had so casually insulted him. He hurried on to cover the lapse. "And, to be frank, I'm none too eager to tackle the return trip just now. So, if it's all the same to you, I hoped I might speak with you."

There was an uncomfortable pause. Stuart thought the Fang would just ignore him entirely and he felt hot words boiling up within him. Just as he opened him mouth to hurl them, however, the scratching noise again fell silent. Without looking up, Arkady raised his right hand to where Stuart could see it. Clutched in his fist was a long, thin bone, its tip sharpened and fire-blackened. Impatiently, he gestured with his macabre pointer to a place not far from his own on the cave floor.

Stuart did not hesitate, although inside he was not at all certain he wanted to place himself within striking range of the fallen Silver Fang lord. By all accounts, Arkady was a formidable opponent, a legendary warrior. But Stuart had more than a passing familiarity with the tales of Arkady's exploits. He was well aware that whenever the Galliards sang of the noble Fang's martial discipline, it was only a matter of time before he would hear of some tragic lapse of temperance that put the entire undertaking at risk. And whenever they told of Arkady's cunning, it was inevitably the prelude to a tale of some undermining lapse of judgment.

But prudence was not Stuart's long suit. Knowing he might well regret it, he walked straight up to Arkady and made a point of settling in right beside the fallen lord. A place much closer than that Arkady had indicated.

If the noble Fang noted this discrepancy, he chose not to draw attention to it.

Silently, Stuart let out a long breath. He was aware that he had passed the first critical juncture in what was already proving to be a much more delicate situation than he had foreseen. What had he expected? For Arkady to be grateful for his arrival? *Well, yes,* he realized. Stuart had pictured Arkady as a prisoner of the Black Spirals. And he still hadn't seen anything to dislodge that first conviction.

But if Arkady was a prisoner, where were the iron bars of his cage? Where were the silvered fetters? After a moment's consideration, even Stuart had to admit that Arkady did not bear himself like a condemned man. There was no sign of the ravages of long internment upon him—the slouch of the head and shoulders, as if from personally bearing up the vast weight of stone above him. The gaunt skeletal tickling of hunger about the ribs. The slow aimless shuffle of feet, unsure of how to measure out their progress now that they could no longer distinguish the procession of days.

Arkady was unbowed.

Stuart studied his companion, but the reality refused to fall into place with what Stuart had envisioned for this encounter. Arkady was still as proud, aloof as any Garou Stuart had ever seen. He showed no sign of being broken by torture or long confinement.

Distracted? Yes, he was that. Arkady scratched obsessively at the cave floor before him with the fire-blackened shard of bone. Its tip left angry black weals across the uneven surface.

Consumed by some gnawing doubt? Almost certainly. Stuart could see the slight tic of the muscles of the Fang's powerful arms, thighs, jaw. He was going through an elaborate kata of slash, parry, counterstrike. But he couldn't quite keep the inner battle contained. Little hints of the conflict kept slipping past his guard, making themselves known.

Contemplating something desperate?

Distractedly, Stuart realized that this corner of the cave corresponded exactly with the location of the foul nest in that other cavern he had so recently quit. It was not a comforting thought.

"If you've come to gloat," Arkady said without looking up, "you should do it quickly. I've killed the last six of you who came trooping down here. And none of them was so foolish as to come alone."

His tone was matter-of-fact, almost emotionless. There was no hint of malice or bravado in his voice. If anything, he sounded very weary.

"Thanks for the warning," Stuart said. "But I haven't come to gloat. Really. My name's Stuart.

They call me Stalks-the-Truth. And I just wanted to talk to you."

At this announcement, one corner of Arkady's mouth curled up in a slight mocking smile. "Stalks-the-Truth," he mused aloud. "Not Finds-the-Truth? A shame. It seems, then, that your tale is fated to be a sad one. A tragedy. All right, Stuart Stalks-the-Truth, if you wish to talk then you should do so quickly. Although I think gloating would be a more satisfying way to spend your final moments."

Stuart frowned. "Look, I've come a long way. And I want to hear your side of the story. At the concolation, when no one else had a single word to say in your defense—"

"Ah, that's better. Now we get to the gloating."

"What? I'm not gloating. If you'd just listen for a minute, I'm just trying to tell you—"

"I said you could talk," Arkady said. "I did not say that I would listen. It was a mistake, I think, to let those first few go. Knife-between-Bones and his companions. If I had killed those first few, the rest of you would not be so bold and I would have some peace in which to contemplate what I must do. But I was so anxious for news then, to hear what the People were saying about me. Perhaps it was a conceit. But it is one I have repented of. I will not make the same mistake again."

"Knife-between-Bones?" Stuart latched on to the name. It was not that he was trying to be brave, to dismiss Arkady's threat. It was more that his personal danger was not nearly so immediate as the sound of pieces falling into place. Stuart did not even have opportunity to reflect that this was not the first time his reporter's instincts for unraveling the tantalizing loose end of a story had put him in grave peril.

Yes, the name was familiar. He had heard it recently, at the concolation…. Of course! He could see the image of the Warder storming into the House of the Spearsreach carrying his grisly pennon—the bloody white wolf pelt hung from a cast-iron spear. His packmate—what was his name?—had given his report to the Jarlsdottir, telling of a party of Black Spiral Dancers who had come under this "flag of truce." The leader of that party, this Knife-between-Bones, had claimed to be a kinsman to Lord Arkady.

"You know him?" Arkady asked casually. "I'm really not surprised. Perhaps I should let you live after all. Perhaps if I left one of you clinging to some shred of life and sent you crawling back home it might convince the others that intruding upon my privacy is simply not worth it."

His train of thought derailed, Stuart looked up irritably. "Look, for the last time, I'm not here to gloat. I'm starting to realize why everyone says you're some kind of…"

For the first time, Arkady looked up and met Stuart's eyes. "What is it that they say about me?"

Stuart felt the challenge in that stare and he tried to hold their eyes locked. But after only a moment, he was forced to look away. It was the intensity of the need in those ice-blue eyes. You would think that someone with a reputation as infamous as Lord Arkady's would just stop caring what others thought of him. Or at least that he would come to affect indifference, if only as a kind of shield against the raw hunger that Stuart saw in those eyes.

Arkady didn't just want to force Stuart to finish his ill-considered insult—which in itself would have been affront enough to justify the spilling of blood that Arkady kept hinting toward. Nor was he simply curious for news—to find out who might even now be on his trail for wrongs real or imagined. No, he honestly, *desperately*, needed to know what others were saying of him. What they were thinking of him. It was a craving—a desire as palpable as that for food or sex or battle.

Poor, unlucky, bastard, Stuart thought, shaking his head in mute sympathy. This Silver Fang really cared what everyone was whispering about him. He needed to wake up each morning and see the admiration mirrored in the eyes of his warriors as they stood on review. He needed to hear the murmur of adoration in the voices of his people as he passed them at their work.

Only vaguely did Stuart begin to get the sense of what this exile, this captivity, must be costing Arkady.

"What do they say?" Stuart repeated. He steeled his courage and gave it to him straight. "They say you're Wyrm-tainted. That you commanded the Knockerwyrm and that it bowed before you. They say that you are to blame for the death of the Fenrir fosterling and all the trouble between the Get and the Gaians. They say you have conspired and connived to seize the Silver Crown, that you trafficked with the Black Spirals to do so. That Albrecht himself told you that you were not to show your face again in that part of the world. And that was all before the concolation. Now they say that you're an exile, an excommunicant, that you're already dead. Fallen in some private inner battle against the Wyrm."

Arkady closed his eyes and inhaled slowly. The gesture was not one of shame and defeat, but rather of drinking deeply, unashamedly, of the echo of his name on other people's lips. For the moment, it almost seemed that it did not matter to him that those whisperings were all words of scorn and condemnation. But then again, Stuart thought, Arkady was a starving man, languishing in a prison of isolation.

After a long pause, Arkady spoke again, without ever opening his eyes. Perhaps he was bracing himself for the answer to his quiet question.

"And what do you think, Stuart Stalks-the-Truth?"

If Stuart were half so concerned with self-preservation as he was with puzzling out what was hidden from him, he would have taken his time and chosen his next words very carefully.

If a man wants to be right in his words or in his deeds, there are only really two ways he can set about it. The first is to assiduously avoid error. Stuart had met these cautious men, those for whom avoiding error had become the holy grail in itself. They acted seldom, fearing misstep, and spoke even less. Better to keep silent and be thought a fool, than to open one's mouth and prove it. And technically they were precisely correct, these smiling silent guardians of the truth—for the man who has never spoken has never spoken falsely.

But Stuart was cut from the opposite cloth. For him, to be right was to tirelessly pursue the truth. It was an active, boisterous thing. Better to aspire to reach the right answer and fail, than to be content with the not-knowing. Grasping for the truth and coming up short was not falsehood, and certainly not so dishonest as to conceal ignorance behind closed doors and closed lips.

"I will tell you what I told them," Stuart said. "A house divided against itself cannot stand. And a man does not cast out devils by the power of the devil. I say that if you have truly found a way to quell the greater wyrms, I can only wish we had a dozen more warriors just like you. Lord knows we have sore need of such skills."

At this Arkady smiled. Not the sideways mocking smile he had shown earlier. But a genuine, unconsidered, *predatory* smile.

Stuart felt his mouth go dry and he began, with excruciating slowness, to edge away sideways. To get out of the reach of those bone-rending canines.

At these close quarters, Arkady surely could smell Stuart's sudden fear. A strangled, choking sound tore free of Arkady's throat. Stuart knew that there was no time for scrambling to his feet. He immediately shifted to a fleeter four-footed form that would stand some small chance of evading the hunter's first lethal spring.

Long out of practice, Arkady's vocal chords struggled to shape themselves around the sound welling up from within him. The pitch changed and the rasping noise resolved itself into a series of short sharp barks and then, finally, rang out clear and pure.

Laughter.

At the sight of Stuart hastily grabbing for his wolf's-skin and scrambling backward submissively, the laughter redoubled in strength.

Stuart got his feet under him at last and bristled. He growled low in the throat and shifted his weight back over his haunches. The opening prelude to a pounce.

Arkady did not miss the motion or its import. He visibly struggled for control and momentarily managed to force a serious look upon his face before the whole effort collapsed back into riotous laughter.

He held up one hand, begging a moment to compose himself. He still clung to his makeshift stylus. "I am sorry," he managed at last, snatching words and quick breaths where he could. "For a moment there, I had the overwhelming urge to throw you the bone. It was an unworthy thought. You have my sincere…"

But by this time, Stuart was laughing as well and struggling back into his more accustomed human form. He waved aside the apology.

"No, you don't need to apologize. You just rattled my pride a little, that's all. But I guess I didn't deserve much better, not after that dose of medicine I handed you. I'm more than willing to cede the field. If you'll just tell me what I came to hear— your side of the story, why you didn't show up at the trial, what you're doing here…"

"Well spoken," Arkady said, at last mastering himself. "I will agree to tell you what you came to learn. *If* in return you will first help me with a small problem of my own. I have come to a bit of an impasse. I can neither advance, nor gracefully withdraw." He gestured hopelessly at the tangle of angry black markings scratched into the cave floor. "But perhaps you can provide some insight that I have overlooked."

"I can try," Stuart replied, unconsciously shifting closer to get a better look at the weird symbols that spread out before Arkady. Already his mind was off and racing after this new mystery.

Chapter 17

"But what does all this mean?" Stuart asked, shaking his head and pushing himself back upright. He lay on his stomach, peering closely at the mad scrawl of runes on the cave floor. His right arm was asleep from where his entire weight had been resting upon it. "It looks like some kind of a map."

"Not a map exactly," Arkady replied. "A battle plan. Although admittedly not much of a battle plan at this point. I keep going round in circles here. I can't see any avenue of penetrating the fortress's defenses single-handedly." He snorted and cast down his crude stylus in an uncharacteristic moment of unguarded frustration. It clattered and skidded out into the center of the diagram. "I'd do just as well presenting myself at the main gate and trusting their tender mercies."

"Whose tender mercies?" Stuart asked, retrieving the blackened shaft of bone. "What is this place?" With the tip of the macabre pointer, he traced the outline of Arkady's meandering runic symbols. If he squinted, Stuart could almost imagine that this wavering coil here was a ring of imposing battlements. That twin charcoal smudges along one side might be a pair of fortified gatehouses. And these angry slashes piled up tightly behind could be construed as a wall of unscalable mountain peaks. Stuart shook his head. The image dissolved back into an unintelligible tangle.

"It is Malfeas," Arkady said simply. "Some have called it the Gates of Hell; others, Sheol, the Bottomless Pit; others still, the Lake of Fire. It has many names. It is the Prison of the Wyrm."

"That's the Prison of the Wyrm?" Stuart exclaimed incredulously. "Somehow I always pictured it being, I don't know, bigger. More cosmic."

"It's not to scale," Arkady said. Stuart looked up, but could find no hint of amusement in the Fang's eyes.

"Actually," Arkady continued, his tone formal once more, "this is merely the *approach* to the realm of Malfeas. Or at least, one approach. The one I have managed to isolate. And that is what is relevant to our current quandary. I have reason to believe my efforts to pass through this portal might be…resisted."

"Why the hell would you want to enter Malfeas?! Are you deranged? Quick reality check here: People don't just go off on little sightseeing excursions to the underworld. And they certainly don't come back from them. Do you really think—"

"As I said," Arkady continued, "I anticipated some resistance."

"Oh, I haven't even gotten started resisting yet," Stuart retorted. "This has got to be about the worst plan—no, I take it back. This is *definitely* the worse plan I've ever heard. You are going to Malfeas. You are *voluntarily* going to Malfeas. You are voluntarily going to launch *a direct assault* on the front gate of Malfeas. Am I grasping the finer points of this plan here?"

"We don't know it's the front gate," Arkady pointed out. "It's one gate. That is sufficient for our purposes."

"It doesn't matter which gate it is! We're talking about suicide here...H" he visibly struggled for control. "Look, why don't we try another tack. Why would you want to go anywhere near Malfeas?" In his own ears, his question sounded quite reasonable.

Arkady gave Stuart a look he usually reserved for idiots and cubs. "I am going to walk the Black Spiral," he said. As if that explained everything.

The only sound in the cavern was the sharp snap of the blackened bone breaking neatly in two against the floor. Stuart still clung to the other half of the splintered pointer. But his eyes were fixed on Arkady.

"Madness!" Stuart hissed, making a sign against evil.

Arkady stood and straightened regally. He brushed at the dust and dirt that still clung to him. "Madness or no, that is what I must do. It is the only thing I can do now. The only way to redeem my people."

"You know what happens to folks that attempt to walk the Spiral," Stuart accused. He rose quickly, as if afraid Arkady would start off straightaway. That he would just walk away and leave him here. "You've seen what they become. The Black Spiral twists them, breaks them, corrupts them. It turns them into something less than human, less than beast. It makes them into—"

Arkady's eyes flashed fire and he wheeled on Stuart. "Do you think to lecture me? On the history of my own people?" He brandished a fist. Stuart watched in apprehension as gleaming claws emerged from that fist.

But something was wrong. Three of Arkady's claws, he saw, were broken off sharply. The stubs that remained were charred, burned black as coal. As Stuart stared, he could see now that Arkady's entire left hand was badly singed.

"You're hurt," Stuart muttered, pressing closer despite the obvious threat. "Here, let me. And I wasn't talking about your people. I was talking about the White Howlers. The Fallen Tribe. The ones who became the Black Spiral Dancers."

Arkady snorted disdainfully. He did not allow Stuart to take hold of his wounded hand, much less to bandage it as was obviously his intent. He gestured angrily back the way Stuart had come. "Do you try to tell me that you did not see the stories carved under the mountain? The condemnations etched into the very heart of the living rock, written in blazing green balefire?"

"No. I just saw the one story rune, and that one I didn't understand. I..." He broke off, slow realization dawning. There had been three runes, he thought. But two had been destroyed. By the gouges of angry claw marks. "The other two stories," Stuart said with growing certainty. "Stories of your kinsmen, of the Silver Fangs. You destroyed them."

"Yes! Kinsmen of mine." Arkady sheathed his broken claws and turned away. "It is not only the White Howlers who have fallen to the Spiral over the centuries. There are those among my tribe, as well. Some of my direct ancestors, may they now rest peacefully, now that, at long last, the final record of their failures has been destroyed. Yes, we have a name for such as these. They are called the Silver Spirals, the noble Silver Fangs who have fallen victim to the Black Spiral. Those who have been turned by the power of the enemy."

"And you would follow in this tradition?" Stuart asked quietly.

He could see Arkady's shoulders hunch in outrage, but the Fang did not turn to face him. "No," Arkady said, his tone clipped. "I would succeed where they have failed. I will walk the Spiral and I will master it. And only then will my forebears be redeemed. They will rest in the knowledge that, although they themselves fell short of the prize in the direct attempt, by their seed the Spiral was mastered and unmade."

"What the hell are you talking about?" Stuart exclaimed. "What makes you think the Spiral won't just swallow you too? From what they tell, your family tree is almost bent double beneath the weight of legendary Garou warriors. Are you trying to tell me that you think you're better than all of them? Better than your father, better than your grandfather?"

"I am the purest of the blood in twenty generations," Arkady said simply, meeting Stuart's eye. "There will not be another twenty. You know that as well as I do. Look within your heart, Stalks-the-Truth, and tell me if I speak falsely. I doubt there will be another two. No, this thing must be done now if at all. And now, at last, I am ready."

"Um, I've seen your plan," Stuart said. "You're not ready."

Arkady pointedly ignored him. "I have reached the point where there is nothing for me to go back to now. You have said as much yourself. That all doors are closed to me. That I am dead to my people. That even my name has been…" he broke off. His eyes dropped. He appeared to study the back of his fist.

Stuart could see the line of broken claws, barely peeking from their fleshly prison. And he knew, as surely as he had ever known anything, what was in Arkady's thoughts. The noble Fang, who had been the last and best hope of his people, the pride of his generation and the last—and he certainly realized this now—the very last of his peerless bloodline. Arkady was seeing only those others now, those who had gone before him into the very depths of hell. The ancestors whose names he had himself expunged.

Freeing them.

Stuart looked up at Arkady, but already his companion was too big for the eyes to take in all at once. A deep surging strength rose up through him, a strength of mountains. All the strength of his forebears, all their pride, all their hope. The tons of rock above him, the prison of granite, could no longer hold him. Arkady was already stepping over the low stile of the mountain range, vaulting effortlessly over the familiar gate, setting his steps on the familiar path. But from somewhere far below, Stuart's tiny voice reached him, called him back.

"There might be a way," Stuart said. "Yes, there might just be a way."

Chapter 18

The pair of Garou that sat hunched forward on the cold cave floor were about as different as day and night. The first was proud, regal of bearing. He was a legendary warrior, a cunning strategist, a man prophesied to rally the Garou Nation to the Final Battle.

The other was a no-account of humble beginnings. A drifter who couldn't manage to hold down a freelance job. A self-confessed and unrepentant layabout.

"Again," Stuart said, sounding more than a little like a frustrated schoolmaster. "The Spiral. There's got to be something we're missing."

Obediently, Arkady wiped the cave floor of its complex diagrams and elaborate plottings. Slowly, he started over again at square one. With a single motion, without ever lifting the blackened tip of the bone stylus from the uneven surface, he drew a perfect, continuous spiral. Nine times the figure looped back in upon itself before vanishing in a final singularity. A crude, coal-black smudge.

"There must be a way," Arkady repeated as if trying to convince himself of the fact. "A way of walking the Spiral without being corrupted. Of striding into the heart of the labyrinth and emerging victorious on the far side. It is prophesied. It must be possible." He struck the cave floor soundly with the flat of his fist.

"Unless, of course, the prophets were just engaging in a little wishful thinking," Stuart said. "Or later scholars were just trying to find a way to explain away the fact that Lord So-and-so had just flipped out and gone over to the other side."

"That's not funny," Arkady said. "I've lost too many kinsmen to that promise for me to start questioning it now."

"Seems to me like an ideal time to start questioning it," Stuart said. "And I can't read a damned thing you're writing anymore. The whole floor here is smeared black and I think my eyes are starting to cross. How about we just call it a night?"

"You said you would help. You said that there might just be a way."

"There might be. But we've been over this a dozen times and I'm damned if I can find it. Maybe in the morning things will be a bit clearer. The late morning," he added hastily.

"Sleep then. I will keep watch," Arkady answered testily. He rose to his feet and began pacing out the interior of the cave. His steps instinctively carried him in an ever-narrowing gyre.

Stuart lay stretched out full-length on the floor, his chin propped up on the back of his hands. "It's no good. Even if you can win through to the Spiral—a doubtful proposition at best— there's still nothing you can do when you get there except repeat the same mistakes made by all those who have gone before you. Once you set foot on that Black Spiral, you are lost. Period. There's no turning back, no turning aside, no escape. It's got you and it's just going to work away at you until you crack."

The winding path of Arkady's pacing brought him back around to Stuart again. This time he brushed past him on the inside and continued his circuit.

"Is that monologue helping you clarify your thoughts, or was it intended for my benefit?" Arkady asked.

Stuart sighed and pushed himself to his feet. "Forget it. Forget I even said anything." He stared after Arkady's retreating figure, saw the scuffled, blackened footprints trailing out behind him like a loose thread. Absently, he followed the path of the tracks backwards, saw the twin sets of prints where they ran closely past him on either side.

But if those prints were the path of the Black Spiral, what was this narrow stretch of floor where Stuart was now standing? With a growing sense of excitement, he took out his pocket notebook. Quickly rifling through to a blank page, he rendered a copy of the infamous nine-gyred spiral. Then he squinted at it closely until his eyes refused to focus on the diagram any longer and everything blurred about the edges before snapping back into sudden clarity.

"There!" he cried aloud.

Arkady stopped dead in his tracks and turned, a look of concern on his face. "Where?" he said, taking a step toward Stuart.

"No! You have to stay on the path," Stuart reprimanded him. "Make your way back to me, but do it the right way. Stay on the Black Spiral."

Arkady sighed, but humored his excitable companion. Soon he stood by Stuart's side once more.

"Now you walk the pattern again," Stuart said. "Just like the last time. Only this time, I walk with you."

"This is your plan?" Arkady asked incredulously. "You would walk with me into the lair of the Wyrm?"

"Uh, no. My mother didn't raise no fools, and there's no way in hell that you're dragging me down to Malfeas with you. This is for demonstration purposes only. Walk."

Arkady shrugged, feigning disinterest, and again began to retrace the black footprints. Stuart kept pace right beside him, shoulder to shoulder. They finished one complete circuit of the room.

"I really don't see what this has to do with…" Arkady began. But Stuart hushed him and urged him on through a second circumambulation. And then a third.

"And the point of this little exercise is?" Arkady asked, at last losing patience.

"The point is," Stuart replied with a triumphant grin, "that I am still at your side—through three complete circuits of the pattern—and I have yet to set one foot upon the Black Spiral."

Arkady stopped dead in his tracks. "But how can that be?" he protested softly.

"Look here," Stuart said, tapping his pencil rapidly against the open notebook page. "It's something I just realized about the nature of spirals. All spirals. Here's the Black Spiral I drew. But there's *another* spiral here, nestled within it. In this case, it's a White Spiral, white for the paper peeking through. It's a negative spiral, sandwiched in between the lines of the black one. And if you were to walk on *that* spiral, like I was just doing, it should be possible—at least theoretically possible—to reach the center without ever taking a single step on the Black Spiral. Without subjecting yourself to its corrupting touch."

Arkady just stared at him. Then a smile split his face. And then he threw back his head and laughed, slapping Stuart heartily on the back. "You are a wonder, Stuart Stalks-the-Truth. Almost I wish you would repent of your earlier decision and agree to accompany me. Are you sure that you are not in the least bit tempted to put your fine theory to the test?"

"Don't you worry about me," Stuart said. "If you manage to pull this off, I'll know about it. Hell, I imagine we'll all know about it. But I've a different path to walk. A road I've avoided for far too long now."

And it was only in that moment that Stuart realized where the White Spiral—if such an improbable thing even existed—must surely lead. It was a path leading unvaryingly home.

About the Author

Eric Griffin is co-developer of the **Tribe Novel** series for **Werewolf: The Apocalypse**. He is the author of **Get of Fenris, Fianna, Glass Walker** and **Black Spiral Dancer**.

His other works include the Tremere Trilogy (**Widow's Walk, Widow's Weeds, Widow's Might**) as well as **Tremere** and **Tzimisce** in the **Clan Novel** series. His short stories have appeared in the **Clan Novel: Anthology, The Beast Within, Inherit the Earth** and the **Scarred Lands Anthology.**

Griffin was initiated into the bardic mysteries at their very source, Cork, Ireland. He is currently engaged in the most ancient of Irish literary traditions—that of the writer in exile. He resides in Atlanta, Georgia, with his lovely wife Victoria and his three sons, heroes-in-training all.

For more information on this series, please feel free to visit the author's website at http://people.atl.mediaone.net/egriffin or White Wolf publishing at http://www.white-wolf.com.

WHERE THERE IS LIFE, THERE IS HOPE

The price of immortality is high. But is there a path that leads to life eternal rather than damnation? The Undying know, and this new breed of mummies unleash their might in the Year of the Scarab!

Land of the Dead
Year of the Scarab Trilogy #3
NOVEMBER 2001

White Wolf is a registered trademark of White Wolf Publishing, Inc. Year of the Scarab is a trademark of White Wolf Publishing, Inc. All rights reserv